Out of Warranty

Also by Haywood Smith

Wife-in-Law

Waking Up in Dixie

Ladies of the Lake

Wedding Belles

The Red Hat Club Rides Again

The Red Hat Club

Queen Bee of Mimosa Branch

Haywood Smith

Out of Warranty

St. Martin's Press ⚎ New York

This is a work of fiction. All of the characters, organizations, and events portrayed in this novel are either products of the author's imagination or are used fictitiously.

OUT OF WARRANTY. Copyright © 2013 by Haywood Smith. All rights reserved. Printed in the United States of America. For information, address St. Martin's Press, 175 Fifth Avenue, New York, N.Y. 10010.

www.stmartins.com

Library of Congress Cataloging-in-Publication Data

Smith, Haywood.
   Out of warranty / Haywood Smith.—1st ed.
      p. cm.
  ISBN 978-1-250-00352-2 (hardcover)
  ISBN 978-1-250-02598-2 (e-book)
 1. Health insurance—United States—Fiction. 2. Satire. 1. Title.
 PS3569.M53728O88 2013
 813'.54—dc23

                                    2012037789

First Edition: January 2013

10 9 8 7 6 5 4 3 2 1

This book is dedicated to all the hardworking people in America with chronic medical conditions who can't afford decent health insurance or copays or medications because they make "too much" money.

May God bless them, because nobody else does.

Out of Warranty

Prologue

Cassie

For a third of a century, I had lived the happily-ever-after of every Cinderella's dreams, which more than made up for my aches and pains. Then my Prince Charming died in his sleep at fifty-eight—just as we were beginning to spend his retirement touring our magic kingdom together.

We'd been so close for so long that I couldn't even remember what life was like without him, and losing him blasted a huge hole in my world and my soul.

I was supposed to be the one who died, not Tom. I had always been the sickly one, with twenty-four surgeries and four joint replacements. Growing up with all my ailments, I was convinced I'd be dead by forty. I never told anybody; I just believed it.

I have a theory about that: baby boomers like me have never really believed we'd get old. Though the term "baby boomers" originally referred to the boom of births after America's troops came home from World War II, I think there's another "boom" that defined our generation far more deeply: the Big Boom, as in "A-bomb."

I still remember when the teachers at E. Rivers Elementary herded us downstairs to the windowless underground hallway beside the sixth- and seventh-grade classrooms, so we'd know what to do when the Russians dropped "the Bomb."

I remember lectures on what would be safe to eat after a nuclear blast (canned goods), and what wouldn't (fresh food, meat, liquids from anything but cans, things in boxes—unless they were stored in an airtight metal container—and dead animals). "No matter how thirsty or hungry you are," our teachers said, "don't eat or drink any of the dangerous things, or you'll die."

I remember hearing "fallout" on the news, then asking my daddy what it meant. He told me the truth with a worried frown (he always told me the truth), and I tucked that away in my closet of fears.

I remember the signs in every public building directing us to the bomb shelter, usually a dusty underground repository for cots, supplies, and emergency equipment. (I peeked in on several.)

I remember when Civil Defense organized the mamas of Atlanta, who dutifully brought their cars to E. Rivers and every other school in town when I was in kindergarten, then evacuated all us kids from the city. E. Rivers went to Sandy Springs, enjoying our unexpected holiday.

When the evacuation drills stopped, I wondered if Civil Defense and our mamas didn't care about us anymore. Then I realized that the bombs had gotten so powerful, even our mamas couldn't get us to safety in time. That one was hard to swallow, I can tell you, even for a precocious kid like me who'd read the newspaper every day since I was five, then skipped first grade.

Then came the Cuban missile crisis in '62, when the richer families in our neighborhood filled their basements with canned goods and canned Cokes, and staples stored in shiny, new metal garbage cans, and the grown-ups were tense and out of sorts. Those of us who didn't have a basement or enough money for doomsday supplies just prayed, whether we were religious or not.

We boomers grew up with the Big Boom hanging over our heads. In the tick of a clock, death was out there, ready to blast us all to cinders, and America along with us.

Dr. Strangelove. Seven Days in May. On the Beach.

It all confirmed the same conviction: live to the fullest and die young.

But that wasn't all.

I remember the lightning bolt of shock and grief that went through me when my third-grade teacher told us our handsome young President Kennedy had been "assassinated," gunned down in broad daylight, along with the governor of Texas, right on camera. Like my parents, I had fallen for the public image of Camelot, hook, line, and sinker, so I was devastated. That awful day, our teachers tried to shield us, but their fear and horror hung in the air of E. Rivers Elementary like a deadly fog.

Some of the boys were glad, because we didn't get any homework that night, but I lectured them severely for their lack of respect. Then, when I got home, Mama hugged me very tight, then drew me close as she sat glued to the TV, crying. When Daddy got home, he hugged Mama for a long time, and his voice was hoarse when he greeted me. The stark, black-and-white TV image of the blood on Jackie's clothes and the stunned look on her face are still graven, vivid and terrible, in my mind.

Then Jack Ruby killed Lee Harvey Oswald, live on TV. Then "they" killed Robert. Then Dr. King.

In the click of a trigger—boom—death was out there, ready to fell the worst and best of us.

Hence, my theory about why so many in our generation deeply and subconsciously believed we wouldn't live to be old. Teetering on the *Eve of Destruction*, our rebels became hippies and rejected the rules. They tuned out and turned on; flaunted free love to the lilting strains of *sha-la-la-la-la-la, let's live for today*. And they took to the streets to keep our young men from getting killed even sooner in a senseless, unwinnable war.

Then there was Kent State, and another indelible image of senseless death.

And later, firefights from across the world, in living color on the news. The boomer boys who went to Vietnam came back with the death-clock ticking even louder, this time inside their heads and hearts.

So I, along with so many of my generation, was totally shocked to reach middle age, which explains a lot about the boomers' major midlife crises. The divorces. The drugs. The drink.

But not my Prince Charming, my rock, my soul mate, my protector, even while so many other boomers were still shaking the pillars of our society the way the Bomb had shaken their personal foundations as kids. Not my Tom, who was good to the bone.

Staring middle age in the face, most of us boomers had to admit, grudgingly, that we *might* live to be old, but we still didn't really believe it, not down deep. We were still just kids inside, no matter what the mirror told us.

I was like that, till my beloved husband died.

He wasn't supposed to leave me in his sleep, a slight smile on his face. How could I live without my best friend and lover, my confidant and cheerleader, my spiritual partner, my protector?

Even a year and a half later, I missed him as sharply as I had after the funeral when I was alone in the house for the first time.

Once the service was over and the estate was sent to probate, my son Tommy had taken his sweet wife Paige and precious little Ethan and baby Catherine back to Charlotte, and my daughter Haley— desperate to escape the emptiness of our house without her father— had driven her father's car back to her life as a would-be actress and preschool teacher in New Orleans.

Neither of the kids had asked me to come with them, so I didn't bring it up, no matter how much I'd wanted to. They didn't have room for me, anyway, either in their houses or their lives.

Mama used to say that Tom and I were so wrapped up in each other that our son and daughter were the outsiders in the family, but I didn't believe that. Not until I lost Tom, and the kids went right back to their independent lives without me, relegating me to a once-weekly Sunday afternoon phone call.

Who knows? Maybe Mama was right.

Tommy was caught up with being a great dad and making his mark in the techno world to provide for his family. And Haley was busy being Haley, with no strings attached, living with a series of complicated men. (Translate: appalling.)

I've always heard, "A son's a son till he gets him a wife; a daughter's a daughter for the rest of your life." But that didn't apply to my Haley. My daughter came into this world a free spirit, independent to a fault and determined to do everything "my byself!" Even as a newborn, she hadn't wanted to be cuddled. And as she grew older, she never could stand my "butting into her personal life." She'd adored her daddy, but merely tolerated me between arguments.

She'd retaliated for my "interference" by packing her things right after high school graduation and moving to New Orleans "because it's so cool and so *decadent*." I'd cried for months about it, imagining all kinds of calamities, but she was an adult in the eyes of the law, so we couldn't stop her. To her credit, though, and our amazement, she'd worked her way through school to earn a teacher's degree while doing community theater and the occasional singing gig.

Now that Tom wasn't around to buffer us, the most Haley could stand of me was fifteen minutes a week on the phone, as long as I didn't start "criticizing" her decisions—many of which were reckless in the extreme—or "trying to control her." (Translate: asking questions.) If she was in a really good mood, she might talk to me for thirty minutes, but that was the best I got.

Deep down in my darkest place, I secretly suspected that my daughter wished that I had been the one to die, not Tom.

Frankly, I did, too. But that wasn't the way things were, and I was left to make the best of it. Like it or not, Haley was stuck with me, and I was stuck with life alone.

I had no normal life to go back to, not without Tom. The worst time for me was suppertime, when he used to come home from work, and we'd share our day and talk about anything and everything over dinner. To ease the silence without him, I'd started watching TV as I ate, but I wasn't really hungry, so I'd dropped thirty pounds, leaving me gaunt for the first time in my previously plump struggles with my weight. Another irony I didn't appreciate.

Hoping for distraction and better health benefits, I tried to find work, but it wasn't as if I could just go out and get a job. Thanks to the Great Recession, people weren't hiring, anyway, especially not decrepit old homemakers in bad health, with no outside-the-home experience.

Still, I'd networked and run down classifieds and checked the state employment listings, but the only interviews I'd gotten had turned out to be straight sales, with no salary or benefits, or door to door. I'd even broken down and tried flipping burgers at Hamburger Heaven. Demeaning though it was, I figured I'd rise to management really quickly, so I'd taken a slot in the 'burbs, where nobody would recognize me, hoping my legs would hold up.

Who knew how exhausting that would turn out to be? The blasted computerized cash register had completely baffled me, and I only lasted for a week before my joints—real and artificial—had complained so loudly, I'd had to quit, much to my nineteen-year-old supervisor's relief.

This wasn't the way my life was supposed to be. I was supposed to be enjoying Tom's retirement, traveling to all the places we'd never been able to go. Snuggling up with him on rainy mornings, eating in our robes and slippers, then going back to bed to read all day, if we wanted to. Going to Friday matinees to see the latest movies before our friends did. Having the best sex of our lives.

Not unemployed, rattling around in my empty house like a loose bearing in the hubcap of a derelict car.

"Don't make any hasty decisions, Mom," Haley kept telling me. "Give yourself time to get used to things. You'll be fine." That was her new mantra, "You'll be fine," especially when some noise frightened me in the night, and fear made me call her.

"Haley's right," Tommy confirmed in our Sunday afternoon conversations (always after Haley's so I wouldn't end up depressed). "All the books say you should give yourself a chance to adjust for at least a year before you make any major decisions. Maybe two."

I'd given it time, but nothing got better.

Things just got worse.

First, not even a month after the funeral, I discovered a bat infestation behind the attic ceiling, which made my arthritis ten times worse and cost more than fifteen thousand to remediate. Fortunately, the homeowner's insurance paid because of an omission in the exclusions paragraph. (Bats are winged mammals, not rodents, thank goodness.)

Then, on the anniversary of Tom's death, I came home from the grocery store and got bitten by a rabid raccoon, right in my garage in the middle of Garden Hills.

Can we say, "Shades of Stephen King"?

I survived the rabies treatments, only to end up sicker than ever, weak as a baby, and all alone, except for Juliette, who was her own kettle of fish to deal with. (Note to children: never, ever give a parent a pet without permission. Ever. Especially a weird one, no matter how appropriate it may seem.)

I coped. I'd always coped with my ailments and put on a smile. Living with pain all your life, you learn to soldier on. But I refused to spend the last third of my life lying in bed, depressed (in spite of the boatload of antidepressants I was on) and weak. So I had made up my mind to find out what was wrong with me, no matter how many doctors I had to go to.

Life went on, and I would, too. And the first order of business was getting well.

Which was what I was doing that fateful day, trying yet another doctor who'd been referred to me by a holistic internist (after four-thousand-dollars-plus of tests), who at least had acknowledged that something was really wrong with me. Not exactly a brilliant deduction, since I could have told him that for free. *Something* had eaten up all my joints by the time I was forty, but at least he didn't think it was all in my head, as the Emory Clinic had.

If you've got to have something weird wrong with you, you'd better be Canadian, that's all I can say.

With nine years left to go to Medicare (or more, if they moved it back), I was stuck in that deadly place for Americans with odd chronic conditions: too rich to qualify for Medicaid, and too poor to afford decent health coverage and all the fees and medications Green Shield insurance wouldn't pay.

Don't think about it, I ordered myself for the jillionth time as I got ready for my appointment with the new doctor. It only makes you depressed.

I was going to get better, and that was all there was to it.

But then, things got worse.

One

Cassie

A fresh stab of loneliness sharded through me as I looked into my ten-times magnifying makeup mirror-of-the-awful-truth, trying to erase the ravages of grief with concealer for yet another day.

Old. I looked old and haggard.

I closed my eyes. *God, thank you for this day and my life, just as it is,* I prayed as a sacrifice of obedience, wondering how long it would be till I could mean it. *Help me, please. I can't do this without you.* That, I meant with all my heart. *I know your love should fill the hole Tom left in my heart, but it doesn't. I'm sorry, but it doesn't.* As always, I sensed God's consoling arms about me, but it wasn't enough.

Focus on today, I told myself as I did every morning, focus on gratitude, the blessings you have, not what you've lost, and you'll get through this. Think of Haley and Tommy, and Paige and precious Ethan and little Catherine. And Mama.

And the house: it was paid for, even though the taxes were ridiculous. And I had what was left of Tom's life insurance, and my widow's health benefits, even though they cost a fortune and

11

didn't cover squat. Still, that was a lot more than some people had these days. And I had new knees and new hips and plates and screws that worked just fine. I needed to focus on that.

Instead, I focused on that honkin' huge zit beside my nose in the mirror.

There's just something so *wrong* about having zits and arthritis at the same time. I broke out the workout makeup, waterproof and thick enough to cover a doorknob, converting the zit to a mere lump that I hoped would be taken for a mole.

Thirty minutes later—dressed, made up, and coiffed—I braved the muggy July heat and left Juliette to do her business in the backyard while I went to the mailbox before heading to my appointment with the new ENT/allergist. In the mail I found a Chico's flyer, catalogues from Vermont Country Store and Harriet Carter, my bank statement, a notice from the Fulton County tax assessor's office, and an explanation of benefits from Green Shield Heath Insurance (or the antichrist, as I thought of them).

Always one to face the music without delay, I opened the bank statement first. Though I knew things had been a lot more expensive lately than I'd planned, I wasn't prepared for the closing balance.

Shoot a monkey!

Half a million dollars of life insurance had seemed like a lot till I'd paid off all my medical bills, plus the refi and equity line we'd done in 2005, and the kids' student loans. I'd also bought a dependable hybrid minivan to last me the rest of my life, which I now suspected would be cruelly long. (Mama was eighty-nine and strong as an ox, in much better shape physically and mentally than I was. It would be just my luck to inherit her longevity along with Daddy's bad bones.)

I looked at the closing balance again and shook my head in mute denial. I was down to only two hundred thousand and facing more medical bills, plus property taxes out the wazoo, thanks to my location in what was now considered Buckhead.

Speaking of taxes, I switched to the letter from the assessor's office, hoping they'd reduced the value of my house to reflect the depressed market. Then I opened it and discovered that they'd reassessed the house, all right: they'd upped it by fifty thousand!

Based on what? Nothing but foreclosures and short sales had sold in our neighborhood for almost a year!

Shoot, shoot, shoot! My blood pressure shot up, making my pulse pound like an anvil in the July heat.

I would have contested the increase, but I didn't have the moxie, and Tom had always fought our battles for us.

Tucking the bank statement and reassessment under my arm, I wheezed as I walked back up the gentle slope of our short drive-way. One more letter left to open.

I ripped the end off the explanation of benefits. For thirteen hundred dollars a month, plus a two-thousand annual deductible and out-of-pocket, my Green Shield PPO should at least cover sixty percent of the four thousand dollars plus I'd spent on tests and IV treatments at the holistic internist's. Never mind that all I'd gotten for my money was some validation and a referral to the ENT/allergist I was seeing that day.

I unfolded the EOB, scanning from the doctor's out-of-network fees to the zero fee adjustment, to the zero payout. Patient respon-sibility: $4,267.53.

What was with *that?* I'd already met my out-of-pocket for the year!

I looked at the code numbers beside the lab fees and treatment charges, then the key printed at the bottom. Disallowed: not standard medical practice. Disallowed: not standard medical practice. Disallowed. Disallowed. Disallowed. Followed by the fatal: non-negotiable.

The antichrist had shafted me completely, not even applying any of it to my deductibles or payout ceiling!

I got so mad, I almost hyperventilated.

Criminal. The insurance company was criminal. And they knew I couldn't go elsewhere for coverage. Nobody would have me. I'd spent well over fifteen thousand just on coverage in the year since Tom had died, and that didn't even include dental or optometrist. And this was what all that money had bought me?

Afraid I might stroke out, I shepherded Juliette back into the blessed cool inside the house. I dumped the mail, then put her away in my bedroom.

Blasted crummy coverage, but what was I supposed to do? I couldn't go uninsured, and it was 2012, so I didn't dare opt for Obama's high-risk pool because of all the court challenges.

"I'll be back later," I called to Juliette through the door. Not that she cared. She slept all day on her pink bed stuffed with cedar chips.

Some company.

On the way out, I grabbed my purse and keys from their hiding place in the bread drawer. I activated the security system alarm, then headed for Dr. Patel's.

At least he was in network. The antichrist would *have* to pay at least seventy percent.

That's what I thought, anyway, before I heard the dreaded "usual and customary treatment" loophole.

Fifteen minutes later, I drove up to yet another expensive parking lot entrance at yet another medical complex in Buckhead, so weak and depressed I could hardly sit up.

Rolling down the window to take my stub, I was smacked with a flood of heat and humidity that wilted me even further. Though I snatched the parking stub the nanosecond it appeared, the wretched machine scolded me with a loud, grating buzz anyway. Blasted machines. They'd leeched the humanity out of everything.

All the parking spaces within a thousand feet of the building were filled, and the lot sizzled in the sun.

I coughed heavily, rattling loose some of the "psychosomatic" gunk (according to the doctors at Emory, who had run a jillion tests, then referred me to a psychologist) in my lungs.

For some bizarre reason, the handicapped spaces were at the far side of the lot. Gasping, I pulled into one (with four joint replacements, you get a handicapped pass, and you need it), sicker than I'd ever been, and lonely to the bone.

Cursed Green Shield.

I got out of my car into the hazy heat, then trudged to the atrium lobby, arriving breathless and light-headed. The elevators—of course—were on the far side of the atrium. Whoever designed this place must never have been sick and alone.

When the elevator doors finally opened, I stepped inside and pressed three as a young mother with a stroller whipped in beside me.

I looked at the child in the stroller. "What a cutie." I studied her big, black eyes and was rewarded with a deeply dimpled smile. "What floor?" I asked her mother.

"Five, please," her mother said with a grateful nod.

"How old is she?" I guessed nine months.

"Nine months," the mother said proudly, bending to stroke her daughter's fuzzy halo.

Bingo. "I have a three-year-old grandson and a ten-month-old granddaughter."

"That's nice," the mother said, clearly not interested.

Embarrassed by her dismissal, I realized I was officially one of those old ladies who bothered perfect strangers in the elevator. Shoot.

At the third floor, I waved to the baby as I got off, then headed for the main corridor. But a familiar bladder sensation caused me to back up and detour to the ladies' room. After four bladder tacks, the last of which was failing, I agreed with George Burns: "Never pass up a chance to pee." The rest of the quote was X-rated, but I agreed with most of it, too, except the sex part.

The last thing in the world on my mind was sex.

After finishing and washing my hands, I braved a series of hall-ways that seemed to be numbered at random, in search of my doc-tor's office.

The Web site had provided directions to the address, but it should have given me a map of the maze inside. Hopelessly con-fused, I halted briefly, lost.

Maybe it was a sign that I shouldn't go to this new guy. Save my money, go back to bed and not get up.

Then I started coughing again. Breathless by the time the spell ended, I steadied myself against the wall, seeing stars.

Maybe I should go to the doctor, after all, even though he might end up bleeding me for tests and start-up fees, pun intended. If somebody didn't help me, I was going to croak, no two ways about it. For all I'd said I wanted to die since the funeral, when it came down to it, I wasn't ready. I couldn't leave my son and daughter orphaned, and I loved my grandchildren to distraction. And what good would the money I had left do me if I croaked from my "psychosomatic" condition?

I decided to take the chance on Dr. Patel. So I'd end up in the poorhouse a few days sooner. At least I would have tried.

I turned down yet another hallway and discovered I'd been going in a circle.

Shoot!

Then I spotted a sign pointing toward a snack bar and set out to get directions, mustering up the last of my energy to put on a happy face for the world one more time.

Two

Jack

Another blasted doctor.

And of course, this new one's office was as far from the handi-capped parking as it could possibly be. Jack's copy of *Pillars of the Earth* felt like it weighed twenty pounds by the time he finally found the door marked FUNGAL INSTITUTE, with SHAMLAN PATEL, M.D., underneath.

Fungal Institute. What were they doing? Educating fungus?

Jack had had his fill of educating anything.

And what had happened to all the American doctors, anyway? The last four he'd been to were from India or Pakistan. Jack didn't trust anybody who could speak a language he didn't understand behind his back.

But he went in anyway, because his lips and fingernails were even bluer than usual, thanks to the heat wave and the Code Or-ange alert.

Inside, the waiting area was spartan and empty of patients: hardly any magazines on the slightly shabby coffee tables; a scat-tering of leather chairs and sofas; a white machine that looked like a square R2-D2 roaring away in one corner and a springwater dispenser in the other. As he approached the reception desk, the metal running foot on his prosthesis clanged on the tile floor, alternating with a slap from the flip-flop he wore on his remaining foot.

In the twenty-five years since he'd lost his leg, Jack had long since accepted it, but every time he went somewhere new, he had to endure people's reactions, which got on his nerves.

He leaned in at the high counter and said to a pert-looking brunette girl at the desk, "I'm Jack Wilson. My pulmonologist referred me." He'd stopped trying to remember the doctors' names. All they did was run expensive tests, charge him a fortune, and refer him to somebody else.

"If you'll just fill these out, please." The aggressively cheerful girl laid the usual clipboard full of forms on the counter between them. Jack eyed them with annoyance. In thirty-two years as a professor, he'd filled out enough forms for three lifetimes. "My doctor already sent over my records."

The girl smiled, undaunted. "We received them, and Dr. Patel has reviewed them. These are to update us about your condition and coverage as of today."

Ah, the magic word: coverage.

The one thing he had was coverage. Jack looked down at the long list of symptoms and yes/no blanks in mouse type. Blasted forms. Then a delicious thought brought a sardonic smile to his face. "What if I refuse?"

Her annoying cheer didn't falter. "Then you are free to find another doctor to help you with your problem."

Rats.

He hated perky little control freaks like the receptionist, but he felt so awful, he really didn't have a choice. "You're sure you take Medicare and are in network for American Supplemental," he accused in retaliation.

She beamed. "Absolutely."

Jack snatched the clipboard and sat down in a singularly uncomfortable leather chair. The top sheet of the papers said that the doctor would scope his sinuses every time, to the tune of seven hundred sixty-nine dollars a pop, and Jack would be liable for whatever the insurance provider didn't cover. And if he didn't sign, they wouldn't treat him.

Medical blackmail! That was a new low. This guy must be a real humanitarian.

If Jack wasn't so blasted sick, he'd walk out.

But he knew he wouldn't, regardless of how much he wanted to leave. He'd earned his COPD by smoking in his professor's cubicle for all those years before he was diagnosed, but lately, the expensive antibiotics his pulmonologist prescribed had only made him sicker. If he didn't do something, he'd die.

Not that he minded dying too much. He actually looked forward to heaven. It was just that, when he got right down to it, he wasn't quite ready to give up on this life, difficult though it was. If nothing else, he didn't want to leave his four kids and six grandchildren to his nutcase of an ex-wife. So he filled out the cursed forms and turned them in.

"The doctor got held up in surgery," the receptionist said cheerily as she accepted them, "so I'm afraid there will be a short wait. May I get you anything?"

Jack grinned again. It had always smoothed things over for him. "I'd love a ham sandwich." And a good, stiff drink.

"Sorry," she said. Her smile breaking at last, she leaned forward to whisper, "No bread within a mile of here. Yeast is a fungus, you know."

Jack arched an eyebrow, then settled on the leather sofa closest to the water dispenser just as a striking woman of probably about fifty blew into the room, bringing with her the scent of expensive perfume and an unmistakable aura of energy, despite her slow step and strained expression.

"Sorry I'm late," she told the receptionist, pulling forms from her expensive purse.

Jack knew all about expensive perfumes and purses from his ex, may she roast for renouncing not only him, but God, when she'd left Jack for a married man at forty.

"I filled these out at home." The Buckhead woman handed the forms to the receptionist, then leaned on the high counter to confide, "I hope your boss can do something to help, or I might just expire on the spot. I'm not kidding. I've already been to five doctors, with no luck."

Oh, Lord. A talker.

Jack had had his fill of narcissists, too, so he buried his nose in the book before this one could zero in on him.

Typical of the self-absorbed, she ignored the visual cue and plopped down on the other end of the sofa, despite all the empty seating in the room. With just one cushion between them, he could hear her wheezing softly.

He briefly glanced from his book to see if her fingernails were cyanotic, too.

They weren't, but that was all the encouragement she needed. She pinned him with a look and asked earnestly, "Have you been to Dr. Patel before?"

He would have told her it was none of her blasted business, but his mother had done her best to inculcate some manners in him, so he responded with a terse, "No," then buried his nose back in the book. As with all the books he read—usually ten a week—he forced himself to read on, though the material had gotten a bit tedious for his taste. He'd had his fill of serious tomes when he was a teacher, but he always finished any book he started. It was the principle of the thing. If the author had written it, there must have been a reason, and Jack was willing to give the writer the benefit of the doubt.

The woman on the other end of his couch cranked her mouth to one side, shifting her focus to the middle distance with a sigh. "This is my first time, too. I've been to the best doctors in town for the last thirty years, and they all end up treating me like a hypochondriac. Never mind that *something* ate up my joints by the time I was forty. If it wasn't for that blasted rabid raccoon . . ."

Even Jack couldn't let a conversational bombshell like that pass. "What rabid raccoon?"

She picked up a magazine, perusing it instead of looking at him. "The one that attacked me in my garage when I got out of my car six months ago." She turned the page. "Doggone thing, right there in the middle of Garden Hills. When I heard it coming at me, I almost made it back into my car, but he cut underneath and glommed onto my left ankle, biting, biting, biting."

Jack dropped his guard along with his book. "How could you tell it was rabid?"

Her brows went up as she paged slowly through the magazine. "Oh, there was no question."

Of all times for her to withhold the details. Annoyed, Jack prodded, "How could you be so sure?"

She laid the magazine in her lap. "Because it came after me like it was shot out of a cannon, and it sounded like this." She placed her hands like a megaphone and roared out a bellowing screech that sounded like a plane crash and a dogfight, rolled into one.

So loud, the receptionist squeaked and a woman in white bolted through the back-office door in alarm.

"Sorry," the raccoon woman said demurely. "I was just showing him how I knew the raccoon that bit me was rabid."

The nurse, or whatever she was, placed a hand to her heart. "Oh. Well, please don't do that again."

The raccoon woman granted her a ladylike smile. "I won't. Sorry I scared you." She picked her magazine back up and continued paging through it as if nothing had happened.

Jack tucked his chin and reopened his book, but he couldn't concentrate.

This was no ordinary woman. No ordinary woman would make that noise in public. Why did he always attract the nutcases? Still, he couldn't stop himself from asking, "Did you have to take the shots?"

"Yep." Again, she focused on the magazine instead of him. "I got so weak after the shots started that I could barely get out of bed. I mean, usually I'm up at six and don't stop till ten at night, but I was like limp spaghetti." Her gaze fixed on a peach-garnished cake in the magazine. "Still am. I called the CDC, but they said fatigue wasn't a side effect of the rabies vaccine. Plus, my yeast infection went out of control."

Jack actually blushed. He knew about women's yeast infections from his ex, and he was surprised this woman had shared such an intimate matter with a strange man. But narcissists always thought everyone was interested in every detail of their lives, even the gross ones.

She looked at him and grinned. "Not *that* kind of yeast infection. My *sinuses*. And my lungs."

He didn't know people had yeast infections in their sinuses and lungs. He changed the subject. "Were you afraid when it bit you?"

She chuckled, lighting up her face and taking years off her. "No." Her grin diminished, but not her humor. "I was royally ticked off. I didn't have *time* for all that nonsense. I was settling my husband's estate." She let out a brief sigh. "When I looked down and saw that thing biting me, I said, 'Dear Lord, whatever are you thinking, letting this poor animal bite me?'" She paged over. "Then I clobbered it senseless with my purse and turned over my garbage can on top of it. After that, I managed to get back in the car and slam the door and call 911."

Most women Jack knew would have gone hysterical. "Did it stay under the garbage can?"

She smiled at him again, as if it were all some joke. "Yep. Once the police and firemen had it trapped, I drove myself to the hospital and told them that I needed antibiotics and rabies vaccine right away, because I have two artificial joints in that leg, and every infection goes straight to your joint replacements. So they took me right in, but it was a while before the vaccine defrosted and I got the shots."

"Shots, plural?" Jack thought aloud.

The raccoon woman held up four fingers and ticked off, "Rabies, tetanus, enough antibiotics to kill a horse, and rabies immune gamma globulin." She winked at him. "Two in the arms and two in the arse."

Way too intimate. Was she coming on to him?

The last thing in this God's good earth Jack wanted was another

25

woman, especially one as gabby as this one. He liked his solitude. And *silence*.

If he got lonely, he read a romance novel—always an historical, and only by a good writer, like Mary Balogh. *The only safe sex is between these covers*, a romance writer had once autographed one of her books for him when he'd stumbled on her signing. She was right.

Flirting women, uh-uh, even when they were as handsome as this one. Jack was firmly set in his independent ways, and he had no intention of changing.

That was always what women wanted men to do: change. Shave before you kissed them. Dress nicer. Clean house. Put the milk back in the refrigerator. Wear something besides shorts and Hawaiian shirts and flip-flops. *Talk*.

Even if he did want a woman at this late stage in his life, he'd been on blood-pressure medicine so long, he wasn't sure he could do anything about it once he got her.

He opened his book again and tried to focus. Halfway down the page, he heard himself ask, "So, how did you find out about Dr. Patel?"

The raccoon woman kept leafing through the magazine. "A friend told me about a holistic internist who cured her of a long-term fungal sinus infection, so I went there and had four thousand dollars' worth of tests and treatments." She turned the page. "The guy's an M.D., but he isn't in network for anybody, and doesn't file insurance. I was desperate, so I paid him and filed the charges myself. Then Green Shield stiffed me completely and applied what little it covered to my thirty-five-hundred-dollar out-of-network deductible." Her features lofty, she exhaled heavily in disgust. "As opposed to my thirty-five-hundred-dollar *in*-network deductible."

Jack hated to have to prod, but he couldn't stand leaving things unresolved. "So, what did he tell you for all that money?"

"He said yeast was causing my arthritis, then sent me here."

Typical. They take your money, then send you to somebody else who can take your money.

The woman laid down her magazine and looked at him. "What about you?" she asked.

She'd answered his questions, so Jack supposed he ought to reciprocate with something. "Similar."

The door to the back office opened, and the woman in white stuck her head out to say, "Mrs. Jones, the doctor will see you now."

Jack arched an eyebrow. Whatever happened to first come, first served?

Mrs. Jones told Jack as she rose, "Nice talking to you."

Talking *at* him would be more accurate. He reopened his book and resumed reading. With luck, he'd never see the woman again.

Nutcases. They always found him.

Three

Cassie

I opened the door to Dr. Patel's office and saw that the place definitely needed a decorator: bland beige tiles; sparse, mismatched furniture, all in solids; no pictures on the beige walls. No flowers. No plants.

The only person there—a scruffy, one-legged man on a sofa at the far side of the waiting room—glared at me as if I were invading his personal space. His linen shorts were creased into a hundred tiny folds across his lap, and he had on a limp Hawaiian shirt and one flip-flop on his only foot. His fake lower leg was one of those high-tech running ones, without a shoe.

Then he buried his nose in *Pillars of the Earth*.

Perfect. Yet another pompous ass. Lately, that seemed to be all I ran into.

Not that I let anything like that deter me from being civil. But I refused to let anybody intimidate me anymore, so I deliberately sat at the other end of the sofa he occupied. Then I picked up a copy of *Southern Living* and started scanning through it. But when he looked over at me, curiosity took possession of my voice. "Have you been to Dr. Patel before?"

His features congealed as if I'd asked him if he slept in the nude. "No." He buried his gaze back in *Pillars of the Earth*, a book that had gotten a bit too long for me when I'd tried to read it, but then again, I hadn't been able to concentrate since Tom died. From the look of it, this guy wasn't having a much better time with it than I had.

Books had always been my blessed distraction and deliverance from pain, but since the funeral, I'd been way too ADD to read for pleasure, which left yet another gaping hole in my life.

I glanced back at my magazine, but it had been so long since I'd had a chance to talk to anybody in person besides the kids or a doctor or a repairman—much less somebody in the same boat, medically—that I looked into the middle distance and confessed to the curmudgeon, "This is my first time, too. I've been to the best doctors in town for the last thirty years, and they all end up treating me like a hypochondriac. Never mind that *something* ate up my joints by the time I was forty. I wouldn't be *here* if it wasn't for that blasted rabid raccoon . . ."

That caught his interest.

We discussed the incident until the nurse stuck out her head and said, "Mrs. Jones, Dr. Patel is ready to see you." Translate: we're going to stick you into an exam room and make you wait another ten to thirty minutes, even though it's already almost an hour past your appointment time.

I dropped the magazine and said good-bye to the scruffy flip-flop man, then followed the nurse back to the exam room, where she squirted bitter-tasting spray up my nostrils, then said, "We'll just wait for that to take effect, then the doctor will be in to examine you."

I'd had to sign a statement that said the doctor would always look up my sinuses with an endoscope, which cost more than $750, every visit, so I prepared myself to kiss another chunk of change from Tom's life insurance good-bye.

There I was in this funky dentist's chair with only a fraction of the money I'd need to stay in my house and keep my health insurance till Medicare and Social Security kicked in, and yet another doctor to pay. This had better be good.

The door to the exam room opened, and in walked a dapper little Indian man no taller than five three, looking through the detailed medical history I'd given them, his nurse in tow. He had on one of those round, shiny forehead reflectors you used to see in old doctor ads in the fifties, and some odd kind of rubber treads that strapped over his shoes. "Good morning, Mrs. Jones," he said without looking up, no trace of an accent beyond the lilting cadence of his speech. "I wish all our patients provided us with such a detailed history. It would make my job a lot easier."

Tom had researched my medical records and done the printed history on the computer. After twenty-four surgeries and all the meds I'd taken, it was the only way I could keep things straight. "My late husband did that for me."

The nurse smiled and nodded. "Very thorough. I'm impressed."

Good. She'd forgiven me for scaring her. I read her name tag. "Thank you, Kay. I'm Cassie."

Dr. Patel closed the file and set it aside, then perched on a rolling stool and faced me. "Mrs. Jones, you are full of yeast." So much for bedside manner. "Probably candida, and some bacterial involvement, as well."

He felt the soft tissues below my jaw. "Please open your mouth wide and stick out your tongue."

When I obliged, he frowned, and drew back. "Yeast on the tongue."

Kay leaned closer and confirmed his diagnosis with a nod.

"But I gave up bread and cheese and sugar three weeks ago, when Dr. Manning told me to," I defended. "And I've been taking the fluconazole he prescribed." An antifungal.

Dr. Patel prepared the endoscope. "That's an excellent first step, but chronic fungal infections can hide everywhere in the body once they're established. Even the brain." He cocked his head like a bird. "Have you been experiencing any brain fog?"

Brain fog? There was a technical term for you.

"I lost my husband of thirty-five years a year ago, with no warning," I said. "Then I got bitten by the rabid raccoon and had to take the shots. Under the circumstances, I figured it was normal not to be able to think so straight."

"Please accept my condolences on your loss," he said without emotion, "but your thinking can definitely be affected by your fungal infection." He wiped the endoscope with a sterile cloth. "Let's take a look at your sinuses. Please lean back and close your eyes."

He ran the instrument up my nose, but I barely felt it. There must have been a deadener in that spray the nurse gave me. I stole a peek at the small TV monitor, then closed my eyes to spare myself the gross details.

The doctor said, "There is a great deal of infection here. We'll culture it to confirm, but as I surmised, you have both fungal and bacterial." He pressed a foot pedal and sucked out a small portion of my brain, then he did it again. "Documenting my diagnosis in this way makes it impossible for your insurance company to deny coverage."

At least he was aware of that. "Good."

Ah, but that was before I got the explanation of benefits forms blazoned with "surgical procedure: not usual or customary treatment."

He put away his brain-sucker, then leaned back and reviewed my records. "My examination and your history suggest that you have a rare genetic form of arthritis secondary to an immune deficiency and an extremely severe allergy to any form of yeast, mold, or fungus."

Hello, this was the South! Mold was everywhere. We hadn't even had air-conditioning when I grew up.

"When you're exposed," he went on, "your body doesn't make antibodies as it should. Instead, the allergens attach directly to your T cells, which violently overreact and flood your system with inflammatory agents. So instead of making you sneeze, the reaction puts your whole body into inflammatory mode and burned up both your pituitary system and your joints."

All because I was allergic to mold? I frowned. "Run that by me again?"

"It's genetic, as I said," he repeated, as if he were speaking to a child, "occurring in one or more of nine genes that govern your immune system. This has been going on all your life. When you were young, your thyroid gland could help deal with the situation, but with age and progressive exposure, it has gotten worse. The chronic inflammation damaged your hormone regulators, which explains the hormone and infertility problems you've had, including your thyroid conversion deficiency."

I'd always been interested in science and biology, so I kept up with the latest developments, and his explanation sounded plausible.

He turned to the nurse. "Kay, give her the pituitary."

Kay handed me a stapled sheaf of papers titled "Pituitary Effects and Chronic Fungal Infections" from the stack file on the wall. "Don't let all this overwhelm you," she soothed. "Just take it in as you can. Everything will be on these sheets, to look at later when you have more time."

Apparently, she was the humane part of the practice. "Thanks."

Dr. Patel went on as if she weren't there. "As soon as possible, I'd like for you to see Dr. William Porter, an endocrinologist I've been working with. Many of my patients need human growth hormone, so he'll need to test you for that and a few other things."

Another doctor? How much was *that* going to set me back?

Was it a law, now, that doctors had to refer you to another specialist? I tried to collect myself.

Talk about good-news, bad-news. Finally, a medical doctor explained what had been wrong with me all my life, why I'd had the joints of an eighty-year-old by the time I was forty. But he hadn't mentioned a cure. "Is there a cure for this condition?"

He shook his head. "No, the condition is not curable at present."

Great. Umpty-jillion dollars for this visit, plus yet another referral, just to find out I had an incurable condition.

Shoot.

My disappointment must have showed, because Dr. Patel hastened to reassure me with, "Do not be discouraged, Mrs. Jones. We have had very good luck managing the condition with diet, medication, and environmental controls." He turned to his nurse. "Kay, give her the rest."

Kay pulled out eight different sets of papers from the stack file, then handed them to me. "These will explain everything. Feel free to call me if there's anything you don't understand, and I'll do my best to answer your questions."

I accepted them, daunted by how many there were, but grateful for her offer of help.

Kay slipped out as Dr. Patel forged ahead with, "Because these infections become entrenched in the lower digestive tract, we find that most of our patients have developed extensive food allergies. There's a definitive test available, called the ALCAT, that actually challenges the patient's blood with various foods, then observes and records the white cell reactions at intervals over a thirty-six hour period. You'll need that test to determine the best diet for you, but I'm afraid it's not covered by insurance."

Of course.

He hadn't mentioned a price tag, which was a bad sign. "And how much will that cost?"

"Two thousand." He didn't even blink when he told me.

Clearly, this guy was clueless about his patients' finances. "And it will help?"

"Immensely. Once we determine the severity and extent of your food allergies, we can come up with a rotation diet that will reduce your allergic reponses. That, coupled with probiotics, mold remediation of your environment, and the MRV vaccines" —whatever that was— "we'll be giving you, can arrest the inflammation and further destruction of your joints."

Ah. A light in the tunnel.

My last appointment with the orthopedist, I'd burst into tears when he'd showed me the latest X-ray of my spine, riddled with bone spurs and degenerated discs. A disaster waiting to happen. If I could stop the damage in my joints before it got any worse . . .

Then it occurred to me that there was one more thing I needed to tell this guy. "You mention allergies," I said. "What about pets?"

Dr. Patel frowned. "I'm afraid most pets harbor mold, not to mention bringing it in from outside. Are you allergic to dogs and cats?"

"Only in the past few years."

He was going to croak when he found out about Juliette. Everybody did.

"Then I'm afraid you must find yours another place to live," he said.

"Oh, I don't have dogs or cats."

He cocked an eyebrow, clearly waiting for me to tell him what I did have.

"Actually, I have a pig. Just a little one, a Dutch miniature, and she's very clean. I wash her every day."

That broke through his cold exterior. His eyebrows shot up like Stan Laurel's of Laurel and Hardy. "A pig?"

"Well, I'm allergic to dogs and cats and feathers," I explained, "so my son and daughter gave her to me after my husband died. To keep me company." When he continued to stare at me as if I were a lab specimen, I added, "So I wouldn't be afraid when I'm alone in the house."

"A pig." He shook his head.

"As I said," I defended, wondering why even as I did, "she's very clean, and very intelligent. Uses a litter box or goes outside. I wash her every night." The worst thing was, most people thought I was trying to imitate Suzanne Sugarbaker from *Designing Women*, but I seriously doubted Dr. Patel had ever seen the show.

Judging from his response, I decided to wait till later to mention the bat infestation.

36

Dr. Patel frowned in thought. "Well, as long as you keep her washed with the antifungal and are meticulously careful with her waste disposal," he said, "I suppose that could be all right. But only if you don't get symptoms."

Part of me was relieved, but the other part was disappointed not to have a medical excuse to get rid of her if I wanted to. "Okay. So much for the pig."

With that out of the way, I shifted the topic back to my medical problems. "If I do everything you tell me to, will I get my energy back?"

He finally looked me in the eye. "Yes. Antibiotics feed yeast, so your body has been seriously crippled by the large doses you had to take with the rabies vaccine. You could not avoid them, of course, but we can counteract a lot of those side effects with antifungal medication and the MRV vaccine. I think you'll be feeling much better by next week, when I see you again."

Next week? Another seven-hundred-dollar visit?

But he seemed so certain he could help me, I was inclined to believe him. Still, I knew from experience that even dedicated doctors could be wrong. What if it just turned out to be a lot of hoo-ha?

I couldn't go on the way I was, though. "Ever since the rabies treatments," I confessed, "I've felt like I was dying."

He looked me in the eye again, his tone dead level. "You were, Mrs. Jones. Many people die from widespread fungal infections like these if they remain untreated."

"Emory X-rayed my chest, then said it was all in my head."

"They were acting on outdated information. Yeast and fungi have the same density as lung tissue, so they do not show up on X-rays. And since most people have yeast in their bodies to some degree, cultures are not definitive. Diagnosis of chronic fungal arthritis is cumulative and exclusive." Whatever that meant.

He went on. "This condition has only been discovered recently, which is why insurance companies don't like to pay for necessary treatments, but we're working to convince them and the medical community. I assure you, we can help you."

Chronic fungal arthritis. I didn't know whether to be glad or horrified. Either way, though, he'd sold me.

"Mrs. Jones?" he asked, breaking me out of my eddying thoughts. "Shall I schedule the ALCAT for you today?"

Might as well bite the bullet. "Okay. I guess."

I saw Kay escort the curmudgeon to the next exam room past mine, and wondered if he'd get the same news—and bill—that I did.

"Very good," Dr. Patel told me. "Kay will take the blood samples, then teach you to give yourself your first MRV injection here in the office, where we can observe your reaction."

Kay appeared with a bloodsucker tray. "What concentration do you think she'll need?" she asked Dr. Patel. "I'm guessing a twelve."

"I think that will be best," he said.

He left as she tourniqueted my upper arm. I looked away when she slid in the butterfly needle, but didn't even feel it. "Wow. You're good."

"Thanks." She undid the tourniquet with a snap, the other hand steadying the vial of blood. After three more vials, she finished. "If you'll come with me to the lab, I'll go over how to give yourself the injections, then you can practice with saline while I make up your vaccine."

"I gave my husband allergy shots for years," I told her as I collected my things and followed.

"Do you have a problem with getting injections yourself?" she asked.

After twenty-four surgeries? I'd be out of luck if I did. "No. I give myself a B_{12} shot once a month."

"Well, this will be much easier, just a tiny injection under the skin."

I sat in the lab chair. "How often will I have to do it?"

"Once or twice a week."

If it would help, I'd gladly do it six times a day.

I'd just given myself the first dose of vaccine when the doctor stuck his head in. "Kay, would you please prep Mr. Wilson while I finish talking to Mrs. Jones?"

So the curmudgeon's name was Wilson. Fitting, as in Mr. Wilson to Dennis the Menace. Only this one was nicer looking, under that unruly hair and stubble.

As the nurse left, Dr. Patel motioned me to follow him back into the exam room, where he inspected the little bubble of vaccine I'd injected just under the skin. "Good. No signs of reaction."

"What about this mold remediation you mentioned?" I asked him.

"Many of my patients also have chemical sensitivities, so conventional mold treatments can leave their houses uninhabitable. For that reason, we use a new nontoxic mold and bacteria killer that also kills MRSA. It's a citrus-seed derivative that's safe for use on fabrics and porous surfaces. Developed by a nurse."

I liked that part, developed by a nurse.

The doctor went on. "You'll find two remediators listed on your mold-remediation sheet. Either of them is qualified. They can explain what's involved." He shot me a warning scowl. "You might be able to find someone cheaper out there, but these are the only two who can guarantee you a safe, mold-free environment when they're done."

Again, my discouragement must have showed. "I know this is a lot to take in," Dr. Patel said, "but it's an essential part of your recovery."

Ka-ching, ka-ching. Dollar signs shot past me faster than male drivers on the I-75/85 connector.

I hated to sound like a broken record, but I had to ask, "For how much?"

"It varies, but if you wish to get better, it must be done. They'll have to take a look to make an estimate. One charges for an estimate, but he's very good, and the fee applies to the cost of remediation. The other gives free estimates."

Three guesses who I planned to call.

Then he dropped the next bombshell. "Meanwhile, you'll need to use allergy encasements and wash all your clothes and bedding and curtains in the antifungal detergent, then store them in airtight bags till your house is clear. And you'll need to wipe down everything—walls, floors, cabinets, furniture, inside and out—with the cleaning solution. Most people use a new garden sprayer. I'll write the prescriptions for the solution. They have it downstairs at the compounding pharmacy. Unfortunately, they do not file insurance."

Of course.

"I'm also prescribing a specific liquid multivitamin," he said as he scribbled away on his prescription pad, "and some strong probiotics, plus some supplements to compensate for the malabsorption issues this condition causes. Take the beta-glucan, thyroid, and glutathione liposomal thirty minutes before you eat in the morning. You won't be able to find these supplements just anywhere, and I want you to use the exact ones I prescribe, so we can be sure you're getting what you need."

More dollar signs sped past my eyes at a daunting rate. But I couldn't go on the way I was, so I would give it a try.

The nurse returned with a little manila envelope and a box of slender syringes. "Here's your vaccine."

I looked inside the envelope and found a small vial of vaccine with a cold pack.

"Keep that refrigerated," the doctor told me as he rose.

Just when I thought it was all over, he added, "For the present, eliminate sugar, dairy, all grains, ferments—including beer, wine, soy sauce, and vinegar—and mushrooms from your diet, and try to avoid carbs. Yeast thrives on carbs and sugar. The Atkins introductory diet is a good way to starve them."

Perfect. I was a celibate, teetotaling, nonsmoking Baptist, so sweets were the only vice left to me, and now he was taking that away. "How long will I have to cut out the sugar?"

"Forever, if you want to get well," he said without a shred of sympathy.

Visions of Baskin-Robbins chocolate ice cream cones and blueberry Dunkin' Donuts made me salivate. We wouldn't even talk about Henri's Bakery's éclairs.

"There's a good book called *Mastering the Zone*, by Barry Sears, that can help you with that. You might want to pick up a copy."

For seven hundred dollars a visit, he ought to give me one!

Suddenly, it was all too much. Books to read, supplements to buy that wouldn't be covered by my insurance or deductible on my taxes, two-thousand-dollar tests, high-protein diets that would cost me an arm and a leg, mold remediation that would probably cost a fortune. No more doughnuts or ice cream, not even a little.

Not to mention the fact that I felt like hell on wheels. Overwhelmed, I wanted to do an *I Love Lucy waaaaah*.

I folded my lips inward in an effort to control myself, but it didn't work. The tears escaped, taking my washable mascara with them down my cheeks.

"Now, now." Dr. Patel gave my upper arm an awkward pat. "Once you get everything going, you'll feel much better. You may even be able to decrease your antidepressants. Depression can be a symptom of this condition, as well as brain fog."

I couldn't help it. I lashed out with, "Maybe your patients are depressed because they've lived with pain all their lives and been treated like hypochondriacs. Not to mention how much all this is gonna cost. I don't have a money bush in the backyard, you know."

The man actually looked astonished, but his nurse stepped in with, "Why don't you come with me to get some springwater?"

I'd rather have a double Whopper, hold the mayo and the onions, but what was I going to do? Burgers were off the list forever—or buns, anyway. But what was a burger without a bun?

I clamped my lips into a crooked line and followed her to checkout.

Sympathetic, she gave me the cup of springwater, but that didn't keep her from further assaulting me with, "You'll need a nasal irrigator, which they have downstairs, and Dr. Patel recommends the Swissair air purifier for your bedroom." She handed me a catalogue turned to that page, but all I saw was the $899.00 price. "You'll find it in here, along with pillow, mattress, and box spring encasements that you need to wash in the special detergent, then put on any beds and pillows you use."

Ka-ching, ka-ching, ka-ching!

The receptionist smiled as she presented me with a bill for two thousand, seven hundred ninety-three dollars. That came out to more than forty-six dollars and fifty cents a minute!

"But he's in-network," I sputtered.

She didn't bat an eyelash.

Counting the cost of the holistic internist, that was almost six thousand dollars in less than a month that wasn't covered by my insurance. Not to mention those prescriptions he'd ordered.

"I know about the two thousand for the ALCAT," I said, "but the rest—I've already met my deductibles for the year."

"Unfortunately, as the statement you signed told you," she said cheerily, "you are liable for any charges not covered by Green Shield, and your current balance reflects your new patient fees and charges. I'm sorry, but that's our policy."

I managed not to tell her what I thought about their policy as I got out my checkbook. Good thing I had overdraft protection that would transfer what I needed from the money market where I kept what was left of the insurance payout. For a juicy fee, of course.

The receptionist went on in a sociable tone. "We've called in your prescriptions to the compounding pharmacy downstairs to speed things up, but you still may have to wait a while. They make them up fresh." As I started to leave, she handed me a business card. "Here's your endocrinologist's information. Be sure to make an appointment as soon as possible."

Lord knew how much *that* would cost.

If that holistic internist hadn't been so sure Dr. Patel could make me better, I'd have told them all where to stick it.

I was officially hemorrhaging money at a fatal pace.

All I could say was, it had better be worth it.

Four

Jack

Jack sat motionless in the exam chair, listening intently as the doctor fired off a huge chunk of medical jargon at machine-gun speed to explain what was wrong, most of it just technical crap. When the man finished, Jack had long since cut to the bottom line: unless he took all of Dr. Patel's medicine and supplements and cleaned up his environment, he was going to die soon.

The trouble was, Jack didn't have the money to clean up his environment. So he thanked the doctor, then charged the two hundred dollars his supplemental didn't cover and headed for the elevator to the compounding pharmacy to pick up the first installment of concoctions. What he'd do after that remained to be seen.

Maybe he'd get better. If not, maybe he'd be lucky enough to die before he had to pay for the drugs.

Five

Cassie

"Mrs. Jones?" the compounding pharmacy clerk called out, heaving two big, bulging white shopping bags onto the counter by the register.

Hoo, boy. You know you're in trouble when it takes two shopping bags to hold your prescriptions. Good thing the bags were unmarked, or every junkie in town would be after me.

I rose and approached her.

She didn't return my smile. "That'll be six hundred and seventy-eight dollars." She'd already explained that they didn't file insurance or take American Express, but it wasn't like I could go somewhere else. I exhaled and got out my checkbook to pay her, hoping this would be a one-shot deal, for the most part. I'd bought enough mold-killing detergent to wash all my bedding, drapes, and clothes, plus enough of the concentrated cleaner to wipe down everything I owned, as Dr. Patel had ordered. Plus the prescriptions and supplements. Plus the nasal irrigator and the candles and the cans of wicking antifungal oil. And the CitriSafe drops.

"No guessing what I'm gonna be doing for the next three

weeks," I muttered as I tore off the check and handed it to her. "Besides going broke."

"If you need more of anything," she said, "just call ahead, and we'll have your order ready in an hour or so."

I lugged the bags into the elevator, and as the doors were closing, I caught a glimpse of the curmudgeon stomping past toward the pharmacy. I almost felt sorry for him, knowing the sticker shock that awaited him. Then I got out on the ground floor and headed back into the heat, forcing myself to look at the situation optimistically as I carried the heavy bags to my minivan.

Once inside the van with the AC blasting, I decided to celebrate finding out what was wrong with me by staging a final farewell to my favorite comfort foods before I descended into a life of deprivation. So I drove straight to Rhode's Bakery on Cheshire Bridge and ordered a dozen of their celestial petits fours, a dozen sugar cookies, and four chocolate éclairs. I washed down the éclairs with a giant Diet Coke from McDonald's, then ate every one of the petits fours on the way home, at the pace of about one for every two blocks. So I arrived home with only the soft sugar cookies left to eat before my final day of feasting ended.

Buoyed by a raging sugar high, I declared war on the yeasty beasties I'd just fed—as of the next day, even though it wasn't a Monday, and all diets should always begin on a Monday, but this was *war*.

I wasn't sure how I would manage without the foods I loved, but I had to try. So, as of the next morning, it would be good-bye bread, good-bye cheese, good-bye dairy, good-bye orange juice, good-bye sugar. Good-bye wheat.

Hello, hope.

If what Dr. Patel had told me was true, I might be able to get my condition under control. Not curable, but controllable, he'd said. I'd settle for that. If I could stop the joint damage, maybe I wouldn't have to have so many surgeries. Or so much pain.

Six

Jack

Every breath felt like his last while Jack sat waiting forty minutes for the blasted compounding pharmacy to fill the bushel of prescriptions and supplements Dr. Patel had given him. It took a shopping bag to hold it all. The doctor was probably in cahoots with these drug pushers.

Don't take Medicare, indeed.

He'd had to max out his credit card to pay for it all, and when he finally got out of there, the parking cost him six dollars!

To make up for the morning's insults, he headed straight down I-75 to the Varsity, then pigged out on two chili dogs with slaw, fries *and* rings, a Big Orange, and three fried peach pies à la mode that tasted nothing like his mother's, but at least were sweet. Full as a tick, he spent the rest of the afternoon scouring all his in-town sources that carried old tractor and lawn-mower parts.

Seven

Cassie

Back home, I pressed the opener to our one-car, detached brick garage and wood shop, then pulled in and punched it again to safely close myself in, the dim interior illuminated by the band of windows at eye level as the door rolled down. Only when I was secure, with my house key in hand, did I get out of the car, then check the driveway through the high windows to make sure no criminals or strange cars were around. Not to mention rabid animals.

Before Tom died, I'd never given a thought to crime. I was always happily content in my house and neighborhood when he wasn't home. But living alone was another matter, and I now lived with fear, hyperconscious of my vulnerability without him.

Getting attacked by the rabid raccoon hadn't helped.

And neither had the pig my kids had forced on me after I'd called one time too many looking for reassurance when I was jumpy at night.

Some help Juliette was. The animal went through her Pig Chow at a staggering rate and could sleep through a train wreck. Plus, she snored.

I looked through the garage door windows again, just to be sure nothing and nobody was waiting outside to jump me.

The odd thing was, despite my hyperconsciousness of being alone and vulnerable, whenever I started to back out of the garage, I still caught myself checking to make sure Tom's Buick wasn't behind me. And it still surprised me that it wasn't there. (I never would have given it to Haley if I'd known she was going to coerce her brother into forcing Juliette on me.)

Satisfied that the coast was clear, I got out the twenty-dollar-a-pound shopping bags of drugs and cleaners. But on my way to unlock the side door and head for the house, I heard a definite thump from my wood shop behind the garage.

I froze, adrenaline sending my pulse racing and my fingertips atingle. Then I heard it again. Somebody was definitely rummaging around in my wood shop.

My tools! I'd spent the past thirty years collecting and learning how to use those woodworking tools, but I wasn't about to risk my safety to save them.

Creeping toward the side door, I fumbled in my purse for my cell phone, then clumsily dialed 911. I tucked the phone under my ear, then struggled to unlock the side door and escape, but just before I pushed it open, I halted abruptly with my hand on the knob. If there was somebody in the garage, couldn't there be somebody in the house, too?

Maybe I should just run. Not that I could really run, mind you, but under the circumstances, I could try. But Juliette was in the house, all nine hundred dollars' worth of her, and I'd just gotten her trained. Not that I'd be so bereft if somebody stole her.

Stymied, I just stood there like an idiot.

"You have reached emergency 911," a recorded voice from

my cell phone announced. "If this is a genuine emergency, do not hang up the phone. An emergency operator will be with you shortly."

Hold? Nine-one-one put me on *hold*! My adrenaline shot even higher, just shy of hysteria.

The recording went on. "Please have your identity, location, and the nature of your emergency ready to tell the operator. If this is a genuine emergency, do not hang up the phone. An operator will be with you—"

A bored woman's voice broke in. "Nine-one-one emergency. What is your emergency?"

"Somebody's broken into my wood shop," I whispered, "and I live alone."

More banging around from the shop. "They're still in there," I whispered, cupping the phone.

"So we have a home invasion," she said.

I didn't care what they called it. I just wanted them to do something! "Send somebody, quick," I whispered, urgent. "Help."

Forget Juliette, my sense of self-preservation told me. Get back into the car and get out of there. Let the police handle this.

"What is your location, please?" the woman asked.

"Forty-two seventy-eight Meadowlark Lane, in Garden Hills," I whispered loudly as I hurried back to the driver's side and got in, accompanied by the sound of something turning over beyond the wood-shop door.

Don't take my tools!

"And is this Mrs. Jones?" the bored voice asked. Caller ID.

"Yes. Cassandra Jones!"

"We're dispatching an officer to the scene right away. If possible, please take refuge in a safe place." A loud clank.

Forget the tools! Don't hurt *me*! "I'm getting into my car to get away."

"Stay on the—"

I hit the locks, then my earring accidentally pressed the hang-up button on the phone as I tried to get the key into the ignition with a shaking hand.

Shoot!

I finally managed to start the car. I released the parking brake, then, at the last second before I backed up at full throttle, I remembered to open the garage door. It rattled loud as a metal barn collapsing in a tornado and seemed to take forever to get high enough for me to escape without destroying my car.

If that didn't scare them off, nothing would.

But then again, it hadn't scared them off when I came in, then closed the door behind me.

Heart pounding in my ears, I laid rubber backing out, but saw no sign of anybody escaping through the yard. I backed to the street, then swerved to park in front of the Pendletons', two doors up, my motor running in case I had to flee the scene.

Nobody was home this time of day. Everybody worked but me and the young mother down at the corner, but her SUV wasn't in the driveway.

The homeowner's association paid for private security patrols. Where the heck were they when you needed them?

As my pulse hammered away with the engine's cylinders, I called 911 back. When they put me on hold again, I hung up in disgust. After a few gasping minutes, my heartbeat slowed. Keeping an eagle eye on the garage and house, I tuned the radio to my favorite consumer guru, Clark Howard, for company as the dashboard clock blinked for *forty-five* minutes before the police car finally arrived.

By then I was really seeing red. What if somebody had been holding me at gunpoint? Or worse, what if I'd been lying, wounded, all that time?

When the squad car pulled up to check my mailbox numbers, I leaped from my car and gave the policeman a piece of my mind as he got out. "Where have you been?" I read his name tag. "Officer Collins, I told y'all I live alone and there's somebody in my garage, and it takes you almost an *hour* to get here? What if it was a murderer? I could be dead!"

Not politic. Officer Collins's features congealed, his eyes narrowing as the heat radiated off his patrol car in waves. "I take it you are Cassandra Jones."

"Yes. And there's somebody in my garage. Or there *was*. By now, they've probably gotten away scot-free with my woodworking collection. It's worth thousands."

"The dispatcher just told me there was a call," he defended. "She didn't say for what."

Brilliant. Your tax dollars at work. "Then why did she bother to ask me?" I snapped. "I told her when I called 911 that it was a home invasion. They don't even tell y'all it's a home invasion?"

"That was the 911 operator," he clarified, "not the dispatcher. We only hear from the dispatcher."

So that was supposed to make it all right?

"Well, there's something wrong when 911 doesn't even tell the police it's a home invasion!" I scolded.

The policeman muttered something unintelligible into his walkie-talkie, then was answered by a blare of unintelligible squawk. He turned and asked for my door keys.

After I got them from the car and gave him the alarm code, he frowned down at me. "Ma'am, I'm gonna have to ask you to get back in your vehicle while I investigate, for your own safety. I'll start with the house."

Juliette! "Okay," I agreed, "but I have a very expensive pedigreed pet inside, so don't shoot her." Let him find out for himself that she was a pig. "Her name's Juliette, and she won't hurt you."

As I got back in the car and cranked up the air-conditioning, the officer headed for the front door, then unlocked it and stood aside as he pushed it open, his gun drawn. He crept inside, gun aiming toward my living room, then closed the door after him.

He must have disarmed the alarm, because I didn't hear anything for long minutes. Then there was a loud yelp inside, followed by Juliette's piercing complaints.

By then, several sidewalk strollers had stopped to see what was going on.

The front door jerked open and the policeman appeared, irate, to yell my way, "You might have told me it was a pig! Thing snuck up behind me and nosed me in the backside. I almost shot it!"

The spectators laughed as I rolled down the window and hollered, "Sorry. I'm working really hard to get her to stop doing that."

"Besides the *pig*, your house is clear!" he fumed, then slammed the front door behind him and headed for the driveway.

Several more spectators arrived to see what was going on.

The new guy across the street shouted from his front porch, "He should have pulled the trigger. Farm animals are illegal in the city." He'd already threatened to turn me in to the zoning board for having a pig as a pet, but Juliette wasn't really a farm animal. She would top out at about forty pounds, full grown.

Frankly, though she was beginning to grow on me, I didn't have the energy to take care of myself, much less a diva pig, so I wouldn't have grieved too much if the zoning board did make me get rid of her. I'd ship her straight to Haley's.

I turned up the volume on Clark Howard and waited to find out who'd broken into my wood shop and what they'd taken. After about five more minutes, the policeman reappeared around the corner of the house and motioned for me to come, his expression grave. "It's safe."

I got out of my car with as much dignity as I could muster, then passed the curious onlookers to follow him inside the open garage door.

"I found your intruder." He opened the shop door wide and motioned me in. There in the corner, hissing at our presence, was a scrawny white cat with orange and black spots on her back, and four tiny kittens with their eyes still closed, curled up on an old moving quilt. "Not exactly a murderer," the officer said and sneered.

Oh.

Clearly annoyed, he pointed to the small gable window above the narrow loft where I stored my precious wide-plank hardwoods. "There's a pane missing up there. She probably got in, then couldn't get back out."

I noticed he was sweating profusely. Well, anybody who has to wear body armor in July has a right to be cranky.

"I'm so sorry, but how could I have known?" The truth slipped out before my brain engaged: "Since my husband died, I've been really scared, alone."

Officer Collins narrowed his eyes again, studying me. "Forty-two seventy-eight Meadowlark Lane." He thought for a moment, then his expression cleared. "You're that raccoon lady, aren't you?"

I exhaled heavily. "Yes. Were you one of the policemen who came?"

He finally smiled. "Nah, but you're famous at the precinct, capturing it, then driving yourself to the hospital and all. You sure didn't act scared, then."

"I wasn't." I hadn't had time to be scared before I was bitten. Then the old, brave me had taken over and trapped the raccoon under my garbage can. It was just things that go bump that frightened me now. "I knew the treatments were one hundred percent effective."

"All the guys admired your guts," the cop complimented.

Perfect. Now that I needed somebody to take care of me, men admired me for my guts, not the rest of me.

"I'm sorry I fussed at you earlier," I offered.

"Ma'am, believe it or not," the policeman said, "I'm very happy that it just turned out to be a cat."

"I'm allergic to cats," I said, "and dogs. Hence, the miniature pig." Not that Juliette was all that miniature. She already weighed thirty-five pounds.

I glanced over at the mama cat's nest. "What should I do about the kittens?"

"You can call animal control or take them to the Humane Society over near Howell Mill and Marietta Boulevard."

I sneezed, just being in their vicinity. Taking them to the Humane Society would involve handling them. But if I called animal control, they'd probably just kill them all, which definitely wouldn't do. I loved cats. "Well, thanks for coming."

"Any time." He briefly tipped the brim of his cap. "Better safe than sorry."

"Thanks. Really sorry I fussed at you."

"If it had been a real home invasion," he had the grace to say, "your criticism would have been justified. I'll speak to my supervisor about making sure we get the nature of the call from 911."

Flushed with embarrassment in the heat, I hurried back to my car and pulled into the garage. Then, holding my breath against inhaling cat hairs, I went into the shop and opened the window over my workbench just high enough for the mama cat to get out. That accomplished, I closed everything else up and headed for the house with my twenty-dollar-a-pound bags of prescriptions and cleaners. I'd get some cat food and a litter box later.

Mortified about my false alarm, I vowed to put it behind me and focus on what the doctor had told me.

Juliette was waiting for me at the door, as usual, clearly agitated by her encounter with the policeman. She leaned heavily against my calf for comfort. "Just a second," I told her. "Let me set the alarm, then I'll give you a hug." I punched in the code, then took the doctor's papers from my purse before hiding my bag and my keys in the bread drawer of our outdated pine kitchen.

Looking the place over with a fresh eye, I realized how dark and shabby the cabinets had become. Maybe this might be a good time to spruce up a few things while the mold remediation was going on. After all, the homeowner's policy would cover the part the doctor ordered, wouldn't it?

I could have the cabinets refaced and redone in white. That shouldn't cost too much. I'd always wanted white cabinets. And some of those new solid-nylon counters would really brighten up the whole room. Forget granite and marble: granite was too cold and unforgiving, and marble harbored germs.

"White counters and cabinets, with a pale sage on the walls," I told Juliette. "What do you think?"

She nodded her head yes and let out a brief, confirming grunt.

That was another reason I didn't mind so much having her around. She was something to talk to.

I'd never talked to myself till Tom died, even though I'd been home alone most weekdays. But after the funeral, I'd started talking to myself all the time, hungry for the sound of a voice, even if it was my own. The radio and the TV didn't count, so I'd gone back to listening to classical CDs and blabbering away about anything and everything, especially complaints.

Now I had Juliette, who was a very good listener and always agreed with me. Maybe she could read my tone, but whenever I asked her if she liked something, she nodded, then uttered a very specific grunt of confirmation. When I asked in the negative, she shook her head side to side and snorted her derision.

I sat down at the breakfast banquette, and she daintily climbed the kiddie stairs I'd put beside it. Then she lay with her head in my lap, heaving a contented sigh.

I rubbed her tummy, patted her jowl, then started to look over the papers the doctor had given me, and as I settled down at last, my adrenaline finally ran out at the same time my blood sugar teetered, sky-high from all the éclairs and cakes I'd eaten, then plunged, leaving me light-headed and inert where I sat, too out of it to get up and eat something.

It would pass, if I just sat there. But suddenly my bra felt like an iron band around my ribs.

The older I'd gotten, the lower my bustline had dropped—along with my bra quotient—so I couldn't wait to lose the tight bandeau. Flipping off my Easy Spirit sandals, I unhooked my bra, then threaded it out the arm of my shirt, as "the girls" headed south.

Aaah. "Free at last," I declared to Juliette, "free at last. Thank

God Almighty, I'm free at last." With apologies to Dr. Martin Luther King, Jr.

Since Tom had died, that was as good as it got for me, physically.

I sat there till I trusted myself to stand without passing out, then nudged Juliette aside and went for a cold Coke Zero and the sugar cookies. When I brought them to the breakfast nook, Juliette climbed in behind me and leaned up hard against my right arm, her snout twitching from the aroma of the cookies. But she used her manners: she didn't go after them; she just begged with her eyes.

"Oh, all right. One for you, one for me." I held out the cookie for her to take, and she nibbled at it with admirable self-control. But I needed my hand back, so I put it down on the table and started to enjoy mine, wanting it to last as long as possible. She politely ate hers beside me. Far be it from me to let on that lard was what made those cookies taste so good, but I still felt a twinge of guilt for making Juliette a cannibal.

We savored them together till they were gone. Juliette got down for a drink from her raised bowl, then climbed back up and settled with her snout in my lap again, and I started to pore through the instructions and reports the doctor had given me, which included three published medical journal articles—two he'd written, and one by a team at Harvard.

They weren't easy to digest, but I managed to get through them and understand the main points, which supported his diagnosis. Then I got to the handout about the mold remediation and made a mental note to call USA Insurance about my homeowner's policy and make sure I was covered.

Surely it wouldn't matter that the house was in trust for Haley and Tommy, and I had a life estate instead of ownership.

I circled the numbers for the two remediation companies Dr. Patel had recommended, then called the first one, based in Carrolton.

"Carrolton Allergy Consultants," a very nice young man answered. When I told him about Dr. Patel's referral, he said he'd be working near me on Thursday and would be happy to come give me a free written estimate at four, if that was convenient.

"Thanks," I told him. "That would be wonderful." Besides my morning appointment with Dr. Patel, I didn't have anything else scheduled for next Thursday—or any other day, for that matter—so I wrote the time on my refrigerator calendar, then called the other company on the list.

At the second company, a rather abrupt man answered and told me he charged a thousand dollars for his oral assessment, but that would count against his fee when he started the job, and he'd itemize everything as he went.

A thousand dollars, and no written estimate? *Itemized as he went?* Sounded like carte blanche to me! Did he think I was an idiot?

"But I'll need a written estimate to submit to my insurance company," I responded as civilly as I could.

The man paused, then said, "I'd be shocked if your homeowner's insurance covered any of this unless you have a specific rider for mold-related damage. I don't know of a single insurer who covers mold without a rider, and most companies won't even offer one."

What?

My chest tightened.

Tom had always taken care of the insurance. I had no idea whether we had a rider or not. I didn't know *what* coverage we had—except for bat infestations. Otherwise, all I knew was how much I paid USAI every month, but I'd find out.

I tried again. "Could you at least give me a ball-park for what a twenty-four-hundred-square-foot, three-bedroom, two-bath on crawl might run?" Not that this jerk would tell me. "I need to know how much this is going to set me back, so I can make financial arrangements."

"The cost varies widely, according to conditions," he deflected. "Moisture is the enemy. Sealing your crawl space can run three thousand or more, beyond whatever work we have to do in your attic and living spaces. We might have to do foundation work or regrading. You may have to replace gutters and outer doors and windows, sometimes even siding or the roof. And we'll have to rework your HVAC system and ducts, removing all the exposed fiberglass. May even have to replace it."

What? And all of it without a cap?

I started to wheeze.

What kind of joker *was* this guy? "I'll have to call you back," I told him, "after I've thought this over."

As if he'd read my mind, the mean mold man responded with an arrogant, "Dr. Patel recommends me because I know what I'm doing, and I guarantee your house will be mold-free, safe, and habitable when I finish. You might be able to find someone cheaper, but not better. Most conventional companies use toxic chemicals that Dr. Patel's patients can't tolerate. You do get what you pay for."

The nerve. "Good-bye." I'd never been so glad to hang up on anybody in my life.

Stunned, I headed for the living room to pace as Juliette settled to watch from her cushion that matched my grandmother's coral silk camelback sofa.

Were we talking ten thousand, or forty? Or worse?

Our house was sixty years old, on a dirt crawl space. Heaven only knew how much mold hid in its walls, much less the crawl space, which definitely had a musty odor.

Maybe the trust should just sell it and get me a mold-free condo. But who was to say there were any mold-free condos out there? I mean, this was the South, second only to the Amazon rain forests in mold production.

But nothing had sold in our neighborhood since the pig protester snapped up the foreclosure across the street for three hundred thousand less than things had been selling for a few years ago.

I stopped in my tracks. What if that foreclosure price *was* fair market value, now?

At that rate, I wouldn't be able to afford a decent condo anywhere near where I lived.

As my favorite consumer guru Clark Howard always said, "Once it's paid for, the cheapest car to drive is the one you're driving, till it's not worth the cost of the repairs." I supposed that applied to houses, too. Ours was paid off. If I had to do this, I would.

What choice did I have? It was a matter of my health.

So I'd end up in the poorhouse a few years sooner . . . or decades, depending on the cost.

"Don't panic," I told Juliette, who was doing anything but. "Wait till the guy comes from Carrolton and gives us an estimate. Then we can figure this out."

I looked down at my new carpet in consternation. Only three months ago, I'd put in a subtle, low-loop gray commercial-grade carpet that you could Clorox without hurting it, on a mold-resistant pad. But now the doctor said it had to go. Brand-new, and it had to come out, because Dr. Patel insisted there was no such thing as a moldproof carpet or pad.

My orientals would have to be cleaned and fumigated by a special mold remediator/dry cleaner listed in the remediation section of Dr. Patel's instructions, then laid down without pads, once the house was safe.

Dr. Patel recommended tile or prefinished wood floors. Tile was too cold and hard underfoot. My balance wasn't as good as it was before I'd had both knees and hips replaced, and I wouldn't want to fall on tile. It would have to be wood, but I had no idea what shape the original floors were in, or how many times they'd been sanded.

I flashed on November of 1973, when Tom and I had finally saved up enough money to cover up the cold, hard, scarred old oak floors with soft, warm wall-to-wall carpet that the kids could crawl on.

"Maybe I could just redo the existing floors," I told Juliette. Holding my nose, I pulled up a corner of the new carpet, sending a surprising amount of dust into the air despite my weekly vacuumings. I coughed and fanned away the cloud of motes in the afternoon sunlight. Then I peeled back the pad and saw that the floors were even worse than I remembered underneath.

"Maybe not." I crossed the room and sank to the down cushion of my grandmother's sofa. I loved that sofa and had made it the center of my décor, but Dr. Patel had said that it—along with all my other upholstered furniture—would have to be reupholstered in vinyl or leather, or gotten rid of.

Obviously a man who didn't realize that a leather Chippendale camelback sofa was a total oxymoron. I couldn't imagine what it would look like, much less cost. Probably cheaper to buy something new. But I'd grown up on that sofa, and it always evoked my precious grandmother. Did they even *make* coral-colored leather, anyway?

Juliette grunted, then daintily climbed up to lie beside me on the down cushion, one of her favorite places. I reached for the cordless phone and called USAI, only to discover that we had great coverage for everything but mold, rodents, floods, acts of war (including accidental nuclear detonations), or bugs of any kind.

I hung up with a heavy sigh.

Then I hunted up the mortgage file and called the credit union to find out if it made a difference that the house was in trust. When we'd refinanced in 2005, they hadn't cared, but a lot had changed since then. They wouldn't do an equity line because I technically didn't own the house anymore, and they wouldn't do one for the trust, either, and neither would anybody else, they said, because the lender couldn't foreclose on a trust. So I was out of luck there.

I hung up with a most unladylike expletive.

Juliette let out a consoling grunt, then buried her nose under my arm the way she always did when I was upset.

"That's okay," I soothed, stroking the coarse blond hairs that covered her pink skin and navy-blue patches. I finished with a nice scratch behind the ears. "It's okay. God will make a way, somehow."

Eight

Jack

On his way to the Varsity after his doctor's appointment, Jack opened a cubbyhole in his brain, shoved everything the doctor had told him inside, and slammed it shut, twisting the lock. As a distraction, he ate, then ran down every lead in every parts place or salvage yard in town that might have what he was looking for. By the time he'd finally run out of energy entirely, NPR had come on the radio, and Jack was stuck in rush-hour traffic on I-400, fuming over not being able to buy the parts to get the lawn tractors at the farm running so he could sell or barter them. His frustration cracked open the cubbyhole just enough to set him seething about how much he'd spent at the doctor's and the druggist's.

Stuck in a miasma of exhaust fumes, Jack wheezed out a long sigh in the evening heat and wondered how long it would be before he got home to Cumming and some semblance of sanity.

Not that Cumming was much better than Atlanta these days. Interstate 400 had become a permanently clogged artery, and the rural refuge he'd found twenty years ago was now a hive of cramped subdivisions, half-empty strip malls, and fast-food restaurants.

He settled in to make the crawl to Mansell Road, where the traffic would spread out a bit. Then everything just stopped.

Wreck. There was always a wreck. People drove like maniacs in Atlanta. Unless it rained; then they all forgot how to drive entirely.

On NPR, the same old news droned out in cultured tones. People were killing each other for greed and power and prejudice; religious fanatics were slaughtering the innocent with the guilty in the name of God or Allah; the government was on the brink of bankruptcy, along with most of America, yet still yammering for more entitlements; global warming was baking the entire country; and the commentators were still blah-blah-blahing about it all.

The western sun beat on the driver's side of Jack's battered '55 Chevy pickup. He turned off the radio, then bent down to the passenger floorboard to retrieve his library copy of *Now You See Her* by James Patterson. Patterson was a perfect antidote for heavy traffic. Simply written and fast-moving, the books weren't demanding, which left enough of Jack's attention free to keep him from running into anybody in the gridlock. So far.

After only half a chapter, though, sweat trickled down his forehead, prompting him to lay the book aside. The cab had to be eighty-eight, if it was a degree, so he turned up the fan on the air conditioner he'd installed back in the seventies, but it didn't help much.

Atlanta was even hotter and dirtier than usual. Thanks to the inversion, every day was an Orange Alert, so Jack was supposed to stay indoors, which he couldn't very well do when he had to drive forty miles each way to see the blasted doctor.

But if his house was making him sicker . . . How do you choose between the devil and the deep blue sea?

Dr. Patel's handouts in the passenger seat caught his eye. Mold remediation, indeed. How much was *that* going to cost him? Jack's pension and Social Security only went so far.

He actually considered trying to get rid of the mold himself. But his previous stabs at deep-cleaning the house had always made him too sick to finish. He couldn't trust just anybody to see his collections because they'd probably come back to rob him when he wasn't there, so he'd given up on hiring maid service long ago. The stuff he needed was where he could find it—well, mostly—but the place hadn't had a down-to-the-walls going-over since he'd bought it with his half of the equity from the divorce.

Twenty years, without a good spring cleaning.

Crud.

Literally. There was dust and cat hair all over everything he didn't use every day.

Inching toward Holcomb Bridge in five-mile-an-hour spates, he considered the alternatives to paying a fortune to those mold remediators on Patel's handout that probably gave the doctor a kickback.

Even if he figured out a way to pay for that, he'd still need some help to straighten things up, first. His kids would be more than eager to oblige, but that was out. Till now, he'd ignored their endless pleas to let them come clean his house. They'd even threatened to call that *Clean House* show, but he'd set them straight.

It was a matter of principle. The house was his, not theirs, and he didn't want them rummaging around in his things and criticizing the way he lived. His ex had done enough of that to last him a lifetime. And the kids would want to throw half of everything away, especially his books. Both his daughters had begged him to get rid of them, claiming the acid paper was constantly deteriorating in a cloud of pulp and dust, which the pulmonologist had confirmed.

But his books were all signed collectibles, and Jack wanted to keep them; use them. Not that he *did* reread them, but he *could*.

If the blasted doctor was right, though, and cleaning up really could make him better . . .

A sudden motion in his peripheral vision brought Jack's attention back to the traffic just in time for him to slam the brakes to avoid being hit by a crazy, weaving BMW that couldn't settle on a lane, as if changing spots would make any difference in the crawling mass of cars.

Pick a lane and stay in it!

Stirred up by the close call, Jack turned the radio back on and busied his mind composing his next op-ed for the paper, dealing with traffic survival and etiquette.

When he finally reached the house at the end of his long, graveled driveway forty minutes later, the two ancient John Deere tractors and three riding lawn mowers he'd been meaning to fix were waiting for him in silent accusation behind the aluminum carport by the kitchen door. "I tried all afternoon to find the parts," he said to them as he got out.

The usual welcoming committee of cats struck up a hungry chorus. "Okay, okay," he grumbled, then opened the kitchen door and let them in ahead of him.

Jack was so hot and tired, he could hardly think.

In the kitchen, fat Dusty reared up and put his paws on Jack's leg, nudging his knee with his jowls as Jack opened the garbage can that held dry cat food from the dollar store. "Okay, old boy," he said as he scooped up the kibble that was probably laced with Chinese melamine, for all he knew. It hadn't seemed to hurt the cats, so far. "Give me a sec."

The tom was useless on the farm, lying around in the shade while the females kept the gardens free of moles and voles and snakes. But Jack admired Dusty's flagrant "papa-san" inertia. He gave the cat's head a good rub, which was the only familiarity the male permitted, probably because he'd been abused. The critter ran for cover whenever Jack had something in his hand.

The females, Schitzo and D.I., were friendlier. They just rolled over and showed their bellies in a gesture of submission. But Jack knew better than to stroke their stomachs. It was a typical cat trap. Just because they acknowledged him as Top Cat didn't mean they'd let him touch their bellies. He'd tried it once with each of them and gotten bitten for his trouble.

Jack poured their food into a divided dish and set it down on the cracked linoleum, then went to the refrigerator and pulled out a root beer and the sausage biscuit he'd brought home from the diner the day before.

Dr. Patel's voice replayed in his mind. *Mr. Wilson, I think we can really improve your quality of life, if you'll only do what's necessary with your environment and your diet. I know there are major adjustments to be made, but you're in the worst shape I've ever seen a patient who walked in here under his own steam. Are you willing to make those changes to save your life? Because if you don't, you'll die before your time, and soon.*

So what else was new?

He took a long, cold swig of root beer.

In spite of himself, Jack looked at the kitchen and dining area with a fresh eye and realized it'd be a lot simpler just to pack a bag and move somewhere clean, rather than go through everything and get rid of the mold. But the real estate market was flat as a flounder, especially for a teardown, even one on twenty acres of prime farmland. There had been a time, just a few years ago, when developers were buying up Forsyth County, that he could have gotten fifteen thousand an acre—maybe twenty. But that was then, and this was now. Like it or not, he was stuck there.

He seriously considered torching the place, but with his luck, the fire marshal would nail him for it. He saw no contradiction in the fact that he'd rather burn everything than let go of it. Still, this was no time to end up in jail as some inmate's bitch, even if his cell was mold-free.

Jack settled into his worn recliner and punched the cable remote to watch the news on BBC, which hadn't gone tabloid like the American press. But the coverage was no better than NPR. Same song, three-millionth verse. So he switched the channel to *Wheel of Fortune*, which he enjoyed almost as much as *Jeopardy!*

All three cats came over to settle around him, shedding as they did.

D.I. jumped into his lap. "No, no!" Raising his sausage biscuit out of reach in one hand, he used the other to drop the cat back onto the floor, but the damage had been done. His lap was covered with orange fur.

Darn cats never learned. He imagined his bronchial tree bristling with a mat of cat hair and coughed just thinking about it.

The phone rang, and he reached over to answer it. "Jack, here."

"I thought you were coming to see me," his mother's voice complained.

Jack exhaled as best he could before responding, "I did, Mama.

You just forgot." It had only been three days. "Remember last Friday? I took you to Denny's, and you got the Grand Slam."

"I do love a Grand Slam," she admitted. "Why don't you come over and take me out to get one?"

She was definitely getting worse. "Is Aunt Junie there?"

"I don't know. Let me look." From his mother's brisk tone, you'd never imagine that she was crazy as a monkey on moonshine. Time passed, and he heard voices in the background. Then his mother returned to the phone. "Yes, she's here." Nothing further.

Jack sighed. "Could I please speak with her?"

"Well, you didn't ask to speak to her," his mother scolded, defensive. "I'll go get her."

Something was going to have to be done about his mother. Aunt Junie could scarcely take care of herself, much less Mama, who outweighed her by at least twenty pounds of lean muscle and another thirty of pure padding. But Jack was in no position to take care of anybody.

"Hello?" Aunt Junie's perky voice said.

"Sounds like Mama's having a bad week."

Aunt Junie paused, then said, "Well, it's hard to tell if she's any worse than last week. Like I told you this weekend, she's been pretty confused for almost a month."

He'd asked Junie to call the doctor about that. "What did the doctor say?"

"She wouldn't let me call the doctor, much less take her."

He tried to keep the exasperation out of his voice. "Mama's crazy, Aunt Junie. She can't make decisions like that. Just tell her she needs to go, and take her. I looked it up on the Internet when I got home, and it may just be a bladder infection that's knocked her off the rails."

"Goodness gracious, Jackson, where did you get a bizarre idea like that?" his aunt scolded. "How in the world could a bladder infection make somebody go crazy? It's the other end, entirely."

"I know it sounds crazy, but it's true. You'll have to trust me on this."

"Well, I certainly can't *make* her go to the doctor. You know how stubborn she can be."

At ninety-six, his mother was still strong as an ox, despite her dementia. She'd probably outlive him by at least five years.

"Put her on the phone. I'll try to talk some sense into her."

The receiver bonked on something solid, then he heard Aunt Junie summoning his mother in her thready soprano. *"Louisa! Jackson wants to talk to you!"*

"I already talked to him! *Wheel of Fortune* is on."

"I think it's important!"

His mother's voice grew louder as she approached the phone. "Why does he always have to call me when my shows are on?"

Because her shows were on all day and night. She lived glued to the TV.

"Hello," she barked into the phone.

"Mama, I think you need to see the doctor. Really. He can give you some antibiotics to help your memory."

"Good Lord, Jackson. If antibiotics could cure my memory problems, I'd have taken them long ago."

"I know it sounds crazy, but a urinary tract infection could really confuse you. It does that with elderly people. Ask the doctor."

"I can't believe you're talking about something so vulgar with your mother. I brought you up better than that, Jackson, and you know it."

"Mama, for me—please just promise you'll go to the doctor with Aunt Junie." He didn't have the strength for another trip to Biloxi so soon after the last one, or he'd take her himself.

His mother let out a shuddering sound of disgust. "Well, if you want me to, all right. But I still think you've lost your mind, saying antibiotics can help my memory. Timothy told me just last night that I need to go back to church, not to the doctor."

His father, who left her years ago.

She rattled on, "And Mama hasn't come to see me for . . . good gracious, I don't know when. I have no idea why she's so mad at me."

Yet again, he had to deliver the bad news. "Mama, Big Daddy and Gram are in heaven. You're just having trouble keeping straight what's real and memories and dreams. I promise," he said, praying it was true, "the doctor can help." His mother wanted to stay in her home until she died, and he wanted that to happen, but if she got much worse, he'd have to look into a facility.

Now, *there* would be a battle royal.

"Please, just go to the doctor with Aunt Junie," he repeated. "For me."

"Oh, all right!" his mother snapped, then hung up the phone.

Grateful, Jack leaned back and watched *Wheel of Fortune*. He didn't have to watch the news, anyway. Judging from what was going on in Washington, the entire government was as crazy as his mother. Fat little comfort that was.

Restless, he turned off the TV and reached for *Pillars of the Earth*, determined to finish the thing. That, at least, would take his mind off his mother and the mold.

He'd deal with what Dr. Patel had said later, when he felt better.

Jack took another long, sweet slug of his root beer, deliberately feeding his yeasty beasties what might be their last good meal, and wondered if the raccoon lady had gotten soaked the way he had at the doctor's office and the druggist's. It pleased him to think she had.

Let her put that in her expensive purse and deal with it.

Nine

Cassie

Bloated from all the sweets I'd eaten, I went to the store for cat supplies and put them out in the wood shop. Then Juliette and I watched *Ellen* and *Dr. Phil*, after which I turned off the living room TV and went into the kitchen for reruns of *NCIS* while I made us both a nice salad with plenty of carrots and spinach to supplement Juliette's Pig Chow. She ate her bowl from her dish on the floor, and I had mine at the table, which I'd sterilized with Clorox Clean-Up after our cookie fest. It was only seven when I finally headed to bed, wanting to put the lid on this very disturbing day. Juliette followed me into the bedroom.

Another reason I hadn't gotten rid of her was that when there's a pet in the house, you don't flinch at every tiny noise, which was Haley's rationale in giving her to me in the first place. The problem was, Juliette had a penchant for mischief, so now every tiny noise in the night meant she might be chewing, rearranging, or destroying something. "Come on. Bedtime."

She headed for her litter box in our bathroom.

I locked my bedroom door behind us. Not only are pigs social, but they're also very intelligent, especially when it comes to getting at food of any kind. She'd broken the lock on the old door, then rooted it off its hinges trying to get to the kitchen, so I'd had to put a steel door on the bedroom to keep her from escaping. Once she was safely locked in, she slept on her big dog bed in the corner, where I could keep up with her.

Unlike a dog, she was far too fastidious to drink from the toilet, so I kept a bowl of water in the bathroom for her, along with her enormous litter box (made from the bottom of an extra large underbed storage container).

After she'd taken care of business, she bumped her snout against the glass door of the big shower we'd put in for Tom when we added the master suite. Never in a million years would I have imagined I'd end up showering with a pig in there every night. Before Juliette, I'd been a bath person.

"Okay. Shower time." I turned on the water, then shucked out of my clothes, ignoring the road map of scars all over my body. I still had a decent shape, but my skin had gotten soft and saggy since I'd lost weight, so I didn't look in the mirror unless I had to.

Juliette waited politely till I got in, then followed and hogged all the hot water, as usual, while I scrubbed her thoroughly with the new mold-killing shampoo that cost twenty dollars a bottle, then doused her in creme rinse. Only then did she move over so I could demold my own hair and skin.

Seeing us with a fresh eye, I realized this arrangement was fine for the short term, but heaven only knows what would happen if I ever did find someone else. *Excuse me, honey,* I'd have to tell him, *but we'll be showering with my pig.*

In my imagination, my gorgeously perfect Mr. Right gripped the towel around his waist, looked at me like I was insane, then headed for the hills—in nothing but the towel—to get an annulment.

For the first time in a long time, I let out a cleansing laugh.

After Juliette and I were clean and toweled dry, I put on my nightgown, then flossed, brushed, put in my bite guard, and motioned her to bed as I climbed into mine, practicing my widow's mantra. "This is home. We're safe in God's hands."

Maybe if I told myself often enough, I'd start to believe it.

Juliette nodded and let out a contented grunt of agreement, then fell sound asleep.

I read till my lids drooped, then turned off the light to the sound of Juliette's gentle snores. It was good to have something breathing in the room, but trust me, a pig is no substitute for a husband.

As I lay in the darkness, the weight of loneliness was so crushing, I finally faced the truth. I couldn't live alone. I needed to try at least to meet someone else. Someone with better health insurance than what I had.

God, I know you can do anything. Please send me a good Christian man to marry. One with decent health insurance, and I will give you all the glory and the praise.

Then finally, I went to sleep.

Four days after my appointment with Dr. Patel, I woke at seven and stretched in my bed, enjoying its warmth and softness in the air-conditioned room. Still half asleep, I got up and went to the bathroom, prompting Juliette to rise and follow me for a drink, then a prodigious pee. In a very good mood, for some reason, I brushed my teeth, then headed for the kitchen. Halfway there, I halted abruptly.

Something was wrong.

I glanced around, but everything was where it was supposed to be.

Whatever it was, Juliette didn't seem to notice. As usual, she made a beeline past me, straight for her feeding bowls in the kitchen.

I remained suspended where I stood. Something. I couldn't put my finger on it, but there was definitely something amiss.

I took two more steps before it dawned on me.

The pain.

It was gone!

For the first morning in twenty years, I felt no pain, no stiffness.

Dr. Patel's vaccine had worked a miracle!

Ten

Jack

Blasted mold guy! A thousand dollars for an oral estimate, with no game plan in writing? No way, José.

The other remediation guy was better, but he'd said it would take at least forty thousand to make the house safe for Jack to live in.

Hell, he could build a nice, new cabin for that, but he didn't have the money.

Not only didn't Jack have the money, he couldn't get it. Not with the market the way it was. He didn't have enough equity.

Maybe he could do the mold remediation himself. Pack up what he absolutely had to have, then call in a dealer to make him a price on everything else in the house. All the treasures he'd bartered and collected over the years, along with the crap. All the oriental rugs, real and fake, he'd never had a place for. The gently used cabinets and appliances he'd found at salvage to redo the kitchen. All the furniture he'd refinished and had reupholstered. His rare-plate collection. Surely he'd make enough to get a new, mold-free bed, a leather recliner, and a table and chairs. That was all he needed really, except his computer and TV.

Could TVs and computers get moldy?

Maybe he'd make enough on his treasures to get new ones, if they did.

The trouble was, the thought of clearing out and starting over was so overwhelming, Jack gave up before he considered beginning. That was the problem with his COPD. When you're not getting enough oxygen, you don't have energy for squat. It was all he could do to keep up his garden, especially in this heat.

But he had no intention of tying himself to an oxygen canister. His kids had been trying to get him to do that for years, but taking the tank was a last resort, and he wasn't that bad off, not yet.

Maybe the doctor visits and vaccine and diet would be enough to help. Jack had to admit, a few days after his appointment, he'd started feeling better than he had in a long time.

When the following Thursday and his second appointment rolled around, he was reading his book in the doctor's office when the raccoon woman came in with a far-too-chirpy, "Good morning. We meet again."

Fortunately, she didn't settle on his sofa, but went to the receptionist and showed her some photos. "Do you know anybody who'd like one of these darling kittens? Their mother had them in my garage, but I'm violently allergic to cats and dogs, so I can't get near them. And if I call animal control, they'll probably just gas them."

If there was anything more presumptuous than telling a complete stranger the inane details of your life, it was trying to pawn off stray kittens.

The receptionist hastily returned the photos. "Sorry, I'm allergic, too." She busied herself with the computer.

Good save.

Jack shook his head, knowing where the raccoon woman—now the kitten woman—would settle next.

She sat far too close for comfort on his sofa and proffered the photos. "How about you? Do they let you have pets where you live?"

None of her business, but to his shock, he heard himself say, "I live on a farm, for the time being, but according to the doctor, it's killing me."

She brightened at that savory tidbit. "Oh, a farm would be the perfect place for these kittens. You could have them fixed, and they'd make nice ratters, I'm sure. Their mother hunts every day and has cleared my whole yard of chipmunks." She waited for his response with palpable optimism.

Jack frowned at the pages of his book, refusing to humor her with a response.

"The funniest thing was," she rattled on, "I heard the mama cat bumping around in my wood shop and thought it was somebody stealing my tools, so I called 911, and they sent a policeman who didn't even know what the call was for. I was *so* embarrassed when it turned out to be a cat instead of a burglar."

"*Your* tools?" he asked aloud, annoyed with himself for encouraging her.

"Yes, mine." She picked up a magazine. "I make furniture. You should see my cherry corner cabinet. Copied it from one at Monticello. Turned out gorgeous, even if I do say so myself. Did a lot of the fine work on an antique treadle band saw."

"Do you sell it?" he couldn't keep from asking.

She smiled. "Oh, no. There's not enough money in this world to pay me for all that work. I just make things for myself, like the corner cabinet, or as gifts for family or extra special friends. I've done several Boston rockers, three quilt chests, and a double dresser— I'll never do all those hand-dovetailed drawers again, though. Talk about tedious."

Jack's interest piqued. He loved craftsmanship and old tools and had an extensive collection. This woman definitely wasn't your usual Buckhead lunch-bridge-and-cocktails matron.

The kitten woman grinned, refilling her lungs for another onslaught. "The funniest thing was when the policeman was searching my house and my pig goosed him. Wish I'd been there to see *that*. He almost shot her, but fortunately, he didn't."

"You have a *pig?* In the *house?*" Maybe she was a pathological liar. Nobody kept a pig in the house, especially in Buckhead.

She nodded. "She's a Dutch Juliette, the only true miniature pig. My kids paid a fortune for her and insisted I take her after my husband died, because I called them too often when I got scared by myself at night."

TMI! TMI!

"But she's very intuitive," the woman rattled on, "and clean. She uses a litter box."

Must have been one heck of a litter box.

Jack hoped she was finished, but she started right back in. "I'm allergic to cats and dogs." She scanned through the magazine. "Fish don't count as pets, and neither do hamsters. I tried one of those golden hamsters, but it was mean as a snake. Kept biting me"—maybe it was trying to get her to shut up—"so I gave it to the local kindergarten."

Jack couldn't resist asking, "So it could bite *them*, instead?"

"No. They trained it, and now it's the most popular member of the class." Her mouth flattened. "Anyway, rodents just pee and poop and eat and bite, so I decided those were out. And don't even mention reptiles." She shuddered.

"So you bought a pig," he said with sarcasm. "A perfectly rational decision, under the circumstances."

"No. I told you, my kids foisted it off on me." Undaunted, she fixed him with an assessing stare. "Are you always this sarcastic?"

"I try to be." He resumed reading.

She teased him by remaining silent for a whole minute before demanding, "Are you here for the mold thing, too?"

He looked up in irritation. "Yes." Now please leave me alone!

She focused on his purplish lips and fingernails. "COPD, too, right?"

Jack frowned. "If it's any of your business, which it isn't."

"I'm very perceptive," she said smugly. "I notice these things."

If she was so perceptive, why hadn't she noticed he didn't want to talk to her?

"Did the vaccine help you as much as it helped me?" she prodded.

Jack closed his eyes in resignation. Maybe he'd get lucky, and they'd take one of them to an exam room. Then he looked over and saw her eagerness to know, so he relented. "As a matter of fact, it did."

"Did you talk to the remediation people?"

"Yes." He exhaled heavily. "What is this? A status review?"

She actually blushed. "I'm sorry. It was just so miraculous to wake up without pain for the first time in forever that I thought something was wrong, at first." She offered him a lopsided smile. "I wondered if I'm a fluke, or if that stuff works that well on everybody."

He softened. "It did help."

"I've been going through my stuff, planning a garage sale before they come to work on the house." She shook her head. "It's amazing what all you accumulate that you don't really need, and it's easier to let stuff go when you know you have to have it fumigated to keep it."

She sized him up. "My late husband was about your size. Forty long, thirty-six waist. He left a lot of really nice clothes. I'm planning to put most of them into my garage sale. It's three weeks from Saturday, but since we know each other, you could come have first refusal the day before."

Know each other? This woman was not to be believed. "No, thank you." Jack shopped at the Goodwill, where he could do so unmolested.

"Sorry. I didn't mean to offend you."

What *had* she meant, prying and keeping him from his book? "You didn't," he clipped out. "I just want to read my book, please, if you don't mind."

"Sure. I didn't mean to bother you. I just wanted to talk to somebody else who had this thing. Compare notes, you know."

Hell. She probably didn't have anybody to talk to at home—except the pig. He put down the book. "So?"

Her features eased. "I knew you were a nice man under all that gruff stuff." She eased back to the other side of the sofa, giving him space. "Did you talk to that awful mold guy who wanted carte blanche?"

That hit his hot button. "Did I ever. What a con artist. A thousand dollars for a guesstimate, and nothing in writing."

"I thought maybe he was just trying to take advantage of me because I was a woman alone."

"I think he tries to take advantage of everybody," Jack grumbled.

"The other guy was very nice, though. Said the job would be

just over forty-seven thousand, including having my crawl space sealed and insulated, HVAC reworked, replacing all my old windows and exterior doors, and both sets of French doors. And the gutters. And part of the roof. And repointing my chimney. And new prefinished floors. Plus new drainage around the foundation." She rattled them off as if they were minor items. She shrugged. "My house is sixty years old. All that needed doing, anyway." She picked up a magazine. "Cleaning and fumigating all my dry-cleanables and orientals will add another couple of thousand."

Only somebody with plenty of money could be so casual about fifty thousand dollars.

Mrs. Buckhead.

For him, that much money was beyond the moon.

"How much of that will your homeowner's pay?" he asked.

"Zip. Nada. Nil." She raised her eyebrows as she exhaled, staring into the middle distance. "We didn't have mold coverage. You have to have a special rider, which, apparently, hardly anybody does, because the insurance companies don't want to offer them."

So much for getting any help from his own insurance, Jack realized. Blast!

He really was in the soup.

"What about you?" she asked.

Fortunately, the nurse rescued him by sticking her head out of the door to the back office. "Mr. Wilson? We're ready for you now."

He wasn't ready to spend another seven hundred dollars, but he had no choice. So he excused himself from the kitten woman, then followed the nurse back for another exam.

The nurse squirted the nasty-tasting stuff up his nose, then left him for five minutes.

Dr. Patel came in and wrinkled his nose. "I can smell the yeast

on you, Mr. Wilson, and the mold, on your clothes and your breath."
He frowned. "How are you doing on your new diet and mold remediation?"

No sense in lying. "I've been taking the antifungal and irrigating
my sinuses. And I cut back on the sugar some and gave up bread,
but biscuits are okay, aren't they?"

"You'll have to check the ingredients for the biscuits. Some,
particularly commercially prepared ones, do contain yeast. But even
without yeast, complex carbohydrates like flour just feed your can-
didiasis. So it's probably better to try the Atkins regimen, or something similar—high protein and low carb, with lots of leafy green
and yellow veggies, and plenty of springwater."

"Whatever." Jack ran through the menu from the diner where
he ate every day and realized he'd have slim pickings there.

Dr. Patel pushed the scope up his nose. "Did you notice any
improvement from the vaccine?"

"Yes, I did. Not a lot, but it helped."

The doctor clicked a photo of his sinuses. "I'm afraid you are
still consumed with these infections. As long as your environment
is moldy, you probably won't improve much. Did you speak with
the people I recommended?"

"Yes, and that first one was a con artist. A thousand dollars, and
no written estimate, indeed."

"He's excellent and does a fine job," Dr. Patel defended, snap-
ping another gross photo. "What about the other one?"

"He was decent enough," Jack told the man, "but did it ever occur
to you that some people don't have that kind of money, and can't get
it? We're not all raking in seven hundred dollars a visit, you know."

"We are talking about your life, Mr. Wilson," Patel said calmly.
"If you do not find a safe place to live, this condition will kill you."

Oh, right. "It's not as if I can just pack up and move, you know. My kids live in central Florida and New Orleans, mold capitals of the world." He didn't mention the son in Chamblee, whose ratty little ranch was almost as moldy as Jack's farmhouse. "What am I supposed to do?" Jack hated having to bare himself to this effete, clueless scientist. "I invested everything I had into my farm, and now I can't give the place away, much less borrow forty thousand dollars against it. The house is a hundred years old, and looks it."

"You are a highly educated and intelligent man. I am sure you can come up with some reasonable alternative," the doctor assured him, as if he had any idea what he was talking about.

"Oh, yeah? Like what?"

"A rented room, perhaps," Patel suggested.

"Right. Have you ever seen the rented rooms around Atlanta?" Jack had, after his divorce, and it wasn't pretty.

"Arizona or Colorado offer some good environments for people with your condition," Patel suggested. "Perhaps you could find somewhere to stay there. An apartment?"

"Perfect. I can hardly get out of bed, but I should pack a bag and go somewhere where I know no one, two thousand miles from my family and friends."

Patel remained unruffled. "The choice is yours, sir, but as long as you live in a contaminated environment, you are on a short trip to the bone yard, and all our other efforts can only make a small difference." Weird, how the guy threw in that slang with his precise diction and lack of contractions.

Maybe Jack should just give up on all this and go back to the farm to die. The trouble was, he wasn't ready to die. There were too many Mexican omelets to eat—without the cheese, if he followed Patel's regimen.

Jack wasn't convinced life could be worth living without bread and cheese and wine.

Yet there were still too many books left to read.

Too many crazy women like the kitten lady to run into.

Too many Internet boob jokes to forward to his friends.

He just wasn't ready to let go.

So he made another appointment for two weeks from then.

Maybe he could come up with something about the house.

Eleven

Cassie

I had no idea how much *stuff* Tom and I had accumulated in the past forty years till I started emptying out all the closets and dressers. It's hard to sort through all the trash and treasures of a lifetime, even when pain is the motivator. Knowing that a purge was medically necessary didn't make it any easier.

I knew it could be done. Mama was proof of that. It had taken her three years finally to face the fact that she needed to downsize to a senior condo. Then it had taken her another twenty months, with constant prodding from her best friend Alice, to go through all her stuff and decide what she could stand to leave behind. The key word is "decide." Making up her mind was hard enough for Mama, one decision at a time. But when faced with all the jillion little ones presented by every little thing she'd deflected into the attic and the basement, she'd short-circuited. Without Alice, it never would have gotten done.

But I didn't have an Alice, or a lot of time. The mold remediators were coming in two weeks, which left me fourteen days to get rid of everything that couldn't be demolded or cleaned, which included all my precious old hardback books and decorator magazines, along with my grandmother's gorgeous coral silk camelback Chippendale sofa with the down cushion.

I couldn't ask Haley or Tommy's wife to come help me. They both worked. And it wasn't as if I could call on a friend to help. Tom had been my best friend. All my gal pals were married, and after the funeral, every one of them had discreetly receded into their couples' world, as if they were afraid I might want their husbands.

Trust me, I did *not* want their husbands. Tom was one in a million. Nobody could fill his shoes.

So I called Mama, even though I knew she'd get the terminal shivers when I so much as mentioned cleaning things out. "Mama," I pleaded, "this is an emergency. The clock is ticking, and there's no way I can do this all by myself. Please tell the Daughters of the King to get somebody else to do the newsletter this week, and cancel bridge and tennis"—yes, she still played tennis, but the slow-mo version—"just this once. Please. You won't have to lift anything. I just need you to nudge me along."

"Why, you're the most organized, decisive person I know," she minced out, "of course you can do this."

She'd become very rigid about her schedule, and her initial response to anything that disrupted her normal routine was always no, but I didn't give up. "Really, Mama. This is too much for me to do by myself."

"No it's not," she huffed. "And anyway, I wouldn't be any help. I'm the *wishy-washy* one, remember?" she said, resurrecting a criticism I'd uttered in frustration when she'd kept postponing her move to the senior condos. "You'll do fine."

"No I won't," I insisted. "Remember how it helped you to have Aunt Alice help you sort through your stuff?"

Mama hadn't let me near that job, claiming that I would "try to throw away all her favorite things."

I played my ace. "Please, Mama. When's the last time I asked you to do something for me?" Not in a long, long time.

There was an extended pause while she finally shifted gears. "Oh, all right," she grumbled. "I suppose I can get Elizabeth Joy to cover for me. But only through Friday. A bunch of us from the place are leaving Saturday for a nature tour of the Tennessee River Valley."

"Will you need time to pack?" What was I saying? Mama always started packing *way* ahead to extend the anticipation of a trip.

"I've been packed for two weeks." Thank goodness. "But if I come over," she qualified, "you'll have to get rid of that *pig*."

"I'm sure Phil and Martin would love to have her for the week." I hoped. Otherwise, it would set me back a pretty penny to board her somewhere. "You'll never see her."

"All right, then," Mama said.

"With you helping me, I know we can get through everything in a week."

"Well, if we don't, you're on your own."

I groveled suitably. "I know, and I really appreciate your giving me that much time."

"See you tomorrow morning at ten." The crack of dawn for her.

"Ten, it is."

I spent the rest of the day emptying cabinets and closets and drawers. Our room would be last. I had to have time to work up to purging my personal belongings, not to mention Tom's. For the moment, I'd just moved his overcoats and jackets from the hall closet to the bed in Tommy's room. Once everything but the master suite was emptied out, I sprayed the closets, walls, and ceilings with mold killer, then took out the drawers and sprayed or wiped them down, finishing up with the insides of the furniture, then the backs and bottoms. The ceiling fans came in handy with drying everything out, but when I looked up, I really saw how old and out-of-date they were, so I added "new ceiling fans" to my list.

I even sprayed myself and Juliette with the mold-killer solution, since it was safe, which she didn't mind a bit, as long as I didn't get any in her mouth or nose. (We are talking seriously bitter with that cleaner and the drops, but eventually, I got used to gargling with the drops in springwater.)

I worked at a furious pace till I ran out of gas and ate a bowl of alphabet soup for supper at nine, only to discover, when I rinsed out the can for recycling, that it contained autolysed yeast for flavoring. Shoot. I loved my canned alphabet soup.

To make up for my lapse, I put three drops of the bitter mold medicine in a bottle of springwater and drank it. Then I went to bed, exhausted.

Mama arrived the next morning on time, and still a bit fuzzy. I had coffee waiting, so after another cup (her third), she woke up enough to get to work.

She rubbed her hands together. "Okay. I need five sheets. We're going to do this the way they do on *Clean Sweep*."

One of my favorite shows. "Okay," I said. "Why don't we start in the attic, then work our way down to the basement? I've already cleared out the kids' rooms."

"Perfect," Mama said. "That's how Alice and I did it. The best place to start is probably all your old financial records. That worked well for me. Do you have a shredder?"

I nodded in amazement at her decisiveness. "Yes. It's in the office. We can plug it in upstairs with an extension cord." Fortunately, we'd insulated and air-conditioned the attic when we'd done the master, and the bat people had put everything back like new. Otherwise, Mama and I would have baked our brains out up there in less than ten minutes.

Once we were in the attic and I started shredding, Mama started sorting through things with relentless precision—maybe because they were mine, not hers, so it was easier to be objective. She didn't ask me, just said, *keep, toss, donate,* or *sell* as a statement, pausing only briefly for my confirmation. There were no undecideds.

I quickly became embarrassed by all the things we'd kept that needed to be thrown away. *Why on this good green earth did I keep that?* became my silent mantra for the day.

There were receipts and records and old files from Tom's job in boxes dating back to 1974. I had boxes of outdated files from parties and Christmases and Thanksgivings past, complete with seating arrangements, menus, and shopping lists and receipts. And every Christmas card list, plus every batch of cards we'd received for the past twenty years, neatly put away in plastic zip bags by year.

"Just keep the photo ones that you recognize," Mama advised about the cards, "and the ones from last year. Toss the rest."

I did, but it tugged at my heart, prompting me to remember those happy seasons with Tom gone by.

In two hours, I had shredded enough old papers to fill a thirty-gallon trash bag.

Once that was done, only a single box of truly important documents, current insurance information, house-related files, and active financials remained to be put into large Ziploc bags and filed back into the empty, mold-free den desk.

Mama eyed the Christmas corner of the attic. "Okay. Now let's cull through all these old Christmas decorations you haven't used for years."

My taste in decorations had evolved over the years, but I hadn't gotten rid of the old ones, just in case I wanted to use them again someday.

Mama shook her head. "You've got enough up here to do a Macy's." She plucked a wreath in a black plastic trash bag from the wall, then opened the bottom and looked inside. "Teddy bears? Since when do you need a giant Christmas wreath with teddy bears?"

"I made it when the kids were babies. I thought they might want it when they had children." Of course, I'd completely forgotten to offer it to Tommy and Paige.

"We are officially deleting 'might' or 'may' from our vocabulary." Mama tossed the wreath to the *donate* sheet. "All this old stuff will be great for the Boys and Girls Club. Or a little church without many funds. Definitely donate."

I considered putting the culls into the garage sale, but it was summer, and everything was outdated, so it probably wouldn't sell, anyway. "You're right."

Suddenly I realized how selfish it was to keep everything hidden away for "just in case," when the decorations could be used for a worthwhile cause. So I started sorting through them with a vengeance that matched my mother's. Even the ones I was still using would have to be treated for mold, then stored in airtight containers with silica gel, so I winnowed out a few boxes of those I could live without, too.

Frankly, my first Christmas without Tom had been a disaster, but I'd decorated anyway, crying the whole time. This one didn't promise to be any better, but I had to try, at least. I didn't want to turn into the Grinch. So I carried all my Christmas *keeps* down to the living room to be treated, and we moved on to the clothes stored in the attic.

If I heard, "Thank goodness you're not that big anymore," once, I heard it a dozen times in the next thirty minutes, but it was true, so I quickly amassed a nice pile for the consignment shop. Just to be safe, though, I kept the very best of my fat clothes to ward off gaining back what I'd lost. Same principle as the baby bed: the minute you sell it, you need it again.

The only real snag was Tom's things. Without comment as they turned up, I moved each box or belonging to the spot where the Christmas decorations had been, to be dealt with later. I was relieved that Mama didn't comment.

"Okay," she said when we'd finished the old papers and decorations and clothes, "let's get rid of all the kids' junk over there." Probably half of what was left.

"Mama, those are their things, not mine," I protested. "I can't just throw them away."

"I didn't say you should," she said in a cheery tone. "This is the fun part. I'll put down two more sheets—one for Haley and one for Tommy—and we'll put everything on those. Then we can get some big boxes from U-Haul and ship them all their junk."

This, from my mama, who'd agonized over every keepsake in her own attic?

She grinned. "They're grown-ups, now. Let them sort it all out."

"Who are you, and where is my mama?" I said with a wry smile.

"Once I got rid of all *my* junk and moved on," she said, "I realized I don't even miss any of it. And so will you." She waggled her eyebrows. "Just consider it payback for their adolescence."

I had to laugh. I'd told Tommy and Haley all about Dr. Patel and my condition, but they'd been so used to thinking of me as a hypochondriac that they'd shown little interest. This should definitely get their attention.

After we'd rooted out all the kids' things in the attic, we lugged everything downstairs to the dining room, then finished up with their old rooms. Then we went to U-Haul for the boxes.

Back home with the cardboard crates, we ate soup I made from tomato paste, a little basil, some garlic, and springwater. I didn't like it as much as my favorite canned brand, but it was decent enough.

Mama took a last swig of her tea, then wiped her mouth. "I wish I could help you out more financially with all this mold business, but I can't. But I do have enough to pay for the shipping to Tommy and Haley, at least." She smiled. "That way, they can be mad at me, too."

"Thanks." Mama had more money than I did, but she was probably going to live to a hundred and twenty, so I understood why she remained so frugal.

She stood up. "Now, let's cram everything into those crates."

By seven that night, we had emptied the attic of everything but Tom's pile, and wiped down what we could from the few remaining *keep*s with mold cleaner.

A night owl, Mama insisted that we go to WalMart for the airtight plastic storage bins we needed ($237 worth!), then joined me for some chicken salad before we loaded the plastic bins with what we'd cleaned. Then we stacked them all at the bottom of the attic stairs.

I could hardly move when that was done. "Uncle. I've got to quit."

Mama patted my shoulder. "Bless your heart. I'll go, then. See you tomorrow at ten."

"How can you be so chipper?" I asked her.

"Zumba," she said, dancing like a native African, which was

pretty funny, considering her hyper-Nordic appearance. "Keeps me in shape, and I love it. You might want to try it."

With my joints, not an option. "If I shook my booty, it would cost me ten thousand dollars at the orthopedic surgeon's." I watched her walk to her car and made sure she backed out of the driveway okay. Then I went inside for a good scrubbing, top to toe, with Juliette in the shower, followed by a long, hot soak in the bathtub and some Advil before I collapsed into a dreamless sleep.

Twenty seconds later the alarm went off, and it was morning. I heaved myself out of bed, took more Advil with my coffee and eggs and bacon and prescriptions, then worked with Mama till nine that night, again.

Repeat three more times, and it was Friday night. We'd gone through everything in the house but Tom's things, cleaning and crating what we could. We'd washed all my curtains, clothes, table and bed linens and towels in the mold-killer detergent, then stored them in giant Ziploc bags in the drawers we'd sprayed, to keep them safe till the remediators finished. We also put encasements on all the mattresses, box springs, and pillows (another $500).

By then, even Mama was showing wear and tear. I walked her to her car, serenaded by July flies in the darkened oaks overhead. "Have fun on your trip tomorrow," I said as she got in.

Mama rolled down her window and looked up at me with a half smile. "After this week, it'll be a piece of cake."

I braced my hands on the edge of her open window, grateful for Dr. Patel's miracle vaccine and the energy I got from my low-carb diet. "I can do the rest by myself." I ticked off my remaining chores aloud. "Take the donations. Drag the trash out to the curb. Set up the garage sale for next Saturday." Hearing myself say it, I realized I probably had more to do than I could manage. "I'm on a roll."

"Good." Mama shot me a soft look. "I know it won't be easy with Tom's things, but it's time. Keep some of his favorite clothes in one of those airtight bins, so you can smell them when you need to remember him." She patted my hand. "I did that with your daddy's sweater and pipe and favorite sport coat. And his pillow."

Tears welled in my eyes. "Thanks." The word came out ragged. "That's a good idea."

"You could call the kids and ask them what of their daddy's they'd like to keep. Or you could just split everything down the middle and ship it to them."

"I'll call them." They were going to be annoyed enough with me when their own junk arrived. I planned to tell them it was coming, of course, but not till it was safely on its way.

"They might say they don't want anything," Mama warned me with compassion.

I managed a crooked smile, missing Tom more than I had for months. "We have stricken 'might' and 'may' from our vocabulary, remember?"

Mama chuckled. "My bad."

"My bad?" I teased. "Where did you pick that up? In Zumba?"

"I'm old, sweetheart," she scolded gently, "not dead. We keep up with the times."

Better than I did. "Good night, Mama. Drive safe."

She waved and backed out perfectly, then headed for home.

I went back inside my empty house filled with things, and burst into tears.

Twelve

Cassie

I gave myself a day off to rest, then tackled what was left with a vengeance. As Mama had predicted, the children didn't want anything of Tom's besides some photos of them, together. So I did as Mama suggested, putting away a few things that reminded me of him. But when it came to the rest, I couldn't part with any of it. I felt as if I'd be erasing him from my life, if I did. So I packed everything neatly in airtight bins and let them stay in the attic. Maybe someday I could let it go, but not yet.

Then I threw myself into pricing everything and setting up the sale in the garage. It was hot, tedious work, but gave me a sense of accomplishment while I waited for the guys from Carrolton to start. I actually began to enjoy cleaning my house down to the bone.

You live in a house long enough, there's an amazing amount of grime hiding out all over the place, and I felt virtuous getting rid of it.

At least I was doing something positive to improve my health. But I got so carried away, I lost track of time and almost missed my next appointment with Dr. Patel. When that Thursday morning rolled around, I was recuperating over my second cup of coffee and *The Today Show* before I looked at my calendar. Whoa! I hastily raked a comb through my hair and covered the dark circles under my eyes, then grumbled as I dressed, which upset Juliette, who always senses my mood. As usual under the circumstances, she traipsed over on her little hooves and leaned heavily against my leg with a worried grunt. "Don't worry," I told her with a consoling pat to her side, "I'll be back soon, and we'll take our walk."

She knew what "walk" meant and perked right up.

I smeared on some lipstick, then dotted some on my cheeks and rubbed it in on the way to the back door. I was halfway to the car when I realized I hadn't set the alarm and had to double back to do it.

So when I arrived at the doctor's office, I was late, harried, and hardly looking my best.

Huffing and puffing from the hike to the building, I was pleased to see my one-legged curmudgeon frowning in his place on the sofa. As usual, I sat at the other end, just to annoy him. Then I noticed his lips were almost blue, and he was really struggling for breath.

"Are you okay?" I asked, worried.

"What difference does it make to you?" he gasped out. "You don't even know me, which suits me fine."

"I have empathy for my fellow man," I explained. "It's one of those characteristics that separates us from the animals."

He shot me one of those "boo to you" looks, then closed his eyes and laid his head back, wheezing audibly.

He was really dusky at the edges of his face. "No kidding," I prodded, "should I call the nurse?" I didn't like the way he looked, and I certainly didn't want him to croak right there in the doctor's office, with help so close by.

"Just leave me alone. Everybody else has," he grumbled.

Uh-oh. Doing that male version of Camille.

Why was it that men refused to get medical help when they needed it, but moaned and wheezed so much that you couldn't ignore them?

My maternal instincts aroused, I got up and tiptoed over to the receptionist to lean in and whisper, "He looks really rough. Let him have the first spot. I can wait."

She nodded.

Then I went back to the sofa where the one-legged curmudgeon sat with his head laid back and eyes closed. When he didn't move, it scared me, so I asked, "How is your mold remediation coming?"

He reared up with a bleary, "I tried to clean out some things, and this is what it got me."

One of those cranky old hermits, no doubt, who probably hadn't cleaned since his wife left him for the milkman because he was so disagreeable. "Don't you have anybody to help you?"

"That's none of your business."

"Did you use a respirator and goggles to protect yourself?"

"What is it about 'none of your business' that you don't understand?" he growled out.

My maternal instincts overwhelmed my common sense, and I heard myself say, "I'm Cassie Jones. They're starting work on my house tomorrow, so I have to go to my mother's, who doesn't want me there. I wouldn't mind coming to help you during the day. And

I have an extra respirator and goggles you could use." I rummaged up one of my calling cards, wrote my number on it, then handed it to him. "Here."

He opened one eye, skeptical, not looking at the card. "I could be a serial killer, for all you know."

"I'm also very perceptive," I told him, "and I can see that you're all thunder and no rain."

He actually smiled, transforming his face to almost decent. "My grandmother used to say that."

"So did mine," I said, smiling back.

He eyed me again, still skeptical. "Are you serious? You'd come to a strange man's house, way out in the boonies, to help clear out?"

My kids were always complaining about my "dangerous" charitable impulses, but God was always putting people in my life who needed some help.

I grinned at the curmudgeon God had sent me. "Honey, I know judo," I lied, "and a three-year-old could outrun you in your current condition, so I don't really consider it much of a risk. Plus, I'm very good at organizing. It's so much easier to do when there's somebody there to help. My mother helped me get rid of my junk."

He cocked his head. "How old is *she*?" As if I were ancient.

"Eighty-eight, and in much better shape than I am." I smiled, remembering Mama's reaction when I'd told her I needed to move in with her for a while. "The first thing she said when I asked if I could stay with her while they remediated my house was, 'When will you be leaving?'"

I looked to the curmudgeon. "What about your mother?"

"She lives in Biloxi with my aunt," he grudgingly admitted.

"What about your father?"

He scowled. "He left my mother thirty years ago. Five years ago, he married his Mexican sitter from the assisted living and moved to the Yucatán." The curmudgeon actually looked surprised to have told me, and even more surprised when he added, "I have a three-year-old half sister, if you can believe it, which I can't. Dad'll leave whatever he has left to her and his wife, I'm sure, but he's happy, and at least I don't have to worry about him anymore."

Interesting attitude, all things considered.

His breathing seemed to have eased as we talked, so I looked at his book and kept up the conversation. "What are you reading?"

He arched one eyebrow with a superior expression. "A biography of Alexander Hamilton."

"Oh, I loved that one. Got an autographed copy. Did you read any of his other books?"

"All of them."

"Me, too. I love a good biography."

He granted me a skeptical, "You read?"

I felt a rush of heat warm my neck. Did I look like the kind of person who didn't *read*? "I used to, everything from James Patterson to Patti Callahan Henry to Kierkegaard to Augustus Caesar. And the Bible. I love the Bible; read it every day."

I felt a stab of loss for the escape that losing myself in a good book had once given me.

"Then my husband died," I went on, wondering why I was confiding in this arrogant stranger. Maybe because we were enduring the same thorn in our sides. "And ever since, I've had some weird kind of ADD. I'll be reading along just fine for a few paragraphs—maybe even a page—then, all of a sudden, the words seem to lose continuity and jump out at me individually, and I totally lose the flow."

I saw the first sympathy the curmudgeon had ever aimed my way. "Wow. That must be awful," he said, his tone and expression sincere.

"It is. Leaves me with a lot of time on my hands. Audio books just aren't the same for me."

He considered me for a moment, then frowned. "You got a piece of paper?"

"Sure." I rummaged through my purse till I found my little tablet, then handed it to him, along with a pen.

He spoke as he wrote. "My name is Jack Wilson. This is my address and cell phone. If you want to come over tomorrow after you get the mold people started at your place, I would appreciate some help. I'll pay you in fresh vegetables."

Ah. Didn't want to be beholden. So male.

But he was still a man, and knowing men as I did, I volunteered, "I'll bring some lunch. Strictly yeast-free and sugar-free."

His brief smile didn't make it to his eyes. "You got a deal."

The nurse stuck her head out. "Mr. Wilson, Dr. Patel will see you first, today."

Twenty minutes later, I was in the exam chair and Dr. Patel had given me the bad news about my ALCAT allergy test results: I was allergic to almost all my favorite foods, including the healthy ones.

How could a person be allergic to *rice*? The wheat, oat, and soy allergies, I could see, but *rice*? I fumed as he squirted the nasty anesthetic up my nose. And romaine *lettuce*, for heaven's sake.

I looked at my copy of the ALCAT results. My most severe allergies were black pepper, for cryin' out loud, and broccoli and whitefish (they use that to make fake crab meat and seafood salad at buffets and the grocery store, which I loved!). And beef. No more medium-rare strip steaks.

The way to my heart was through my stomach, too, and this was bad news, indeed.

Dr. Patel pushed the scope up into my sinuses. "I strongly advise you to use a good nutritionist to help you work out your rotation diet."

"Rotation diet?"

He nodded. "Your food allergies developed because the infection in your lower tract allowed food particles that were too large into your bloodstream, so your body developed antibodies against them. Food stays in your system for three days, then you need to give your body a day to rest before you eat that food again. After we get your system cleared out, you'll be able to try adding back some of the foods listed on the mildly allergic column, one at a time. But the ones on the severe and moderate columns are out, for life."

Most of the foods I loved!

So much for breaking it gently. This guy needed an interpreter who had some bedside manner.

Then again, I guess there wasn't any point in sugarcoating the truth, pun intended.

Clicking photos of my now-clearer sinuses, he went on. "You're doing a very good job with your irrigation, by the way." Then he added the straw that broke the camel's back. "Also, chlorine interferes with your medication and destroys the cilia in your tract, so you need to start drinking only springwater. Mountain Clear is a good company. They use glass bottles and stainless lines in their dispensers, which is safer than plastic."

How much was *that* going to cost?

I'd have to make my tea and coffee with springwater, then drag them with me. Could we make this any *more* difficult?

My expression must have reflected my dismay, because he added, "The nutritionist I recommended is very good. She can help you work all this out."

"Will my insurance cover that? I have Green Shield PPO."

"I'm afraid not," he said without emotion. "Since this diagnosis is so new, a lot of the treatments and necessary dietary supplements aren't covered under customary medical treatment protocols, so they're denied."

Perfect. "How much does this nutritionist cost?"

Dr. Patel's nurse chimed in with, "A hundred fifty for the first consultation, then a hundred a week for your phone sessions until you can handle things on your own. It's well worth the money."

I started guesstimating how much this was all going to cost. Fifty thousand dollars' worth of mold remediation. Special food. Bleemin' *spring*water. Special detergent and cleaners and shampoo and drops. Jillions of supplements that weren't covered or deductible on my taxes. Liquid vitamins that cost sixty dollars a month. Seven-hundred-dollar office visits.

I had a vision of Tom's insurance money being sucked into a giant eddy of twenty-dollar bills that fed the greedy maw of the medical/insurance monster, and the specter of destitution reared up, ragged and grinning, in the background.

Just then, Jack Wilson stuck his head into the exam room on his way to check out. "See you tomorrow."

Dr. Patel and his nurse's curiosity was palpable.

"What time?" I asked.

He shrugged. "Whenever. I'm not going anywhere. Just not too early." Then he disappeared.

"Whenever" suited me fine, as I'd become a "whenever" kind of person since Tom had died.

At least going to the curmudgeon's would provide a distraction from all my new restrictions, and I didn't have to worry about any man/woman complications. Jack Wilson was Mr. Wrong, personified. The man was a people-hater who looked like a bum, for heaven's sake.

But there was a chance—a very slim one—that we might be able to become friends. After all, he was an avid reader. And a host organism, like me.

Thirteen

Cassie

I got home from the doctor's that afternoon and—not wanting to wear out my welcome with my sweet gay neighbors—I boarded Juliette at an elegant pet hotel in Buckhead to the tune of sixty dollars a day. For that, though, they said they would potty-train her. To go on a real potty, I swear. I'd believe that when I saw it. At any rate, she was the most popular animal in the place, with humans and pets alike. By the time the mold people finished with my house, she probably wouldn't want to come home.

The next morning, the mold remediation crew arrived on time at nine, as promised, followed in rapid succession by the flooring people, the roofers, the foundation people, and a huge truck full of new windows destined for the garage till they could be installed. But I still had some things left over from the garage sale to deal with, so I had to scurry around to make room for the windows. I'd bitten the bullet and gotten really good ones, which had upped my budget from fifty thousand to sixty-five.

How that nice mold man from Carrolton had managed to get all the subcontractors to show up on time was a mystery to me, but I was glad. Good thing I'd moved my car to the street, so I could get out.

So I handed over my house to the nice mold man from Carrolton, along with my keys and the alarm code on the back of one of my calling cards. "Please keep this in confidence and remember to set the alarm whenever you leave," I told him quietly as I handed it over, "even for a short time."

Not that there were any valuables left inside. My jewelry and my sterling silver and computer were packed behind the rear seat of my minivan with my favorite summer clothes, ready to go to Mama's, along with my small bookshelf component system and two little flat-screen TVs.

"Don't you worry, ma'am," the nice mold man reassured me. "We'll treat your house like our own."

Whatever that meant. "Just be gentle with it, please." I waggled my cell phone. "Call if you have any questions."

I finished loading all the cleaning supplies and masks and rubber gloves and goggles into the middle seat, along with the five old sheets I had used with Mama, then checked the rear section of my minivan to be sure I hadn't left behind anything I'd need. If you pack for a week, you might as well go for a month, so there wasn't a square inch left unoccupied in the storage or the seats, but I'd loaded up everything on my list, including special food and spring-water.

Mama had told me to be on time when I brought everything over to her condo, because she had to meet with the altar guild at St. Phillip's at eleven, and she wouldn't give me a key because of my unreliability as an adolescent. Never mind that I was fifty-five.

I got in the car and buckled up, then punched Jack Wilson's address into my GPS. When I saw the dot outside the map of Metro

Atlanta, I let out a low whistle. He wasn't kidding when he said he was out in the boonies. It would take me at least forty-five minutes to get there—assuming there wasn't a wreck on I-400, which was assuming a lot. I'd have to hustle over to Mama's, dump my things in her guest room, then schlep all the way back to Whole Foods on Paces Ferry to pick up lunch.

But I'd promised to bring lunch, so schlep I would.

For a car its size, my Chrysler minivan got pretty good mileage, so I wouldn't have to spend too much on gas.

The one-legged curmudgeon had said his house was small. I figured one day, two at the most, and we could get things in order. But that was before I saw Jack Wilson's house—or warehouse, to be more exact.

When I got to rural Forsyth County and found the dented mailbox with Jack's numbers painted crudely on the post, I turned in at the dirt driveway, then stopped and peered into the thick woods that hid the rest of the way.

Was I crazy to be doing this?

What if Jack Wilson really was a serial killer?

He was antisocial enough to qualify.

Nah. His eyes had harbored no malice, just irritation. In his condition, who could blame the guy?

In the end, my conscience won out. I'd promised to help, so help I would.

Lord, I'm trying to do a good deed, here, so please don't let me get killed. Or maimed. Or worse.

Lucky for me, God honors even reckless faith.

So I pressed the gas and bumped along the rutted road till the woods ended at a huge, dried-out pasture that surrounded one of the saddest-looking little farmhouses I'd ever seen. It had once been turquoise, but the paint had peeled and faded to a pale green wherever the sun hit it. As I approached, I noted that the aluminum windows were ancient jalousies, shaded by peeling aluminum awnings. I heard a rusty window unit rattling away in a futile effort to subdue the waves of heat that rose from the ground and the roof.

An ancient, beat-up old green pickup with a rusty riding lawn mower in the load bed was parked under the dented aluminum carport on the near side of the house. I would have figured the curmudgeon for a junker like that.

As I came nearer, two scruffy-looking cats reared up from the load bed and yawned, then jumped out to check out my car.

Perfect. Just what I needed: cats. I grabbed one of the respirators from the backseat and resolved to put it on before I got out.

There was a barn in back, against some more woods, with a daunting collection of overgrown, rusty farm equipment scattered around it.

Very creepy. Like the set for one of those awful teen hack-and-sack movies, where everybody ends up dismembered.

Remember, Lord, I'm on a mission of mercy.

The only thing that didn't look seduced and abandoned was the large vegetable garden out back. That was as tidy and well tended as anything I'd ever seen in Amish country.

So Jack was a gardener, and an impressive one, at that.

That was a relief. I was a gardener, too, and I'd never met a true gardener who wasn't a decent person, so I decided to park and get out.

Just in case, though, I cut onto the verge, then backed in ahead of the old green truck, so I could make a quick getaway if I had to.

I got out, pressing the button to open the side door, then put on my cleaning apron and—just to be safe—stowed my cell phone in the apron pocket, ready to dial 911 if anything dire happened. Assuming 911 didn't put me on hold again, but this was the country, so maybe they weren't as busy as calamity-ridden Atlanta.

I put on the respirator, with its two hot-pink, moldproof canisters on either side of the mouthpiece. Because of the cats, I donned goggles, too, then put on my rubber gloves and got out to gather the cleaning things. When I couldn't hold anything more, I clunked up to the side door and bumped it with my plastic pail. No bell.

I was really hot in the goggles and respirator, so when nobody acknowledged my bumps, I set down the pail and rapped loudly on the door. "Yoo-hoo! It's me!"

My voice barely escaped the respirator.

I waited some more and was just about to turn to leave when the door jerked open, and two more cats streaked past me. Jack looked down at me in consternation. "Callie?"

"Cassie," I corrected, then pushed past him, the state of his house distracting me completely. Piles and piles of stuff were everywhere.

Holy hoarder!

This was going to be a lot more complicated than I'd bargained for.

"You look like something from a UFO," Jack said as he closed the door behind me.

I glared at him through the goggles. "I came to help you clean, not make myself sick."

I put down the pail and tossed the other respirator at him. "Put that on. No wonder you can't breathe. This place is *lethal*." Dust and cat hair coated everything. I shivered, just thinking about it.

Jack scowled, but put on the respirator.

I tossed him the goggles. "And these." Where in the world was I supposed to spread out those sheets? Stuff covered all but a few trails to his recliner, the kitchen, and the bedrooms.

The house was small, with one common room and only two bedrooms, but it sure was firmly packed. Crammed bookcases took up all the wall space, but I couldn't see all the titles for the stuff piled in front of them. More books stood in teetering stacks amid the rest of his junk. I spotted a very eclectic selection of titles, from classical to mysteries to spy thrillers to literary.

"What is all this *stuff*?" I hollered through the respirator.

"Part trash, part treasure," he admitted with a shrug. "And I'm the only one who knows the difference."

"Okay," I told him. "Here's the plan. I have five old sheets in my car, one for what you absolutely must keep, one for what you want to donate to charity, one for your garage sale, one for what needs to be thrown away, and one for undecided."

I looked at all the things he'd let pile up in his house. Was it pathological, or from neglect? I'd find out when we started.

He at least didn't veto the sheet idea, so I went on. "Why don't you back your truck out of the carport, so we can spread things out under the cover, in case we get an afternoon storm?" We should be so lucky.

Jack nodded. His response was muffled by the respirator: "Your mouth to God's ear." We were six inches low on rain for the year. "I've had to hand-water my vegetables from the well for the last month."

Whoa! Talk about hot, heavy work, especially for a man in his condition.

He rummaged up his keys, then went out to move the truck. I followed with the sheets. When he walked back into the stifling shade of the carport, I handed him one end of the *toss* sheet, then proceeded to spread it and all the others out with his help. We anchored them with cracked clay flowerpots from a stack leaning by the stairs.

The cats immediately lolled right in the middle of every one, but Jack didn't chase them off. Instead, he stroked and petted them with soft words I couldn't hear for the respirator.

If there's one thing that really gets my goat, it's people who spend all their affection on pets, then treat the human beings around them like dirt. Strike three, you're out, for Mr. Jack Whatsisname. (I'd already forgotten his last name, maybe as a result of brain fog. Something common . . . Smith? No. Something to do with tennis. Wilson!)

Jack Wilson moved very naturally on his gleaming, sci-fi artificial lower leg, but I was too polite to ask him what had happened. Still, I couldn't help wondering.

I went to my car for the last of the things we'd need: two laundry hampers. I handed one to Jack. "Start with this. Decide on a category—*keep*, *toss*, or *sell*—and fill this with stuff from the house, then put it out here. Once we get going, it should move pretty quickly." I saluted him. "Okay. Let's find those treasures."

Jack looked at his container askance. "Did you order your husband around like this when he was alive?"

What nerve!

Smarting, I stormed over, snatched his basket and flung it to the ground, then gripped his Hawaiian shirt with both my rubber gloves and got into his face. "I didn't have to order anybody while my husband was alive. He was the kindest man I've ever known, and he took care of me and our home without my having to ask. So don't you dare mention his name again."

"Jeez Louise," Jack said, "I didn't say his name in the first place, but if that's how you want it, okay."

I let go of his shirt and stepped back, my heart still pounding from his unexpected attack, not to mention my reaction. "Okay." I shoved his basket back at him, then left him to his own devices while I got the vacuum and the garden sprayer with the mold cleaner in it from the minivan. "We'll start in the kitchen." Good thing I had half a gallon of Clorox Clean-Up left to tackle the grease in there.

"Aye, aye, your bossiness." Jack saluted with lowered brows, but did as I asked.

First, we had to get everything out. Only then could I scrub the floor and walls, then tackle the pile of pots and dishes in the sink. Did the man ever wash anything?

If it weren't for Dr. Patel's vaccine, I wouldn't have had the energy to start such a big job, much less finish it. But all we had to do today was make a dent in things.

It must have been at least eighty-five in there, despite the window units, which didn't help.

Three hours later, I'd filled up and thrown out two huge contractor bags of plain old trash and garbage, and stacked up five feet of old newspapers Jack had been saving to read later. When I pointed out that "later" never came, he finally surrendered them to be recycled. Outside, the *undecided* pile of old appliances, clothes, books, ancient bills and bank records, and furniture was huge, and the *toss* pile was the smallest. A few things that I doubted anybody would ever want—including a broken hobby horse—lay on the *donate* sheet, and the *keep* heap was almost as high as the *undecided*.

I didn't challenge Jack about the undecideds. That would come later, after he'd had time to adjust to getting stuff outside. One step at a time.

By lunchtime, we'd managed to clear the kitchen floor and a third of the dining area, which convinced me that the curmudgeon's hoarding was situational, not pathological. Though he was definitely a slob, it soon became clear that he didn't see his things as an extension of himself. For the most part, he saw his stuff as investments and things that needed to be recycled instead of tossed into the landfill.

So he was a *green* curmudgeon, which still didn't justify the state of his surroundings.

I was shocked when he showed me some of his plate collection and told me how much each one was worth. He held up one with an eagle crest in the middle. "This is a genuine Romanoff plate, prerevolution, commissioned for the marriage of the last czar."

"Nicholas." I stared at its emblem and intricate gold work. "How do you know that it's real?"

"I had it appraised at the Smithsonian," he said through the respirator, which seemed to be helping his breathing. "Did you know they used to do appraisals for any citizen who made an appointment?" He carefully placed the plate on the now-clean dining room table where we'd put his other valuables. "Not anymore, though. But when they did, I drove to Washington many times to have my finds verified."

His artificial foot lifted when he said it, but he didn't seem to notice.

I motioned to the still-grimy items on the table. "Where did you buy all this?"

Jack shrugged. "Garage sales. Estate sales. Local auctions. That's my hobby. That, and old tools. I've got a barn full of old tools. And tractors."

That piqued my curiosity. "Could you show me your tools, once we're done with all this?"

He snorted inside his respirator. "Careful. Your greed is showing."

"I don't plan to steal them," I snapped. "I just want to see them."

Noting that it was already one o'clock, I changed the subject. "I'll set up lunch." At least the table was clean, and half clear. We ate baked chicken and green beans with bottled springwater to wash it all down. Then we went back to work and didn't come up for air till the sun hovered above the trees. I looked at my watch and was surprised to see that it was eight o'clock.

My stomach let out a huge growl, to which Jack responded. "I reckon I'd better feed you."

No way was I eating anything that came from that kitchen. But I was suddenly starving. In deference to Jack's obvious lack of funds, I picked two relatively inexpensive choices where I could stick to my diet. "Do y'all have a Golden Corral or a cafeteria any-where around here?"

"Yep." Jack pulled off his respirator and rubbed the deep lines it left on his face, then scratched the stubble of his beard. "Brand-new Golden Corral in Cumming, over by the mall on the other side of 400."

At least I'd be close to the route home. I removed my own res-pirator, then felt the impressions graven into my own skin. The respirator straps always trashed my hair, so I knew I looked like an apparition, but I didn't care what Jack thought. Only the people in the Golden Corral. "I'll follow you."

"Give me a minute to change my shirt."

I needed to go to the bathroom, but my one trip to that hell-hole had convinced me I'd suffer genetic mutation if I went back. "I'll wait in the car."

I could comb my hair and freshen my lipstick on the way, then use the bathroom at the restaurant.

Leaving my cleaning things, I braved the cats for the safety of my minivan.

Once I got into the minivan and turned on the air-conditioning full blast, my body reminded me how hard I'd worked all day by seizing up. I debated heading straight to Mama's, but decided I needed to eat first.

Jack came out wearing wrinkled linen shorts, a red designer flip-flop, and a fresh designer Hawaiian shirt. He waved, then got into his truck and circled around to lead the way. Twenty minutes later, I pulled into the last free handicapped space in the jammed restaurant parking lot.

At least I could fill my empty stomach from the buffet with legal foods. Green beans, chicken, melons, salad, tomatoes, deviled eggs, and black-eyed peas waited inside.

I was parked, putting on lipstick in the van, when Jack knocked on my side window, scaring me. I got out in a huff. "Don't ever sneak up on me that way." I headed for the entrance. "I almost had a heart attack."

"Sheesh. I *came* up to escort you inside," he protested, "I didn't sneak up." He held open the entry door for me. "Are you always this jumpy?"

None of his business. Every joint ached from my day's labor. Inside, I excused myself, then took my place at the end of the huge crowd waiting to get their trays and pay. "I'm starving."

"You left your stuff at my house," he said loudly.

God forbid somebody thought he was referring to my personal effects. I didn't look at him. "I'm not done cleaning, and you know it. We are far from finished." I always finished what I started, no matter what.

Wincing, he let out a gravelly, strangled cough, whether in response to what I'd said, or from his COPD, I couldn't tell. "The job might not be finished," he gasped out between coughs, "but after today, I might be."

"You'll feel better when we get rid of all that dust and decaying paper, then vacuum with my HEPA filter Oreck and spray everything down with the mold killer." I still had several boxes of the giant Ziploc bags I could donate to the cause.

"Nazi," he muttered.

We shuffled along in silence till we got to the middle of the snaking line, where Jack let rip with a huge burp, and people all around us glared.

Jack reared back and looked at me in disgust. "Patsy! Really. I swear, I can't take you anywhere anymore." He moved away from me.

Most of me was mortified and seriously ticked off, but some primordial remnant of my six-year-old self actually thought it was funny. Maintaining a dignified expression, I stepped close to ask him in a low voice, "Are you always this crass and juvenile?"

He had the nerve to grin. "Every chance I get." He waggled his white, shaggy brows. "I might be able to muster up another one, if I really try."

I glared at him with narrowed eyes. "Don't you dare."

His answering expression was noncommittal, so I remained on

tenterhooks till we ordered our drinks, then he paid for our supper—with a Platinum Visa.

Poor people didn't have Platinum Visas.

Maybe he was one of those misers, who never spent a penny of the fortunes they'd amassed.

But I was too hungry and achy to speculate. I just got my food and set to eating it. When Jack went to the salad bar, our pretty little dark-haired waitress came over with two bottles of cold springwater and whispered, "Mr. Jack, he is a saint. When my car quit, he pay for the fixing, every bit, so I no lose my job." She set the springwater at our places. "He say no tell anybody," she confided, "but I tell you; he a very good man." Then she hurried away before he spotted her.

So the curmudgeon had a soft side. Imagine that.

Or did he have an ulterior motive? She was very pretty.

I finished the rest of my food while Jack laid into his salad.

I stood to leave before the aromas from the dessert bar wooed me into sin. "Thanks for supper. I'll be back tomorrow morning about eleven." I looked at Jack's dusky fingernails. "If I were you, I'd get a room in one of these new hotels we passed. Until we finish, you really shouldn't go back home."

He glared up at me. "It's my house, and I'll sleep there if I want."

"Suit yourself." I left a double tip. "But don't expect any sympathy from me."

"I didn't ask for any in the first place," he said, his face red with suppressed anger.

I leaned in close, my purse tucked under my elbow. "See you tomorrow." It was a challenge.

He scowled, picking up the gauntlet. "Okay."

Boy, there'd better be some jewels in my crown for this one.

I left without saying good-bye. When I finally got to Mama's, she fussed at me for not calling to say I'd be late.

"Sorry." I headed for the tub to soak and wash the mold and dust from my hair. "I'm whipped. Gotta run." I took three Advils, then scrubbed myself almost raw in the tub. I went to bed with wet hair and slept like the dead, then woke up looking like Medusa, and got ready to go clean the dragon's den for another day.

Fourteen

Jack

The raccoon woman had a point about the house, but there was no way Jack would ever tell her he'd gone straight to the newly renovated La Casa after she left.

"Only one, for the one night?" the sissy clerk asked, scanning Jack's Goodwill clothes and disheveled state with obvious condescension.

Jack shot him a nasty look. "Yes. One."

The clerk let out a brief sigh of resignation, but kept one brow arched, as if Jack had just walked up to the guy's house, rung the bell, and asked to use his bathroom. "Very well."

Who the heck said "very well" anymore?

"That'll be thirty-nine dollars for the night, plus seven dollars tax, which brings the total to forty-six dollars," the pompous twit announced.

What a rip-off. Jack wasn't going to spend but eleven hours there.

When Jack didn't respond immediately, the clerk added an icy, "Will that be cash or credit?"

Jack whipped out his Visa Platinum. "Credit."

Instead of impressing the clerk, the card made the guy even more suspicious, as if Jack had stolen it. "I'll have to see your driver's license, please."

With narrowed eyes, Jack produced his license.

The clerk seemed disappointed when the names matched and the charge was approved, but he remained suspicious. He handed Jack his card with a perfunctory, "Thank you for staying at La Casa, Mr. Wilson." He scanned briefly for any baggage. "We have someone who can help you with your luggage, if you wish."

Jack scowled, deliberately adding fuel to the little clerk's concerns with a sinister, "No luggage." A slow smile spread across his face. "If I'm still alive in the morning, I'll need a wake-up call at eight."

The clerk's lips twisted with worry, his brows drawing together. "Are you ill?" Clearly, the last thing he wanted was somebody croaking in one of their rooms.

"No more than usual." Jack stuck out his hand. "My key, please."

His expression still worried, the clerk nodded and handed over the key card.

Jack headed for his room, still fuming over the cost and the fact that he had to get up at the crack of creation to make sure the raccoon woman didn't beat him to the farm the next day.

Sore, worn out, and coughing, he found his room. Then he stripped, took off his leg, and hopped into the bathroom for a shower. He turned on the shower and waited till it was steaming hot, then got in and sank down to sit on the tiles, letting the spray pelt away, the vapors loosening his cough as he washed himself. When he felt better, he pushed up to a crouch with his hands on the tiles, positioning his good leg under him, then waited till he could muster enough energy to stand and turn off the water.

Every time he suffered the indignity of having to get up without his prosthesis, crawling like an animal, he still felt angry that his own negligence had cost him his leg. He'd worked on hundreds of combines in his time, and knew they could eat him alive. He'd only daydreamed for a few seconds. It hadn't even been a paying job, just a favor for his friend Joe Mason in Dothan. Whole, one minute, incomplete the next. Not long after, his wife had left him.

Obviously she'd wanted somebody who still had all his parts. It wasn't fair, but who said life was fair? And Jack was the one who'd been careless.

It still burned him up.

He knew the anger didn't accomplish anything except giving him indigestion, but he felt it just the same as he had that day twenty-five years before.

Not that sulking did any good. So he hopped out, dried off, then hopped to bed to lie down, aching and coughing all the way.

Jack turned off the bedside light and lay under the sheet, lulled by the air conditioner but aggravated by the shards of light that crept through the blackout curtains from the parking lot. He hated light pollution. Night was supposed to be dark, except for the moon and stars. That had been one of the reasons he'd bought the farm. It was dark there—or had been, until they'd built those blasted gas stations two blocks away. Now their unnatural reddish glow crept all the way to Jack's, except on the clearest of nights.

He closed his eyes and willed himself to stop coughing and go to sleep.

Jack still believed in mind over matter, despite years of evidence to the contrary. It gave him some sense of power over his renegade body. So he never relied on pills or meds unless he was really, really bad. And he always held off calling the doctor until he couldn't manage for one more day. Then, as soon as he felt better, he ditched the prescriptions and went back to mind over matter and the natural way. Once those blasted doctors got you on that appointment/ prescription merry-go-round, there was no end to it.

Jack's last thought before he finally drifted off at one-thirty was that maybe this Indian guy, Patel, might know what he was doing. Jack could hope so, at least. Time would tell.

He fell asleep and dreamed of sex with nameless, faceless big-busted women who asked no questions and had no limits to their expertise.

He was just having his way with the third—or was it the fourth?—when he looked at her face and saw the raccoon woman glaring at him in accusation.

Shock and guilt brought him straight up in the bed at the same instant the phone rang with his wake-up call. Heart pounding, he fumbled with the receiver, then slammed it back down on the phone. With sheer force of will, Jack swung his good leg off the side and stood till he got his balance so he could hop to the bathroom to relieve himself, then shower again.

The image of that accusing face went with him as another bout of coughing set in the way it did every morning.

Damned COPD. But it was his own fault, smoking all those years while he repaired farm equipment to put himself through college, then after.

The shower revived him only partially. Coffee would do the rest.

Still, he didn't feel as bad on this particular morning as he had after trying to clean house without the respirator and goggles.

He owed the raccoon woman for that. But that didn't mean he wanted her in his dreams.

He dried off and donned his running leg. Then he dressed and went down for the breakfast buffet, which offered nothing Dr. Patel had said he could eat, so he ate what he pleased: doughnuts, some cantaloupe, and lots of black coffee.

Until he got the house cleaned and demolded, Dr. Patel's diet was moot, anyway.

Jack got up for a refill from the buffet, then sat down at one of the little tables with a complimentary newspaper and second cup.

Like it or not, the raccoon woman would be back at the farm cracking her whip at eleven. It was humiliating enough, that he really needed her help.

He didn't like asking for help from anyone. He'd always managed on his own, from the time he went to the local college back in Mississippi till he'd earned his doctorate in English lit, paying his way by fixing farm equipment. He hated to rely on anyone now, but the fact was, though he had reams of acquaintances, he had no real friends. Real friends took time away from his books and his hobbies. And his privacy. So there he was, relying on that controlling raccoon woman who showed up, uninvited, like a scolding schoolmarm in his erotic dreams.

The truth was, she was probably only helping him so she could feel superior. Another man to control, now that her husband was gone. Jack knew all about women like that, the do-gooders who did charity work because their husbands made enough money to keep them idle. And this one was a widow; probably rolling in insurance money.

Well, let her feel superior. He didn't really have a choice but to accept her help.

After breakfast, he drove home and tended the garden, picking a peck of Early Girl tomatoes, a few seedless cukes that weren't really seedless, and a sack full of Champion bush beans as pay for the woman's help. When that was done, he stuck them in the ancient veggie fridge under the carport. Next, he went inside and grudgingly put on the respirator and goggles and rubber gloves. Then he set to work, chipping away at Stone Mountain with a teaspoon. He was on his third laundry basket of *keeps* when suddenly, he saw his house the way she must have seen it.

Holy crow.

The chaos and squalor took what was left of his breath.

Good Lord.

Jack sank to his worn recliner, laundry basket in hand.

How had things gotten this way? How had he let them?

Granted, he'd felt like hell for the last four years, but *street people* took better care of their *boxes* than he'd taken care of this place.

No wonder that Buckhead woman felt superior. She was.

He suddenly felt like Han Solo caught in the trash-masher in *Star Wars*, with the walls closing in on him. Shame and claustrophobia overwhelmed Jack, making his stomach roil. He'd never be able to get this ancient house clean enough to make a difference. It was too old, too rotten.

And everything piled inside . . . His things owned him, not the other way around.

The stacks seemed to swell even larger, sucking all the oxygen out of the whole house. A thousand little decisions he'd refused to make now loomed before him, an impossible task.

He should pack a bag and go, leave it all behind. Take what he absolutely needed and walk out.

But where would he go? Not to the kids'. They'd try to tell him what to do all the time and make him babysit.

Jack loved his grandkids, but only in small doses.

He'd reared his children, already. Let them take care of their own kids. More than that, Jack refused to burden them with his illnesses. And most important of all, he refused to give up his independence.

No way around it. He'd have to stay where he was and make the best of a bad situation.

He was still a man. He had to take back control of his environment.

So he began to purge with a vengeance, piling the *sell*, *donate*, and *toss* items outside.

An hour later, he'd just collapsed in his recliner in exhaustion when he heard the raccoon woman drive up.

Blast. She'd be all fresh and rarin' to go, and he was already done in.

Jack grabbed his inhaler and took a couple of shots, then rose to open the door.

She didn't say hello. Just glanced back at what he'd accomplished in the carport and said, "I'm impressed. Seriously."

"Well, don't get your hopes up," he said. "I'm already whipped."

"Sit, then," she said, no criticism in her voice. "I'll pick things to hold up, and you can render a verdict: trash or treasure."

Jack nodded, grateful.

In the next three hours, they cleared half the room, with only a dozen valuable items added to the treasures on the dining room table, and mountains of "trash" in the carport.

Jack looked at the table and shook his head. What had he been thinking, holding on to all that junk outside, when the only things of real value didn't even fill up a tabletop?

Aside from his autographed books, he didn't care how she designated the rest—*toss*, *donate*, or *sell*. He was just glad to see it disappear.

Suddenly, the raccoon woman heaved a great sigh through the respirator and sank into a dining room chair. "Whoa. Gotta sit."

The genuine fifties clock on the wall said it was almost two. "You need to eat," he said, hauling himself out of the recliner. "Come on. I'll take you to the diner."

She didn't get up. "Can we get anything that's legal to eat there?"

Jack considered. "Baked catfish. Green beans. Sliced tomatoes."

She rose with surprising grace. "Okay, then, but we go Dutch."

No way. Jack had to repay her somehow. He'd buy her lunch, but there was no sense arguing about it till the check came.

He led her outside to his truck, then opened the passenger door, but she balked before getting in.

"Oh, good grief," she said when she saw the interior. "This is worse than the house."

Jack looked at it the way she must see it, and had to admit she was right. He had only a vague knowledge of what was under all the junk mail he'd tossed behind the seat. And whenever he hit a bump, things shifted, releasing a fresh cloud of dust and cat hair.

Blast.

She faced him. "We'll take my car this time. When we get back, we'll clean out the truck, and you can drive the next time." Assuming there would be a next time, which, clearly, she did.

Typical. She never suggested or asked, just gave orders.

Jack didn't like it, but he could see she was serious, and he knew the truck would only make both of them feel even worse. "Only if you let me buy your lunch."

She shook her head no even as she said, "Oh, all right, Mr. One-up."

"I'll navigate," he responded.

They got into her immaculate minivan, then passed the trip in surprising silence, except for when he told her where to turn.

She didn't speak to him again till they settled at their table with their lunches at the Midway Café. "You have quite an impressive collection of books," she told him.

Jack nodded, squeezing lots of lemon on his catfish.

"I noticed a lot of equipment manuals for farm machinery," she prodded. "Are you a mechanic?"

Jack was glad he'd stored his diplomas away in the fireproof box, under lock and key. "Among other things." Let her think he was a mechanic, if it made her feel superior. "How about you?"

She actually blushed, focusing on her lunch. "I haven't worked since I married Tom. He was old-fashioned about that, and I didn't mind. I loved taking care of him and our children, full-time. When he retired, we had so much fun traveling. But now that he's gone, I don't think I could get a job anywhere, especially in this economy."

"What about the library?" he suggested. "You like to read."

She looked down again. "I tried, but with the budget cuts, they're firing people who've been there for years." When she looked back up, he saw a glint of despair in her eyes.

"Do you *need* to work?" he heard himself ask, appalled that he'd done so, but curious, nonetheless.

She cocked a sardonic smile. "I'll answer that after I've paid for everything Dr. Patel ordered."

Jack had to give her credit for her honesty. Not that it was any of his business.

For some inexplicable reason, though, he felt bad about embarrassing her. Jack reviewed his repertoire of jokes and finally came up with a clean one, just to lighten things up. "Did you hear the one about the woman who told her psychiatrist, 'I need your help. My husband thinks he's a refrigerator'?"

The raccoon woman eyed him with suspicion.

Jack went on, anyway. "So the psychiatrist says, 'Don't worry. That's pretty harmless. Just ignore it.' But the woman says, 'I can't. He sleeps with his mouth open, and the light is keeping me awake.'"

The raccoon woman let out an exasperated sigh. "That's supposed to be funny?"

For creeps' sake. Didn't she have a sense of humor? Jack bristled. "That's classic Henny Youngman." Along with most other things, Jack remembered every joke he'd ever heard or read. Lately, though, it took longer to call them to mind.

"You want funny, I'll give you funny," she said, arching a brow. "Orson Bean. A lawyer shows up at the pearly gates, and Saint Peter offers him a deal. 'We don't usually accept your kind, but this week, there's a special. You do your lifetime in hell, then you get to come back up here for the rest of time.'" She nodded. "The lawyer thought about it, then said, 'I'll take the deal.' So Saint Peter says, 'Done. I've put you down for 212 years in hell.' The lawyer yells, 'But I'm only fifty-five years old!' Saint Peter smiles at him. 'We go by billable hours.'"

Jack paused a second, letting the punch line sink in, then actually laughed. The joke was subtle and intelligent, but the boob jokes he swapped with his online cronies were a lot funnier. "Mine's funnier, but you get the prize for droll."

She eased, focusing on her food. "I like a man who's a good sport."

"Then you won't like me," he said, inspecting the bite of turnip greens on his fork. "I hate losing."

She stirred Splenda into her unsweet tea. No springwater at the diner. "Well, cleaning out your truck and house isn't a competition. When it's finished, you win. And when it's mold-free, you win again."

Jack knew better. "And you?"

"I win when the workmen finish with mine." She sipped her tea. "I've washed or wiped clean every single thing in that house with Dr. Patel's special cleaner. Now it's the mold remediators' turn to do the rest."

Jack's interest perked up. "What about your clothes that aren't washable?" Not that he had but a few.

"Sent to the special cleaners to be done, then fogged," she said, talking neatly past a bite of fish stashed in her cheek. "Along with my oriental rugs."

"Do you always talk with your mouth full?"

Crestfallen, she went ruddy with embarrassment, but waited till she was finished chewing to speak again. "Sorry. Living alone these past months, I've completely forgotten my table manners."

Now, why did she have to go all wounded like that? Jack felt like he'd kicked a kitten. He changed the subject to, "After we finish at the house, I'll take you out to see my tools and my tractor collection in the barn."

She cocked her head, alert. "What kind of tools?"

Clearly, she hadn't been paying attention when he'd mentioned them before. "All kinds. Been collecting them for years. A hobby. I go to garage sales most Fridays and Saturdays, looking for good deals."

"That's how I got a lot of mine, too," she said with pride.

Probably not a man's definition of a tool collection, but since she was helping Jack out, he decided to be nice. "You said wood-working tools. How many do you have?"

"All the usual power ones, plus a nice collection of manual and wheel- or treadle-operated ones. Veneer cutters and patterns. Carving knives. Specialty saws. Some that go back to the seventeenth century." The confidence had returned to her voice. "I love working in the shop. Or, I used to. Dr. Patel says I'd have to have my whole shop mold remediated and wear a respirator and goggles to keep working out there. I'm not sure I can do the fine work in all that gear."

For the second time, Jack felt really sorry for the woman. "That's harsh."

Her lids lengthened, gaze downcast. "Well, I want to feel good again. Guess that's just one of the sacrifices I have to make."

Ah. The martyr. "Bummer," Jack said, focusing back on his food.

"Actually, I'm so glad to be able to get out of bed again," she said with a frankness Jack didn't believe for a minute, "that I try to be grateful and focus on the good things, not the inconveniences."

Now, the Pollyanna. Please. Was this woman delusional, or what?

But Jack knew better than to tell her that life's a bitch, and then you die. She'd probably just witness to him, which he didn't need.

He waited till she was finished to take her check and rise. "It'll probably take us the rest of the day to clean out my truck," he told her. Lord only knew what was under the seats. "We're liable to find something dead in the cab."

"That wouldn't surprise me," she said with an affable smile as she got up to follow, "but we'll both feel a lot better when it's done."

Jack stopped in his tracks, regarding her with a mixture of suspicion and curiosity. "Why do you care whether my truck makes me sick or not?"

She didn't flinch, just responded with a level, "It gives me something positive to do for someone else. That way I don't think. I don't—" Her eyes went wet, but she stiffened herself against the tears. "It keeps me distracted." She looked at him askance, with only the slightest hint of a smile. "Why? Do you want me to find somebody else to terrorize? I will, if you want me to," she said lightly.

"No," he answered with a speed that surprised him. "I need your help." The words surprised him even more. "There. I've said it."

She shook her head, the smile widening. "And the world didn't come to an end. Imagine that."

Jack stepped up to the register to pay. "But I'll pay you for it, more than just vegetables. Maybe with tools. I have some nice scoops and chisels from the late seventeen hundreds."

"We shall see, Jack Wilson," she said archly. "We shall see."

Fifteen

Cassie

It didn't surprise me that there was nothing of any real value in the cab of Jack's truck, just delayed decisions by the dozens. More old newspapers. Junk mail. Overdue library books. Old shoes. Mismatched socks. Three bottles of dollar-store liquid laundry detergent with just a little left in each. Numerous empty Nehi and root beer cans and bottles. Wrappers from every imaginable fast food restaurant. Two muddy jackets that were so stiff, they could stand on their own. And a mounted rabbit head with antlers.

Jack had to think long and hard about letting that last one go, but sanity prevailed.

Was this what happened to men when they had nobody to take care of them?

I wouldn't venture to guess. Jack Wilson wasn't your average man, to put it mildly. He was a misanthrope, but he seemed to have a sharp mind, especially for a mechanic. I mean, how many mechanics have copies of Aristotle and Plato and Kant on their bookshelves? And a genuine *Oxford Unabridged Exhaustive Dictionary of the English Language* that traced the words back to their origins?

That one, I'd like to try to buy off him, but clearly, he didn't like to part with his books. There were only a few in the *donate* pile outside.

Once the truck cab was finally empty—but still caked with dirt, cat hair, and dust—I walked back to the load bed. Even late in the afternoon under the shade of the oak by Jack's carport, it was still so hot, I had to take off my mask and rub my face with a clean paper towel before replacing it. The grooves the respirator had smashed into my skin felt permanent. But the sooner we got back to work, the sooner we would finish, and I could go back to the air-conditioning at Mama's. "Okay. Let's clean out the load bed, then wash everything down."

Inside the back of the truck, the rusty riding lawn mower sat flanked by two long metal runners a foot wide, almost buried under a jumble of assorted boxes with their tops folded shut (empty? hard to tell), at least a dozen old paint cans, and a disreputable collection of worn tools rattling around.

I bristled to see the tools treated so badly, but it was none of my business. Still, you could tell a lot about a person by how they treated their tools.

Jack hadn't said anything when I'd announced we needed to clean out the back of the truck, but his posture slumped like a sulking toddler's as he opened the tailgate with a rusty *skreek*.

I pointed to the metal runners. "Are those for getting the lawn mower out?"

He turned his respirator my way, one possessive hand patting the dusty bag on the lawn mower. "I was going to fix it, then sell it."

"Why didn't you, then?" I knew the question was really a criticism, but the nice thing about being around a totally inappropriate man was that I could say what I thought and ask what I wanted to, without having to consider the consequences.

His answer was defensive, of course. "Couldn't find the part on the Internet. Yet."

I looked around at the junk piled in front of his barn and the piles of stuff in the carport and saw decades of "I was going to" fill-in-the-blank, but I didn't comment.

True, he was handicapped by his illness. But the difference between a man and a woman in similar circumstances is that the woman will usually get things done anyway, even if she has to pay somebody.

Jack pulled the runners to the back of the tailgate and positioned them at the right width to provide a ramp for the lawn mower.

"How long has it been in the truck?" I challenged.

"None of your business," he growled through the mask, then removed a couple of chocks wedged behind the mower's rear tires. Then he put one foot on the end of the truck's rear bumper and heaved himself up into the load bed with such great effort that he went red as a tomato. He motioned me toward the front of the truck as he mounted the mower. "Now, get out of the way."

I stepped back, expecting him to start the thing, but he didn't. Instead, he twisted around and pushed off with one foot, steering the back wheels onto the runners. Once the tires crested the tailgate, the thing rattled backward down the runners at alarming speed, then bumped across the sloping yard, with Jack barely hanging on.

"Jack!" I ran after him, unsure what I'd do if I caught up, but feeling it necessary to do something. I went as fast as my arthritic joints allowed, but he was still careening away from me pell-mell, his forehead bright red.

Finally, Jack turned the wheel enough to steer the thing into a wide one-eighty, where it lost momentum as it backed up the slope and slowed. It finally stopped when I caught up to him.

I jerked off my respirator and inhaled a lungful of dust that arrived in his wake. "Are you okay?"

Jack got off, dusting his clothes. "Why'd you get so hysterical? I've done that a hundred times."

Oh, right. And if you believe that . . .

"Come on," he said, heading back to the truck. "Let's wash the truck. Then you can do your mold thing."

He moved the truck over to a sunny patch of dried grass, then disappeared around the corner of the house. He came back dragging a hose with a formidable black nozzle on it. "Open the doors, will ya?" he called through the respirator.

I obliged, then stepped out of the line of fire when he aimed for the hood.

Jack turned the ring on the nozzle, and a powerful blast of water struck the oxidizing paint, blasting away bugs and dirt. Then, without so much as a fare-thee-well, he turned the stream on the truck's interior.

Not necessarily the best thing for the wiring, but I kept my trap shut. It was his truck, after all, and he claimed he could fix things.

After he'd cleaned the seats and walls and blasted the roof liner, he blasted a tide of dirt and fur and food and bits of paper out of the far door.

I had to admit, the interior looked and smelled a whole lot better when he was done.

"We'll let it dry out before you do your mold thing," he announced, pulling off his respirator and tossing it aside. Then he dialed the nozzle down to a spray and soaked himself, reveling in the cool water as he stood in the baking afternoon sun. "Aaahhhh." He stuck the nozzle into each sleeve of his shirt, then down the front. Then down his shorts!

I might not have been there, for all the consideration he gave me.

Fortunately, his Hawaiian shirt of the day remained opaque, as did his Goodwill shorts, so his modesty remained intact, but my face was flaming. And I couldn't help noticing that he was thinner under his baggy clothes than I had imagined—except for his middle-aged slight potbelly.

He shot me a wry half smile. "Like to cool off?" His eyes went straight to the part of my white shirt that covered my bust.

Randy old goat. "No, thank you," I said with enough ice to freeze Lake Lanier. "I'm going back inside to bag up some more trash."

He waved the hose my way, but the spray didn't reach. "By yourself? That's my stuff, you know."

I glared at him, unable to say why I was so upset by what he'd done. "Trash is trash. I'll leave the rest for you to decide." God forbid, I should be able to make a simple decision.

Men.

Well, maybe men.

Tom had been the only man I really knew, and he was a gentleman, in stark contrast to Jack Wilson.

At least, that's how Tom had always been with me.

Surely he hadn't secretly been as crass under the surface as this guy was.

Surely.

Sixteen

Cassie

Hey," I called as I dragged into Mama's. "I'm home."

Mama came around the corner looking like a glossy ad for Talbots. "Good Lord! You look horrible." She took hold of my shoulders and inspected the semipermanent imprint of the respirator. "You must stop wearing that thing. Those marks may never come out."

"Buy me a full-face respirator, and I'd be happy to oblige," I told her, then pulled free and headed for the guest bath. "I feel like Pigpen in Charlie Brown. Gotta take a shower."

Mama must have agreed, because no sooner had I stripped than I heard the vacuum approaching the door. I was so tired I could hardly stand up and lather away the grime. Just to be safe, I washed my hair three times—once with the antifungal shampoo and twice with my favorite John Frieda—then tried to undo the damage with some conditioner.

When the hot water started to give out, I moved like a hundred-year-old crone as I stepped out, dried off, then twisted my hair into a towel and donned my terry-cloth robe.

The combination of being clean and warm in the cool air-

147

conditioning sent me straight to bed. I was lying there when I heard the vacuum approach the bathroom, then echo off the tiles as Mama sucked up the last remnants I'd tracked into the house.

She finished by barging in to give my carpet a quick once-over, then turned off the infernal machine. "Cassie, I don't think you should go back to that place. I only have to look at you to see it's making you sick again."

She was right, of course, but my usual automartyr kicked in. "Mama, the guy's got awful COPD, and the mold remediators couldn't begin to do anything with all that stuff in his house. He just needs somebody to help him sort things out. You know how hard it is to make all those minor decisions on your own."

"So he needs you for a slave?" Mama never minces words.

I sat up on my elbows. "Not a slave. A helper. As far as I can see, he has nobody and very little money."

Mama's eyes narrowed. "Did this man ask you to help? Because it takes some nerve, asking a complete—"

"He didn't ask me. I volunteered." Mama would never understand, but some inner compulsion made me try to explain, anyway. "We both have the same condition, and when he tried to clean up on his own, I saw how sick it made him. I swear, Mama, I thought he was going to expire right there in the doctor's office. So I offered to help." I tacked on, "It's not like I can do anything till my house is finished, anyway. It's good to have a project."

Mama remained unconvinced. "I'm your mother. I'm looking at how this affects you, and I don't like what I see. You're sick enough already, without rooting around in that pigsty." She went sly. "Tell him you're not coming tomorrow, and I'll spring for a mani/pedi and lunch at the Ritz."

She knew how to tempt me.

Frankly, I wasn't sure I could manage another full day in my current condition. "One more day, and we'll just about finish. Then I'll take you up on your offer. But that doesn't mean I'm not going to go back to help him with his garage sale."

She cocked a skeptical eyebrow. "Whatever." That battle would be waged another day.

So I went the next day, and sure enough, we got close to finishing. As I was getting ready to leave, I leaned out of the driver's window. "I think you can manage the rest by yourself, now that everything's been washed and sprayed."

He didn't seem relieved or disappointed. "Okay. Bye." With that, he turned his back and walked away without a word of thanks.

What a jerk! After all I'd done.

I stomped the gas and raised a huge cloud of dust on my way out. Served him right.

The next morning after a late breakfast, I drove Mama over to check on my house, and was horrified to find the doors unlocked, the living room floor half laid, dust everywhere, and the hallway littered with mangled, insulated ductwork under a ladder that led to the plenum in the ceiling. Only three windows had been replaced. Two were completely missing, wide open to the elements— and to the mold!

So much for our good beginning.

I called the nice mold man and got his voice mail. "Hi," I said. "It's me, Cassie Jones. I'm at the house, and I found it completely unlocked, and nobody's here, and it's filthy and looks like there hasn't been any work done today. Could you please call me back on my cell?" I gave the number, then hung up.

Memories of the time we'd added the master bedroom and bath loomed in my mind. It had taken three times longer than it was supposed to and cost five thousand dollars more. Even though we'd checked the contractor's references thoroughly, having him supervise had just meant there was one more person for us to call and complain to. Tom had ended up having to contact the subs directly to get them to finish, and they'd constantly tried to badger more money out of him before the job was completed.

But it wasn't as if I had a choice, here. The work had to be done, and I had to deal with these people on my own.

Lord, how I missed my husband.

Don't get me wrong, I'm all about women's rights, but when you've been under the protection of a truly godly man, being without it feels awfully naked and vulnerable.

My emotions must have showed, because Mama came up behind me and circled her arms around my waist, giving me a peck on the ear. "It isn't easy without them, is it?" Even fifteen years after Daddy died, her voice still echoed her loneliness.

Tears welled in my eyes for both of us. I leaned against her head. "No."

She gave me a little squeeze, then broke the embrace, her tone brisk again. "Well, life goes on. You'll get through this and be back in your house eventually." She kicked a stray piece of insulation out of her path with her crocodile ballet shoe. "The truth is, I've actually enjoyed having you with me at my place. So far."

Maybe because I'd hardly been there. I smiled, anyway. "That's just because I put your dirty dishes into the dishwasher."

Mama smiled back. "That, too." Teetering far too close to the brink of sentimentality, she changed the subject. "Come on. Let's go do something about those wretched nails of yours."

"I sure hope the contractor calls me back."

He did—when my nails were wet. "Ooh," I said to the nail

woman when I saw his number come up on the screen. "This call is really important. Could you please punch *talk*, then put the phone to my ear? Thank you so much."

How Jerseylicious can you get? Not that I ever watched.

The woman obliged.

"Hello?"

"Mrs. Jones? I'm sorry I couldn't get back to you sooner."

I struggled to hear over the din of the shop.

"The electrical inspector dropped by when he saw we were working on the house, and he found some serious problems with the electrical that have to be fixed before we proceed. He said it's a miracle you haven't had a fire. I've been trying to find somebody who works on old houses, but a lot of electricians don't want to bother with that anymore, so my choices are limited, and not cheap."

Perfect. The contractor for the bedroom addition had said we needed new wiring, but by then the renovation was so out of control, the last thing we'd wanted was to tackle something else. So we'd told ourselves we'd take care of it later, then promptly forgotten it.

Now "later" had dropped into my lap like a ten-ton boulder of granite.

Only years of self-control kept my response to, "Rats!" I tried to remain calm. "How much is that going to cost?"

"To do it right? Well, you're seriously overloaded for the current system. The electricians will have to replace that with a much larger service, double your previous. Then we'll have to thread all the new wiring. Copper wiring's not cheap, but I strongly recommend it."

Perfect. I needed a boutique electrician. And copper wiring.

People were stealing copper wire from office parks, it had gotten so expensive.

This didn't bode well. "Bottom line?"

"Eight to ten thousand," he said, "but that will bring the house up to current code, and then some. When the market recovers, you'll be able to get more for the place if you ever want to sell. If you don't, you can at least sleep at night without worrying about a fire."

Fire was the one thing I *hadn't* worried about when I went to bed, but unless I dealt with this now, I'd have to add that fear to rapists and burglars and Peeping Toms.

What choice did I have? "Okay. Find someone and give me the estimate."

"I'm really sorry about this," he said with what sounded like genuine concern. "I'll do my best to keep the cost down to a minimum."

The manicurist holding my cell phone shifted, impatient, but I was too preoccupied with "eight to ten thousand" to care.

"Thanks. Oh, and one more thing: the whole house was unlocked! And some of the windows are missing entirely. You promised to keep it secure."

"Sorry. I left the door open this morning for a couple of the electricians to come in and give me an estimate. I'll have the window people put those in immediately. It won't happen again."

Why didn't I believe that? "Okay. I'm trusting you to make that happen."

"Sure thing." He hung up.

Tom, Tom, Tom, why did you leave me?

I knew the thought was irrational, but I had it anyway. It wasn't as if he'd gone out for milk and not come back.

152

I leaned back, frowning, and nodded to the woman with the phone. "Thanks. Could you please press *end*? Thank you so much." I made a mental note to tip her really well.

Mama leaned over from the next foot throne. "What was that all about?"

"The wiring in my house is shot," I told her. "Could start a fire any minute, according to the electrical inspector. So I have to re-place the service and rewire."

Mama scowled. "And you just took their word for that? Cassie, the trades will try to milk single women for every penny they can. You need to call that inspector and make sure he really said that. And bring in some other people for estimates. Find out if they're telling you the truth."

I knew she meant well but felt compelled to defend myself, anyway. "I know it's true, because the contractors who did the new master told us the electrical needed replacing back then. Tom said we'd have it fixed later, but the renovation took so long, the last thing we wanted was to deal with another sub. Then time passed, and we both forgot."

Mama was clearly horrified. "So you just ignored a hazard like that?"

Another button, pushed. "Yes." I made a stab at humor. "It made going to bed so exciting every night, knowing we might wake up in flames."

Mama's brows shot toward the ceiling, her expression aloof. "There's no need to be sarcastic, Cassandra." She always called me Cassandra when I hurt her feelings, which was hard to avoid.

I reminded myself that our time together was just beginning. With the electrical added on to the mold remediation, heaven only knew when I'd be able to go back home. "I appreciate your concern,

Mama, really, I do. Tell you what, why don't you go on Angie's list or Kudzu and find me some good electricians who do old houses? That would be a big help."

"Oh, no," she responded immediately. "I couldn't possibly do that." Mama waved her newly painted nails. "What if they turned out to be awful?" She pointed a scarlet talon my way. "People get their relatives to go online and do fake testimonials," she added. "Did you know that? I couldn't possibly take that responsibility."

Welcome to my life with Mama.

I prayed that God would convince the mold man to get someone reasonable and reliable, then surrendered the matter to heaven, wondering how long I'd be stuck at her condo.

If it's a test, God, please help me pass it with flying colors, because I really don't want to take it again.

Seventeen

Jack

By the time he got to the elevator in the doctor's building, Jack swore they'd moved the whole place a quarter mile farther from the parking lot. Cleaning up his house had come close to killing him, but he'd finished it on his own without using the bossy raccoon woman's supposed system after she'd bailed out on him.

Never mind that most of his stuff was now out in the barn. He didn't live in the barn, so that was okay with Jack.

Not that clearing out all the crap had helped much without the remediation. If Dr. Patel didn't do something drastic, and soon, Jack might not be living anywhere much longer. His wheezing echoed loudly in the stainless steel elevator. He leaned against the wall and let his head fall back, eyes closed, as he struggled for air.

When the third floor dinged, Jack summoned himself upright to brave the trek to the office.

The only thing that would make things worse would be to find the raccoon woman sitting in the waiting room. She'd want to ask him about his house, and he didn't have the breath to talk to anybody.

Not that he had to say much, even if she was waiting for him. Three days of working with her had confirmed his assessment that she didn't care what anybody else thought, just kept rattling off whatever popped into her head. He was still smarting from her tart assessment of his living conditions, even though she'd been right.

Jack opened the office door to the roar of the air purifier, and sure enough, there she was on the sofa. In his spot.

Blast.

She frowned, brows shooting upward. "Wow, Jack. You don't look so good."

He glared at her. "I have good reason." He sat in one of the chairs farthest from her, but couldn't keep from spending his precious breath on, "Do you always insult people when you see them, or is it just me?"

She actually colored. "I'm sorry. That was terribly rude of me. I was just worried about you."

He let loose a gravelly cough, then strangled out, "Why? I'm none of your business. A stranger, and frankly, I'd like to keep it that way."

She sighed, aiming one of those woman looks at him that said, "Poor thing."

Jack picked up a golfing magazine because it was close by, and used it as a shield. He hated golf—expensive, time-consuming, and frustrating, even for the pros—but he read on, anyway.

Diverted, the raccoon woman did what blathering women everywhere did when they didn't have someone to blather to: she dialed her cell phone. After a brief pause, she said, "Hi. It's Cassie Jones. Were you able to get the final estimate from the electrician?"

Pause.

A stunned, "What?" followed.

Jack sneaked a brief glance over the magazine. All the color had drained from her face.

"But you said ten thousand, max. That's double—"

Jack could barely hear the drone of the voice from her phone over the roar of the air purifier, but he could tell it was male, and rapid-fire.

The raccoon woman slumped where she sat, shrinking visibly. "I understand, and I appreciate the research you've done, but I'll need to get another opinion before I—" She stopped, cut short. "Yes, but I only have so much money to last me, and this would—" Another forced pause. "I know you can't move forward without it, but I can't just—"

More explanations buzzed into the air.

"I'm sorry, but I'll have to think about this. I'll call you back." Clearly, the person she was talking to wasn't ready to hang up. She scowled, the phone still to her ear. "I know the subs are lined up. I just can't okay such a huge expense without time to check into it." She raised her eyes skyward as the drone went on, more emphatic, now. "I do appreciate the time you've spent," she said, annoyed. "Really. I just have to think this over. Good-bye." She hung up on whoever it was, presumably her contractor. Leaning forward, she placed her palms on her knees and breathed heavily, her eyes closed.

Jack couldn't resist. "Boy. You don't look so good."

Her lips folded inward as she struggled to regain her composure, but her response flashed anger and frustration. "Why do you care? I'm a stranger to you," she quoted him to himself.

"I'm empathetic. It's one of the higher functions of the species," he quoted her to her.

She glared up at him with a fierceness he didn't expect. "I have good reason to look awful. Between the mold remediation and having to rewire my house, not to mention the jillions of dollars I've had to spend on prescriptions my insurance won't cover, plus special food and supplements and cleaners and treatments from Dr. Patel, plus the gawd-awful rates I'm paying for the bleemin' health insurance that refuses to pay ninety percent of what I need, I'm going to end up stone broke in my mold-free house, with no prospects of a job in this economy, and years before I qualify for Medicare and Social Security."

More than Jack wanted to know, but he only had himself to blame for kicking open Pandora's box. "Sorry." He retreated to the golf magazine. "Good luck with that." At least she had the money to pay for it.

"Right." The word was steeped in bitterness.

She sighed heavily, then laid her head back against the couch, eyes closed. "I hate being alone. I hate it."

Against his will, Jack saw her vulnerability and amended his opinion somewhat. She was sick, too, and probably doing the best she could—albeit with a never-ending sound track—trying to cope, just the same.

"Then why don't you try to find somebody else to be with?" he suggested, against his better instincts. "Somebody with health insurance. And money."

She shook her head, mouth crimped. "It doesn't work that way. All the good ones are taken. And those that aren't want some young chickie-boom, not somebody over-the-hill and high maintenance, like me."

Jack kept his eyes on the magazine, nostrils flaring. "If I made some gross generalization like that about women, you'd brand me as a sexist."

"I saw your stack of Internet boob jokes," she retorted. "You are a sexist."

Jack bristled. "Boob jokes do not a sexist make. I'll have you know, a lot of those were sent to me by women."

She rolled her eyes. "Lord help us."

"Anyway, how can you *know* what men are out there unless you try to find out?"

She chuffed. "Now you sound like my children."

"Maybe they're right," he challenged.

"Well, it's not like I'm surrounded by eligible men." He could see it annoyed her to have to defend herself. "All my friends are couples. And I don't think bars are a very good place to look for dates. I don't drink." Now, why didn't that surprise him? "So there you are."

"Bars are passé, anyway," he said.

She pointed to him. "Oh, and I tried that big singles group at Artie Stayley's church, and everybody there liked hiking and jogging and kayaking and bike riding. When I said I liked reading and gardening, every man at the table looked away. Fifty may be the new thirty, but for me, it's the new eighty. Nobody wants somebody handicapped."

Jack managed to refrain from telling her that he'd had plenty of offers, in spite of his obvious handicaps. But then again, he had a good pension and health insurance. That was more than enough for most women, but it certainly wouldn't be for this one. This woman was high-strung and definitely determined to make somebody over into her late husband's sainted image. With a constant narration, to boot.

"Have you tried the Internet?" he asked her. "There are some legitimate Christian dating sites."

"I only know how to do e-mails," she shot back.

"Cop-out." Why was he bothering to talk to her about this, anyway? As she'd said, it was none of his business. But he always had been susceptible to damsels in distress, usually to his detriment. Time to put an end to this useless conversation.

He looked back at his magazine, wondering how many phosphates had been released into the environment to make the fairways at Augusta look so green.

Propitiously, the office nurse stuck her head out of the door. "Mrs. Jones, the doctor will see you now."

The raccoon woman stood. "Did you finish getting your house cleared out?"

He'd known she couldn't leave without asking. "Yes. Why do you think I look so bad?"

She shot back, "It made me sick, too, you know." She scowled at him in indictment, probably expecting a thank-you for three days' work—three days he hadn't asked for in the first place. Well, she wasn't going to get it.

Jack kept poring over the magazine till he heard the door close behind her. Then he claimed his rightful seat on the sofa.

Fifteen minutes later, Dr. Patel listened to his chest with his stethoscope, shaking his head. "I am very concerned about you, Mr. Wilson. I'd like to call in a pulmonologist immediately."

"I have a pulmonologist, thank you," Jack replied, "and trust me, he's in no hurry to do anything immediately."

"Then I strongly advise you to go to the facility I recommended in Arizona, at least until we can get your fungal infections under control and remediate your environment."

"They don't take Medicare, and they're not in network for my supplemental." Why should he have to explain this to the man? Did Patel think everybody was made of money?

"What good is money to a dead man?" Patel challenged.

It galled Jack to his soul to have to admit, "I don't *have* any money. I'm land-poor. So I can't have my house remediated or pay some aristocratic spa in Arizona for God knows how long. Do you think I have a mint in my backyard?" He didn't pause for a response, because Patel didn't show the slightest sign of emotion. "And I'm not alone. There's a major recession going on out there. Or hadn't you noticed?"

"Depression is one of the side effects of this syndrome," the man said blandly. "Are you on any antidepressants? Because if you are not, I can write some for you that will not interfere with your other medications."

That did it. "Didn't you hear me?" Jack shouted, feeling his blood pressure rise. "I'm broke, I'm dying, and I'm stuck in a house that's killing me even faster. That's not depression. It's just the facts." Jack got up and stormed out before he said something he'd regret.

On the way out, he passed the raccoon woman standing with her checkbook open at the front desk as the clerk said, "That will be three hundred and forty-seven dollars for today. The compounding pharmacy downstairs will have your prescriptions ready by the time you get there."

Lord knows how much that would cost her.

The clerk glanced up to see Jack jerk open the door to the waiting room. "Mr. Wilson, you need to make another appointment and check out before you—"

Propelled by rage and adrenaline, he crossed the waiting room in three strides, then slammed the outer door behind him, cutting off the rest of what she was saying.

They knew where to find him. Let them send a bill. He'd take his own sweet time paying it.

Blasted doctors.

Eighteen

Cassie

I waited till Mama left for bridge to call Cindy, the nerve center of our couples friends. The phone rang. And rang. Maybe I'd get lucky, and she wouldn't be there. But after ring five, she answered, breathless. "Hello?"

"Hi, Cindy. It's Cassie. I'm sorry, did I get you out of the north forty?" Code for the bathroom.

Cindy laughed. "No. It's these cordless phones. I never can remember where I put them. What's up?" Before I could answer, she tacked on, "We need to have you over for supper sometime soon."

We both knew the perfunctory invitation was motivated by guilt, not a desire for my company, so I didn't even address it. "Actually, I called to ask you to put out the word that I'm ready to start seeing people. Not that there are many decent, eligible Christian men out there, but my kids have convinced me it's time for me to move on." Liar, liar, pants on fire.

Cindy didn't hesitate. "Ohmigosh, I know just the guy, a friend of Bill's. Lovely man. His name's Wade Milton. We've been pals with him and Maryanne since we were all starting out."

Maryanne? I said eligible.

Cindy gushed on. "She died a little over a year ago, and Wade just told Bill that he wants to start dating. This is fate." I heard a rustle of papers. "Hang on. Where is that cell?" More rustling. "Ah. Let me call Bill and see what we can set up for y'all to come to dinner. Better yet, we'll eat out, then see a show. Now, where was that ad for the show?" More rustling. "That Beatles tribute on ice is in town. Ha. There it is: *Rain*. That's it."

On ice? I'd thought it was a musical.

Cindy's leader-of-the-pack triumph resonated in her words. "This is so perfect. I'll call you as soon as I know."

"Okay." I hung up and sat, shocked that it had been so easy.

But God did everything perfectly. At least, that was my initial reaction, before I met Bill's friend.

Cindy called back just thirty minutes later and invited me to double with them on Friday night.

Whoa, whoa, whoa. Way too soon. "That will be fine," I heard myself say. "Should I meet y'all at the restaurant?"

"Heck, no," she retorted. "Wade's a gentleman. Old-school. He'll pick you up."

I wasn't at all sure how it would feel to have him come to get me at Mama's, the well-heeled geriatric Mecca of Atlanta. Not to mention bring me home.

At least I wouldn't have to worry about his asking to come in.

But I couldn't think fast enough to come up with an excuse not to have him pick me up. "Okay, then. I'm staying at Mama's at Canterbury Court till my house is finished. He can meet me in the main lobby of the original building. What time?"

"The show starts at eight, so why don't we say six, so we'll have plenty of time to talk over dinner?"

Uh-oh. Six was when all the wheelchair people got out of dinner. Definitely not the best first impression. "Six, it is," I heard myself say. "I'll be ready."

"Good. He's very punctual. Wear that pink jacket," she instructed. Cindy never could pass up the chance to tell people what to do. "You look wonderful in pink. And your black satin camisole. I love those with your pearls and cross. You look like a princess in those."

This was starting to feel way too high school. "Okay. If you say so."

That night after I checked on the progress at my house—very little—and visited Juliette, who didn't even seem glad to see me, Mama let me into her unit with a grin of pride. She motioned to her tiny kitchen. "Look, sweetie," she said. "I cooked. Everything's from that list on the refrigerator"—my ALCAT test results—"so you can eat it."

Uh-oh. I'd convinced Mama to quit cooking for me two years ago for a darn good reason: she couldn't taste anymore, so she overcooked and overseasoned everything. I didn't want to hurt her feelings, but—

She read my expression. "Don't worry. I followed the recipes in that *Zone* cookbook of yours exactly." She plunked a bottle of hot sauce on the table next to her daily glass of cheap, wretched red wine from the Kroger. "It's a bitch, not being able to taste anything anymore."

I came over and gave her a big hug. "Thanks. I love you, Mama." She felt so frail. Or was it me, now that I was down to skin and bones? Either way, it made me sad.

I decided to tell her the big news. "Guess what? I have a date."

Mama pulled back in amazement. "Already?"

I had mentioned I was thinking about it. "Well, it just sort of happened. I called Cindy Calloway to put the word out, and she fixed me up right away."

"Fix-ups are definitely the best," Mama announced, as if she knew the first thing about it. As far as I knew, she hadn't dated since Daddy died. "That way, you at least know something about them." The microwave dinged, and she headed over to take out a dish of green beans, then added almond slivers and ghee. I was impressed.

"Who is he?" she asked as she set them on the table.

"A friend of Bill's from way back. Widowed over a year. New to this, like me."

She motioned for me to sit. "Sounds perfect."

Then why wasn't I happy? "Yes, it does."

It was too soon, that's why. I hadn't looked at another man since I'd married Tom, and I didn't want one, now. I wanted Tom.

Blasted health insurance, making me sell myself, for all practical purposes.

Tears welled from the backs of my eyes.

Mama served herself a chicken breast boiled in diet Italian dressing, one of her favorites that looked awful but actually tasted pretty good. I didn't mention that the vinegar in the dressing was poison.

"Wear that pretty black-and-white damask jacket you have," she said. "And your big black silk rose. And that hot-pink camisole. You look so nice in that."

What was it, about my clothes? I knew what I liked and what liked me. Did she think I'd suddenly forgotten? "Cindy told me to wear my pink jacket with the black satin camisole."

Mama laughed. "Listen to us, telling *you* what to wear, as if it were your first date."

I sighed. "It feels like my first, I'll tell you." I calculated. "I haven't been on a date since 1977. And according to all my divorced friends, the rules no longer apply. This is pretty scary."

Mama smiled. "You'll do fine, sweetie. Just think of it as something you have to get out of the way. Every time will get easier, I promise."

I wished I could believe her.

Tom. I want Tom.

When he'd looked at me, made love to me, he'd seen the girl he'd fallen in love with, not the scars and dents I'd accumulated over the years. And in my heart of hearts, I knew what a rare and wonderful man he'd been. Could anybody else live up to him?

The odds were against it, a million to one. Knowing that, I missed him so much, I could barely breathe.

Mama took my hand into hers. "Will you bless it for us?" she asked.

Afraid I'd break down if I spoke, I shook my head in denial and managed to get out, "You."

She bowed her head. "Bless us, oh Lord, and these thy gifts, which we hath received from thy bounty, through Jesus Christ our Lord, in the name of the Father, and the son, and the Holy Ghost." She crossed herself. "Amen."

Why she'd switched from her usual Episcopal blessing to a Catholic one was beyond me, but it was a recent affectation. Maybe she had a new Catholic friend.

"So," I asked, "met anybody new here lately?"

"Actually, yes." Mama salted the schmoo out of her food, then peppered it black. "A cute girl from Indiana just moved in and joined the bridge group. We needed some new blood. She's only sixty-seven, a real live wire." Mama helped herself to beans, then pushed them my way. "Came to be near her kids, so I thought I'd show her around, make her feel welcome. I gave her the grand tour of Buckhead, then took her to the Ritz."

If Mama's driving hadn't scared her away, nothing would.

Mama splashed pepper sauce on her beans. "I think we're going to hit it off nicely, so I took her to my Great Books Club. She used to be an English professor."

"What's her name?"

"I have no idea. I stopped doing names at eighty-six." Mama focused on her food. "She's probably the same way. Never calls anybody by name, either. I'll go to the main office and find out, then write it down."

Mama had no trouble making new friends. Maybe I should have moved to Canterbury Court instead of remediating the house. But my grandmother, and now my mother, had moved there to live out their last days, and I wasn't ready to consign myself to that. Frankly, I wasn't sure I'd ever be.

Of course, Mama had said the same thing, and so had Nana.

Mama looked and acted twenty years younger than she was, and so had my grandmother. If I could ever get some weight back on me, there might be hope that I would, too. Before Tom had died, people always said I looked like I was in my forties. It was just my insides that wore out early.

Now, people who hadn't seen me since the funeral regarded me with shock and sympathy.

Shoot. I'd probably lost my youthful edge forever, along with my husband.

What man would want a woman as flawed as I was?

It occurred to me that I'd never asked Mama, outright, if she'd ever considered going out with anybody after Daddy died. "I know you've never said anything about it," I asked, "but did you ever consider dating after Daddy died?"

Mama finished what she was chewing, then dabbed her mouth with her cloth napkin. "Actually, I did, but I didn't want to say anything unless I found somebody nice. Louella McElroy set me up with the first guy, a retired executive friend of her husband's from college. He was very sweet, but the trouble was, he'd never left home and lived with his mother. We are talking serious issues, there." She cut another dainty bite of chicken. "Still, I got to go to dinner and the symphony with him a few times, which was nice, and a couple of musicals at the Fox, so it wasn't a total loss."

"So what happened?"

"First, he always wanted to come in after we got home, if you get my drift. I set him straight about that, but I could tell he thought he'd wear me down eventually. Then he took me to meet his mother, who was enthroned in her bed with a nurse around the clock, and so possessive it was creepy. Way too *Great Expectations.* So on the way home, I told him not to call me back till she died." Mama laughed. "Confounded him completely."

"Did she ever die?"

Mama shook her head. "Nope. She's a hundred and four, and he's still dancing to her tune."

"Was there anybody else?"

"A few, but they all were either alcoholics or wanted a nursemaid, or both. No, thank you." She took another ladylike little bite, chewed it up, then dabbed. "I know you worried about my being alone, but I'm not like you. I do fine by myself."

I didn't, and we both knew it.

Hungry, I broke my diet and helped myself to a piece of vinegar-poisoned chicken, hoping it wouldn't ruin my regimen entirely.

Mama pointed her fork at it. "I used Four Seasons salad dressing mix on that. Made it with lemon juice instead of vinegar, like your diet says."

Would wonders never cease. "Thanks, Mama. I really appreciate that." Actually, it tasted great.

She focused back on her food. "You'll do fine Friday night, honey. Just fine."

I wished I could believe her.

"Just don't say too much the first time," she added. "Let him do the talking. Men like a little mystery. It's very appealing."

Perfect. I was about as opaque as a pane of glass. My face telegraphed my every emotion. It was one of the things Tom had said he loved most about me, the fact that I was so transparent. So honest.

Now, all of a sudden, I was supposed to be mysterious? "Mama, I have no intention of lying." Well, not about anything but my real reason for dating.

"I'm not asking you to lie, sweetie. I'm only saying it's best not to tell everything on the first date. Men are hunters. Leave something for him to discover."

Like the awful truth of my situation and my health? She had a point. "I'll try."

Mama did a credible imitation of Yoda. "There is no try. Do." She never ceased to surprise me.

Enjoying my reaction, she granted me a smug smile. "We had a *Star Wars* marathon in our theater this week."

Reverting to mother mode, she pointed her fork at me. "And definitely don't talk about Tom. That's very off-putting."

"I'm not an idiot, Mama." Never mind that I'd be thinking about him every second, comparing, remembering our first date, when I'd fallen so hard I couldn't see straight.

Ooooooh, I wasn't ready. But I probably never would be, so there you are.

The rest of the week I spent trying to find a decent electrician to rewire my house, but all the bids I got were higher than the one my contractor had come up with, so by Thursday afternoon, I surrendered and told him to go ahead.

When Friday came around, Mama treated me to a wash and blow-dry, a manicure, and a cosmetic makeover at her spa. I didn't even want to know what it cost, but she insisted. When they were done with me, I thought I looked like Tammy Faye Bakker, but Mama insisted I was subtle and elegant.

Back at her place we went through my outfits, and she ultimately agreed with Cindy that my pink shantung jacket and the black satin camisole and black Chico's travel pants looked best, accessorized by a gold serpentine belt and my triple-strand pearls and cross. I had a pair of dressy flats with a little gold buckle on them, so I wore those, earning Mama's seal of approval.

When it came time for me to go down to the lobby to wait for Wade, Mama wanted to come along to sneak a look at him, but I managed to dissuade her. When I got there, the wheelchair brigade was in full force by six, as I had feared.

The main doors opened and a nice-looking man with gray hair and glasses came in—not handsome, but not bad-looking. He had on a rough silk navy sport coat, white pinpoint oxford shirt and tasteful tie, and lightweight camel-colored summer wool slacks with an expensive drape.

So far, so good.

I stood up, gripping my black lizard clutch for dear life.

After scanning the area, he focused hopefully on me with a most gratifying smile of approval.

171

Maybe I didn't look like Tammy Faye Bakker after all.

He navigated past the wheelchairs to greet me. "Cassie?"

I stuck out my hand to shake his, feeling self-conscious that my short nails shone like pink-painted dimes below my favorite gold bracelets. "Hi."

His handshake was just right: dry, and not too hard or too limp. "Wade Milton." His approving smile broadened. "Bill neglected to tell me you were so attractive."

He wouldn't have said that if he'd seen me naked, but still, I flushed like a girl. "You're not so bad, yourself."

Oh, please. *You're not so bad, yourself?* Could I be more inane?

"My car's right outside." He placed his hand in a respectable spot on my lower back to guide me toward the exit. Through the tinted double doors of the lobby, I saw his black Mercedes waiting.

Points for the Mercedes—not because it was expensive, but because it wasn't a red sports car or a Porsche.

He held the doors for me as we went outside into the blaring heat, then he opened the passenger door to the tasteful, immaculate camel Mercedes interior with lots of wood on the dash.

So far, so good. The man had classic style. Points for the style.

Supremely self-conscious for the first time in decades, I sat as gracefully as I could, then swung my legs inside, reminding myself to keep my knees together and my toes pointed, the way I did as a teenager trying to impress some boy with my grace and good breeding.

He closed the door behind me with a solid click, but didn't slam it.

Classical music played softly on his satellite radio.

Points for the music.

Inhaling the cold air from the vents, I fastened my seat belt as he came around and got in.

"Cindy decided we should eat at Brookhaven," he said as he buckled up, "so we can hear each other." He put the car in gear. "Bill and I have played nine holes there every Saturday morning since we started our practices in the seventies."

Points for the country club. Points for stability in occupation and friendship.

Deduction for the golf. Too many golfers I knew used it as an excuse to escape their families—very expensively. But then again, in retirement, that could be a plus, give them something to do out of the house.

We pulled up to the red light at Peachtree Road. "Do you golf?" he asked with a definite note of anticipation.

Double deduction for hoping if I played.

"Sorry," I said, trying to keep my tone light. "I'm not any good at sports." I started to explain why, then remembered Mama's admonition. Going into my health at that point would be lethal to any prospects, so I stifled myself.

Then I second-guessed myself. What was I doing, anyway, being so judgmental? Points for the car, the style, the music? Please.

Who cared if he had a nice car and played golf? The question was, what kind of man was he? He seemed nice enough.

As the silence between us stretched out, I suddenly felt completely tongue-tied. I hadn't made small talk with a man in two generations.

We headed north for the two blocks it took to turn left toward the club. At least I wouldn't have to try to come up with something to talk about on a long trip to the restaurant.

He concentrated on the road with a slightly grim expression, probably feeling the same way.

I decided to take the bull by the horns. "You'll have to forgive me, but my last date was in 1977. I'm afraid I've forgotten how to do this, so please bear with me."

He shot me a relieved grin before focusing back on the shady street in the elegant neighborhood. "Ditto, in spades."

I didn't want to bring up his wife's death, but I was curious. Instead I asked, "Do you have any kids?"

He nodded, visibly grateful for the safe topic. "Three. Two sons here, and a daughter in California. All grown and on their own. The boys are in practice with me."

"How does that work out?" I asked, realizing how nosy it was as the words came out.

He grinned. "Fine. They do their thing, I do mine, and we all make money."

Points for working with his sons and getting along—assuming his sons would say the same thing. And points for making money, especially in this economy. Slight deduction for bragging about it.

Shoot. There I went again. If he'd been rating me that way, I'd be furious.

"What kind of law do y'all practice?" I asked.

"General. Real estate"—translate: foreclosures—"some corporate. Divorce. Estates. Trusts. The usual." He shot me a sidelong glance as we turned onto the access road to the club. "How about you? Any kids?"

"My son Tommy lives in Charlotte with his wife and my two grandchildren, a boy and a girl. My daughter Haley is still finding herself in New Orleans. She wants to be an actress."

Too much detail! He didn't even mention his kids' names, much less grandkids.

Minus points for me.

Oh, for crying out loud, why couldn't I just relax and go with the flow? Which was a stupid question, because I knew perfectly well why I couldn't relax. I was a one-man woman, and my man was gone. I didn't want to be there.

Stop that! Mama's voice commanded in my head. *You'll never find anybody with that attitude. This is a start. Just a start. A simple date. Period.*

We pulled up to the entrance and two valets opened our doors, one handing Wade a receipt in exchange for his keys.

Feeling naked and exposed, I got out and stood very straight, sucking in my stomach as I waited for my date to escort me inside. Then I realized I was a fifty-five-year-old woman who looked like I'd been in a POW camp, for crying out loud, not some debutante. My posture deflated.

Wade put his hand on the small of my back and leaned in to murmur, "It's okay. You look beautiful."

So much for being mysterious.

Once inside, the maître d' escorted us to Bill and Cindy's table. They both rose when we arrived, Bill to shake Wade's hand with a wink, and Cindy to give me a hug and a whispered, "You look mah-velous."

Frankly, I would have preferred the chaos of a Buckhead restaurant to the near-funereal silence of the club. Noise can cover a lot of gaffes, but there was no hope of that here.

The busboy arrived with water. Suddenly I was very thirsty, but rather than make an issue of it, I just gazed longingly at the icy, chlorine-laced glass. Fortunately, the bar waitress approached immediately and asked me, "And what can I bring for the lady to drink?"

"Do you have springwater?"

She nodded. "Still or sparkling?"

"Still, please, and no ice." There was probably chlorine in the ice.

"Bottle or half liter?" she asked, her tone discreet.

All the others were staring at me with opaquely pleasant expressions. "Half liter, please." I looked toward the others. "I'm a heavy drinker."

They all let out a halfhearted chuckle, then Cindy ordered a refill for her bourbon and branch. Bill had the same. When the waitress got to Wade, he jerked his head slightly, as if his collar were a bit too tight, then said, "Double Glenfarclas, the twenty-five. Neat."

Glen-anything meant scotch. Deduction for the double.

Shoot. There I went again.

I shifted uneasily in my seat, realizing that I'd never paid much attention to how much or little our friends drank. Tom had always nursed a single gin and tonic or glass of wine all the way through dinner. The fact that Cindy and Bill were already on their second drinks did not bode well.

The waiter came up and introduced himself, then told us the specials. To my vast relief, one was grilled cod amandine with sautéed zucchini and whipped cauliflower. God was smiling upon me.

He left to give us some time to consider.

Wade leaned over. "What looks good to you?"

Ah, old-school. He'd order for me, but was considerate enough to ask what I wanted. Points for the old-school manners.

"The cod, I think," I said as casually as I could manage. "I love grilled cod." Before I could edit it, "Without any pepper. I'm allergic to pepper," came out.

Shoot!

"Great." He nodded, scanning the menu. "I think I'll have the rib eye." He looked back at me, his nostrils flaring. "Rare. How about an appetizer?"

The question sounded like a proposition. Flustered, I responded with, "Have one, if you'd like. I'll save my appetite for the main course."

Uh-oh. Had that sounded suggestive?

He shot me an intense stare accompanied by an oddly hungry smile. "I think I'll save my appetite for later, too."

A definite double entendre.

Huge deduction for the double entendre. I was not physically attracted to this man in the slightest, and I didn't want him to think I was.

Or was I just imagining that he did?

Oh, help. I was so bad at this.

I fled to Cindy for safety. "So, what looks good to you?"

She leaned over and whispered, "You and Wade," then let out a suggestive chuckle.

Bill looked from me to Wade, then aimed a pointed glance at Cindy. "If y'all will excuse me for a minute, I'll be right back." He headed for the restrooms we'd passed on the way in.

Cindy asked Wade about his most recent interesting case, which he discussed without mentioning any names, but still, I felt uncomfortable that he spoke so freely about privileged information. But he and Bill were lawyers, and I supposed lawyers and their friends talked shop. Wade was halfway into his story about some crazy old lady who set up a trust for her caregiver nurse, excluding all her children, when Cindy's cell phone rang.

"Sorry." She picked it up, not even looking at the caller ID, and told me, "I need to get this. We left the plumber working on a leak at the house," as if she was reciting a script. She answered, then put on an exaggerated look of dismay. "Oh, no. Really? But we're right in the middle of dinner." She turned her phone to her shoulder and leaned toward me, her hand on mine. "The pipe burst, and we have to go home right away." She said into the phone, "We're on our way. The shutoff is at the meter near the street. We'll be right there."

Cindy hung up and grabbed her purse at the same time I grabbed her arm. "Can't the plumber turn the water off by himself?" I insisted. "He's a plumber."

She had staged this; I could tell. Planned it, so they could leave me and Wade alone.

"Please don't go," I pleaded. Turning my head so Wade couldn't see, I grimaced at her as I gripped her forearm even tighter. "It would be such a shame for y'all to miss dinner and the show."

"I'm sure y'all will be fine without us." Cindy pried my hand free, then gave me a dismissive pat as she stepped neatly out of range. She turned to Wade. "Bill gave you the tickets, Wade, didn't he?"

Wade nodded, frowning slightly at my reaction. Cindy gave him a peck on the cheek as she left. "Y'all have fun. Don't worry about us." She waved a toodle-oo, then hustled to the entrance, where Bill met her with a conspirator's smile.

Perfect. Not.

Nineteen

Cassie

Bill and Cindy sent us a look like doting parents, then turned to leave.

I shot daggers at their retreat till Wade's sigh brought my attention back to him.

His expression was guarded.

"I promise," I blurted out, "I had absolutely nothing to do with that."

He looked down, swirling what was left of his scotch, which wasn't much. "I have a confession to make," he said with an apologetic smile. "I did."

I stared at him in surprise.

His smile leveled out. "It was Bill's idea. If I gave him the signal that I was interested, he said they'd get out of the way so the two of us could go out alone."

I didn't like subterfuge. Major deduction for the subterfuge. "That's sneaky. I do not like sneaky. I like honesty."

He cocked a wry expression. "Well, I *am* a lawyer."

Unsure which way he meant that, I was appalled at the chuckle that escaped me. "Cad."

"Oh, I'm not a cad," he hastened to say. "I'm an old-fashioned gentleman, not a cad. And I promise, you are safe with me, dear lady."

That remained to be seen.

The waiter came back, glancing around when he didn't see the others. "Is everything all right?"

"Our friends were called away," Wade explained, "but we're ready to order. The lady will have the grilled cod, hold the pepper on everything, and I'll have the rib eye, medium rare, baked potato all the way, and the chef's salad." He looked at me. "Would you like a salad? They're all very good."

"No, thank you."

"Some wine?" he asked.

I started to say I didn't drink, but curbed myself to, "No, thank you. Just water."

"Bring our food all at once, please," Wade instructed, "and bring us a bottle of that nice robust white I had last week. And two glasses." He winked at me. "Just in case you change your mind." He handed the menus back to the waiter with a smug smile.

A bottle of wine! After a double scotch? *Major* deduction.

And another one for *in case you change your mind*.

If there was one thing I couldn't stand, it was people who wouldn't accept that I didn't drink.

Of course, I hadn't *told* him I didn't drink, but still . . .

I busied myself with my napkin to keep him from seeing my reaction.

He's nervous, Mama's voice said. *Cut him some slack. Men drink when they're nervous. He hasn't been out since 1977, either.*

Yeah, I countered, but he's driving.

He hasn't drunk the whole bottle yet, she retorted. *See how it goes. Relax.*

"I promise," he repeated, "I'm not the big, bad wolf." He finished his drink, then motioned for another.

So much for seeing how it went.

I struggled to keep the fixed smile on my face.

Cabs took forever in Atlanta. Maybe I could walk home from the club. It wasn't far, and it was still light.

But it was also ninety-five degrees.

Wade's second double arrived in no time. Forearms on the white tablecloth, he gripped it tightly, but didn't dive in right away. "It's been really hard since Maryanne died," he volunteered. "We were best friends. Married right out of college."

I softened a bit. "How did she die?" Oops. I felt myself flush. "I'm sorry. I shouldn't have asked that. You don't have to—"

He looked into his drink. "Breast cancer, stage four when she found it. She fought it, but it kept popping up other places. The worst was in her spine. They gave her so much radiation that she was paralyzed for the last year, in a wheelchair. We had great help, but it was so hard on her, the pain, the loss of dignity." He took a gulp of the scotch, then seemed to come to. "I'm sorry. Bill told me not to talk about her. Didn't mean to be a wet blanket."

I softened toward him. "It's okay," I told him. I looked down, swirling my cold glass of springwater. "I was lucky. Tom was never sick. He was my best friend, too. And then one morning, he just didn't wake up." I peered out over the manicured greens and fairways. "Sometimes I still can't believe it."

I took a swig. "I still dream about us, and I'm always so relieved

181

to see him, but he never says anything, and then I realize it's just a dream."

Wade covered my forearm with his hand. "I have that same dream about Maryanne. Exact same dream."

We had that in common, at least.

Just when things were threatening to get way too depressing, the food arrived, looking and smelling fabulous.

"No more talk about that," Wade said. "Let's talk about now. How are you keeping yourself busy?"

I debated what to tell him and settled on, "I had some problems with my house, so I'm renovating. New floors, new doors and windows. New roof. Foundation, all that. It's a disaster. That's why I'm staying with Mama."

He lifted the bottle of wine and tipped it toward my empty glass. "You're sure you don't want any?"

"Certain, thank you."

He poured a glass for himself. "Where do you live?"

"Garden Hills."

"I didn't figure you for a place like Canterbury. You're way too young."

"Thanks. I feel the same way. Where do you live?"

"Just around the corner, but now that I'm alone, I've seriously considered getting a condo. Big houses are so much trouble to keep up. But the boys don't want me to move. So I'll probably just stay. It's where they grew up."

The fish was delicious, as were the vegetables. After a few silent bites, I tried to pick up the conversation. "It's been too easy just to hole up in my house for the past year. Maybe that's why God allowed this renovation, to blast me out of my cocoon."

Wade didn't comment on my mention of God, and I couldn't

get a read on his reaction. I tried again. "Cindy said you and Bill are friends from church."

Wade wiped his mouth, then took a hefty swig of wine before replying. "Yep. We were both confirmed at Christ the King. Been there ever since."

I'd had no idea Bill and Cindy were Catholic, but I'd never made it a point to ask anybody about where they went to church or synagogue. Whether Wade's being Catholic was a plus or minus depended on what kind of Catholic he was: a man of faith, or mere ritual. But then again, you could say the same thing about a lot of Baptists.

I started to ask him how he felt about a personal relationship with Christ, then thought better, clobbered into silence by a metaphysical glare from Mama.

Okay, okay. First date. At least he went to church.

"So, read any good books lately?" he asked with a twinkle in his eye.

When we started to talk about books, the conversation finally fell into place. Even though I hadn't been able to read lately, there were still plenty of authors we could discuss, and discuss we did. So well, that I forgot to check on how much he was drinking, and I couldn't see how much was left in the dark green wine bottle by the time we finished.

"Dessert?" he asked.

Boy, would I love some, but I made myself say no.

After he signed the check, he rose from the table, rock solid on his feet. "You're very good company," he complimented, his speech unslurred. He pulled out my chair without faltering in the slightest. "Let's go sing along with the Beatles."

Caution wavered. I was having a good time, and he seemed

unaffected by what he'd had to drink. I decided to watch how he walked to the car and make up my mind there.

As we proceeded smoothly through the dining room, I wracked my brain for some excuse to give if I needed to beg off, but nothing came to mind except a migraine, the lamest of all lame excuses.

Still, it would have to do. But Wade seemed completely sober, so I hesitated only briefly before getting into the car. If his driving showed the slightest hint of impairment, I'd tell him to drop me off.

But it didn't, and neither did our conversation. We started talking about our favorite golden oldies, and before I knew it, we were at the arena downtown. But no sooner were we seated in our fabulous loge seats than he asked me if I wanted anything to drink. "Wine? Beer?"

"Diet Coke, please," I said, worried about what he'd choose for himself.

I was relieved to see him return with two large fountain sodas, mine diet, his regular. He dragged on his straw a few times, then reached into his expensive sport coat and pulled out a flask.

Help, help. A flask drinker!

His eyes on the stage, he poured most of the contents into his Coke, stirred it with his straw, then replaced the lid and stashed the flask away.

My mind raced with contingencies. Cabs from downtown to Buckhead cost a fortune—if you could get one. Mama never kept any cash, and I hadn't brought but forty dollars and no credit cards.

Royally annoyed, I debated begging off then and there, before he could drink any more, and insisting he take me home.

But then he'd probably tell everybody in Buckhead I was an

impossible prig. And if he didn't, Cindy would, may she break out in zits for doing this to me.

What to do, what to do?

Help, Tom. I wanted Tom.

Then the lights went down and the music started, and it was too late. I'd try to get a cab later. Furious at myself for not acting sooner—for caring what anybody said about me, including this attractive, intelligent, well-to-do *lush*—I forced myself to concentrate on the music and the show. Eventually, to my surprise, I started to relax.

I was on my way out of the bathroom at intermission when I had a brainstorm: call Cindy and Bill to come get me. That was it! This was all their fault, in the first place.

I punched up my directory before another thought stopped me.

Shoot. Cindy and Bill were liable to be just as tight as Wade was. Shoot, shoot, shoot!

I couldn't call Mama, because she didn't drive so late anymore.

Surely, there was somebody I could call.

Then I realized there wasn't. Our good couples friends were probably already settled in.

I didn't have a best friend to call. Not even a close one.

Stunned, I realized I didn't have anybody, really, but my family, to call in the middle of the night. That hit me so hard, I went immobile.

"Cassie?" Wade's voice came from just behind me over the roar of conversations in the lobby, the smell of scotch strong on his breath. "Are you okay?" Wavering slightly, he took my arm and steered me toward our seats.

How could I have been so stupid, letting myself get into this predicament? I should never have let him bring me down there.

Now it was too late. Against all my better instincts, everything I'd ever told my daughter about dating, I heard myself say, "I'm fine. Just fine."

My self-confidence evaporated, on the spot. I might as well have been a teenager at a frat party with a BMOC. I let him lead me back to our seats for the rest of the show.

Despite all he'd consumed by the time we got out, neither Wade's step nor his speech faltered. So like a fool, I let him put me into the car and drive me home. I prayed for traveling mercies and angels of protection the whole way, but my trust in God was tempered by the knowledge that it was my own foolish fault that I needed help in the first place.

Wade's only concession to his condition was that he took Peachtree instead of the expressway, and stayed five miles an hour below the posted speed limit, leaving plenty of room between us and the other cars.

It dawned on me that this man had been drinking and driving for a long time, to have adapted so well. But even so, we drifted out of our lane several times, to varying degrees. By the third incident, I couldn't keep quiet anymore. "Wade, you're drifting. Please pull over and let me drive."

He cocked a bleary half smile and speeded up. "Relax. I'm fine. Just fine. Never even had a ticket."

I tried two more times to convince him, but each time, he just speeded up more, so I eventually lapsed into terrified silence and prayer.

When we finally pulled up at Canterbury Court, I leaped out of the door with hasty thanks and fled inside, leaving him standing there, half out of the car, in dismay. I didn't look back, just hurried to the elevators, heart pounding all the way up to Mama's floor.

Once I got there, I collapsed into one of the tasteful upholstered chairs across from the elevators, head in hands, and thanked God for getting me home in one piece.

Mama. How would I ever keep this from Mama?

I couldn't. She'd see it in my face.

Dear heaven. I was fifty-five years old, and I didn't know what to tell Mama about my date, for crying out loud.

Shoot.

She'd be waiting up. I knew she would.

Shoot. Shoot. Shoot.

Twenty

Jack

Jack clicked on his e-mails and saw that he'd gotten at least ten more naked pictures from fat, desperate, middle-aged women in Cumming, Indiana, evidenced by "Let's Play" in the subject line. Served him right for clicking that button on the dating Web site he'd been exploring. For some reason, the dating service had shown him as living in Indiana instead of Georgia, which was a very good thing. The last thing he needed was to have women like that recognize him where he lived.

Not that it would have made any difference. As a matter of morality, Jack had long since restricted himself to merely looking at pictures of naked women instead of bedding them, and reading about sex instead of doing it.

In the strictest sense, he knew he probably shouldn't be doing either, but he was only human, and he *was* still a man—albeit not as much of one because of his blood pressure medicine—so he prayed for mercy and figured God would understand. After all, God was responsible for the testosterone in the first place.

Frankly, the "Let's Play" pictures were punishment enough. He didn't even open them anymore.

Jack abandoned his e-mails to cruise the Net for information about chronic fungal infections. Since his first appointment with Dr. Patel, he'd printed out and read more than thirty articles and medical papers about the subject, and though there was some issue as to which came first, the chicken or the egg, when it came to adrenal fatigue, nothing he'd found contradicted what the doctor had told him. The truth was, he was still hoping to discover something credible to debunk the expensive, complicated regimen Patel had ordered, but Jack was beginning to suspect he wouldn't.

Letting out a forced wheeze, he scanned the books he'd cleaned, bagged in plastic, and put back into their demolded shelves. And the remaining stacks around them, safe in their plastic containers and bags. The trouble with clearing out was, it only called attention to the wretched floor. And the wretched cheap paneling on the walls, and the destitute, bare-bulb nature of the place in general. Even though he'd saturated everything left out in the open with the antifungal spray, he knew that millions of tiny, micron-sized particles were seeping in from above and below and all the cracks, then reproducing in the warm and humid air he breathed, settling all over everything he'd cleaned, and multiplying inside him.

There was something decidedly macabre about being a host organism. It gave him the creeps.

Granted, he'd felt better since he'd finally left off the complex carbs and sugar altogether, but he couldn't remain in the house much longer.

He'd finally broken down and called four people he knew to come out and bid his collections. The results hadn't been good. Pleading the economy, every one of them had told him the bottom had dropped out of the collectibles market, then offered him only a pittance, even for his plates. So much for his treasures. The vendors hadn't even been willing to look at what was in the barn.

No money there.

Jack paged through the Google listings about chronic fungal infections, not finding anything new. Then he tried a couple of other search engines, but still, no luck. Frustrated, he shut the computer down and headed for the refrigerator for a root beer. He was halfway there when he remembered there wasn't anything cold to drink in the fridge but springwater. No more sausage biscuits, either. He couldn't eat any grains while taking Patel's new oral vaccine for reasons the doctor had explained that went in one ear and out the other.

What he needed was a solid concrete house somewhere. Two rooms, a bath, and a microwave would be enough. Maybe he could find such a place on the Internet, somewhere near the sea but not too hot. Offered by a seller willing to trade.

After all, P. T. Barnum had said there was one born every minute. All Jack needed was one who would swap for the farm.

Frowning at the springwater he retrieved, he went back to his computer to search "seller financing" and "near beach." While he waited for it to boot up, he decided to broaden the search to the Yucatán or Central America. Maybe he'd find something not too far from his father.

But deep down, he knew that nobody would want the farm, any more than anybody would want him. Not even those fat, desperate exhibitionists from Cumming, Indiana, once they knew his situation. And God knew, Jack didn't want them.

At this point, what he wanted was to go to sleep, then wake up in heaven, like Cassie's husband.

It would be so much simpler for everybody.

The fact that it didn't happen annoyed him intensely.

The phone rang.

He picked it up and checked the screen. His mother.

Jack sighed and collected himself before answering, "Hi, Mama."

"Jackson," his mother barked out, "why haven't you come to see me? Mama and Daddy haven't, either, and I must tell you, I'm getting vexed with the lot of you."

Jack knew the answer before he asked, but he felt compelled to say, "Did you go to the doctor with Aunt Junie, Mama?"

"When?"

Jack rolled his eyes. "Just lately."

"Heavens, Jack. I have no idea."

"Could I please speak to Aunt Junie?"

"Not till you tell me why you and Mama and Daddy haven't come to see me."

Same song, millionth verse. Jack tried to keep the despair and aggravation from his reply. "Because I live in Cumming, Georgia, and it's a long way from here to Biloxi."

"Well, what about Mama and Daddy?"

He hated this. Hated it. "Mama, Gran and Big Daddy are in heaven. They died fifteen years ago. You just forgot."

She responded with a dismissive, "Hmph."

So much for trying to reason with a crazy person. Why did he bother?

Because he loved his mother.

If she could endure living that way—believing everybody who loved her had abandoned her, except Aunt Junie—Jack decided he should be more grateful for his own trials. At least he had his mind.

"Could I please speak to Aunt Junie?" he repeated.

His mother paused, then said, "She's not here."

Alarm brought him alert. "Where is she?"

"Those men came and took her."

Jack straightened the recliner to bolt upright. "What men?"

"You know," his mother said with a mixture of confusion and exasperation. "Those men who come."

Extrapolating everything from gang members to morticians, Jack stood, his pulse pounding. "How long has she been gone?"

"I really couldn't say," his mother answered lazily. "Frankly, I think she was exaggerating. She's always exaggerating about her ailments."

With any luck, "those men" were paramedics. Jack got out his Biloxi phone book and started hunting for the hospitals. "Mama, I need you to listen to me very carefully. Do not leave the house till I get there, okay? It's very important. I'm coming to see you, but it will take a while, so I need you to stay where you are and watch your shows till I get there, okay?"

"You're always bothering me when I'm trying to watch my shows," she said. "I have to hang up now, Jackson. *Price Is Right* is coming on."

Please, God, don't let Aunt Junie be hurt or dying. Or dead. Jack dearly loved his aunt, but the idea of losing his mother's caregiver overrode even that.

"Okay, Mama. You just watch your shows. I'll be there to visit soon."

Blast it all. Just blast.

He started calling hospitals.

To his vast relief, he located his aunt and was able to speak to her doctor. She'd fainted, but they said it was probably due to dehydration, and they were giving her IV fluids. His mother had been the one to call 911, much to Jack's surprise.

At least she'd had the wherewithal to do that.

Jack explained the situation, and the doctor promised to call in Social Services to get his aunt home when the treatment was finished. After he hung up with the doctor, Jack called the senior sitting service he'd used on occasion to give his aunt a break. They promised to send someone right over to stay with his mother till he got there.

That accomplished, he threw a few clothes and audio books into his duffel, then headed for Biloxi. High as gas was, he could probably fly cheaper, but he'd need transportation when he got there.

Blast. Just what he needed. Another long trip with a fast turnaround so he could make his appointment with Patel.

Assuming things down there didn't get worse.

Like it or not, he was going to have to do something permanent about his mama.

Twenty-one

Cassie

Pleading fatigue when I met Mama at the door after my date, I staved off her questions by overusing the word "nice" in varying forms. I was too upset with myself to go into what had really happened, and after I escaped to my room, I lay there fuming, second-guessing myself till two in the morning, when *Punkin Chunkin* ended, marking the onslaught of the infomercials on cable. I turned off the set, but couldn't go to sleep till three.

So I was still twisted in my sheets, a pillow under my knee, when Mama's phone rang at ten the next morning. Grateful it wasn't mine to answer, I flipped over and covered my eyes with my mold-remediated lovey pillow to shut out the noise and light.

The door opened abruptly. "Cassie," Mama sang as she came to sit on the bed, "it's for you."

Please don't let it be Wade. I rolled over with a chuff of annoyance, eyeing Mama through one slit as I accepted the phone with, "I've got it, Mama. Please close the door on your way out."

Clearly disappointed, Mama frowned, but did as I asked. I waited for the knob to click before venturing a gravelly, "Hullo?"

"Wade just called," Cindy said. "He said y'all had had a great time, then you suddenly jumped out of the car and ran inside. Did he do something wrong?"

Shoot.

What should I say? She'd set me up with the man, so she'd probably take it personally if I told her he'd gotten plastered. "Just a second, Cindy," I deflected. "Mama just woke me out of a dead sleep, and my brain's not engaged." True enough.

Quick. Think of something that wouldn't burn any bridges with Cindy and Bill.

Help. I was a horrible liar. Think. What had made me run away?

My mouth came up with something before my brain did. "Bladder attack."

"Oh. Is that all?" Cindy laughed in relief. "I was afraid maybe he'd said something stupid or put the mash on you."

"No, he didn't do that." No thanks to her and Bill, for deserting me. The next came out on its own. "But he did have a lot to drink."

Cindy sighed. "Oh, that." She paused. "He told me he had a few too many." Try a *lot* too many. "He regrets that. He was really nervous, being his first date and all. And he really likes you."

Then why hadn't he called me himself to apologize?

Heck, he might not even remember keeping me hostage on the trip home.

"Well, *I* was really nervous riding home with him," I retorted.

"He's really sorry. Please don't write him off because of one misstep." Try a dozen, which was probably how many drinks he'd totted up. "Y'all are so good together," Cindy coaxed.

Yeah. All three of us: Wade, me, and his booze. Not!

"Listen, speaking of bladders," I hedged, "I really need to go."

Pun intended. "I appreciate your checking to make sure everything is okay, but I've got to hang up."

"Just give him another chance," she insisted. "Please. For me and Bill. Let him take you out to dinner. He'll be a model citizen, I promise."

Shoot, shoot, shoot. All my instincts said no, but all my instincts always said no when it came to this dating business. Still, I could refuse, but that felt so confrontational, and I had no stomach for confrontation. "Oh, all right. But if he gets drunk again, I'm calling a cab."

"Fair enough," she conceded. "Is tonight okay?"

I made for the bathroom. Would tonight give him enough time to sober up?

"Or tomorrow night," she prodded. "Either works. Any night you want. Name the day."

"Monday," I said, knowing he'd have to come from work, so he'd probably be sober.

"What time?" she asked.

This was so high school. "Six-thirty." Too early for him to get fortified. "But if he blows this one, I'm out of it."

"He won't. I promise."

I hung up, angry with myself for giving in, but hoping Cindy was right.

Monday night at six-thirty on the dot, Wade arrived to collect me with a sheepish smile. "Sorry about Friday." He took my elbow on the way out. "Can we start over?"

Seeing his sincerity, I relented. "Okay."

He grinned in relief. "Great. I know a fabulous little place that just opened up in Midtown. Amazing seafood. They even have scamp."

Getting into the car, I perked right up. I loved scamp, my favorite Gulf game fish. "I didn't know anybody but me and Captain Anderson's knew about scamp."

"I've spent my time at Captain Anderson's," he said as he got in. "We had a double unit down near St. Andrews Park for years. Ate at the captain's almost every night. Kept the place till the kids were teenagers, and we wouldn't fit anymore." He started the car. "By then, mondo condo had surrounded us, so we got a beach house on Captiva. Still have it." He pulled up to the light. "The whole family gets together there the week after Christmas every year."

A beach house was nice. Very nice.

He seemed stone sober. Relaxing, I settled back, and we swapped reminiscences of the panhandle from our own children's growing up. The only difference was, Tom and I had been renters, not owners. To my pleasant surprise, both of us naturally included our late spouses in our recollections, and it didn't feel awkward at all.

When we reached the restaurant, I excused myself, then came back to the table to find Wade with another double scotch, but this time, he'd ordered scallop and artichoke dip and pita chips to go with it.

At least he was eating with his drink. I tried not to drool over the fabulous-smelling dip and ordered a Diet Coke to fill my stomach.

We continued to talk about growing up in Atlanta, and I thought things were going really well.

When I looked over the menu, I didn't find anything that wasn't battered, breaded, or fried, so I asked the waiter if they could grill me some scamp with olive oil and lemon juice, hold the pepper, and he was happy to oblige. After what Wade had done Friday night, I wasn't so self-conscious about my diet anymore. But as the evening wore on, he seemed to withdraw a bit, preoccupied with something.

He drank a couple of glasses of wine with dinner, but that seemed okay. After we'd eaten, he started to tell me something, then thought better of it and asked if I wanted dessert.

I turned it down with, "I can't eat sugar, but please, have one yourself."

He frowned. "Are you diabetic?"

"No." I felt the color rise from my neck to my ears. "It's a long story, one for another day." I pointed to the little menu. "That flan with strawberries looks really good. Why don't you have that? I'll have a cup of decaf."

Once again, he hesitated, and I sensed he wanted to tell me something, but he ordered the French silk pie, instead.

Things got progressively more awkward till we got to the car. I had no idea what was going on, but I did my best not to make a big deal out of it.

Wade put me into the passenger seat, then circled around and got in. But when he reached for the keys, he halted, then turned to face me, propping his left arm on the wheel in an open, vulnerable stance. "Cassie, I really like you." He looked down in the gentle evening light. "I'd like to see you. But there's something I have to get off my chest, first."

Uh-oh.

I nodded, worried what was coming next.

He looked down again. "You said you wanted honesty. I've been thinking about that a lot since I made such a fool of myself Friday." He met my carefully arranged expression with one of guilt. "This has been eating me alive since Maryanne died, and I can't begin a relationship with it hanging over us both." He turned haunted eyes toward mine.

Uh-oh. Lord spare me from a lawyer in a fit of conscience.

Turning his head in profile, he peered through the windshield. "Maryanne had been so sick for so long, and I was so lonely and depressed. I slipped into drinking too much. I met Eunice at the nineteenth hole. I didn't mean for what happened to happen. She started out consoling me, and that was all it was for a long time. But then, one night . . ." He looked to me for understanding. "I slipped. I knew it was wrong, but it just happened. I was so lonely . . ."

I could not believe my ears.

Cheating didn't just *happen*, like the weather! He'd betrayed his wife when she was dying!

What had made him think he could drop a bomb like that on *me?*

Wade swiveled back into his seat and laid his forehead on the steering wheel, hands gripping it tightly. "There. I've said it." He let out a hard breath. "What a relief."

Holy mother of Maloney!

This idiot had cheated on his dying wife with a woman named *Eunice,* for heaven's sake, then dumped that into my lap on our second date?

He shot me a sidelong glance of torment. "If I could take it back, I would, and I swear, it will never happen again."

Right. *Once a cheater, always a cheater,* echoed through my mind.

I tried my best to appreciate his honesty and trust, but it didn't help. Mentally, my old-fashioned, hypermonogamous self cocked her hip and let out a sarcastic "un-honh" worthy of Flip Wilson's Geraldine.

This was so wrong in so many ways that words failed me completely. Friday night was a walk in the park compared to this. I couldn't believe he thought I'd even *consider* a relationship after his self-serving confession.

I stared straight ahead and focused on keeping my voice even. "Please tell me you didn't tell your wife."

"God, no. I'd never do that to her."

He'd just cheat on her. When she was dying.

My stomach roiled, but I knew there wouldn't be any sense in confronting him. Obviously, he'd thought he was doing the right thing by confessing.

"Wade, I really enjoyed dinner, but I'm worn out. Could you please take me home?"

Clearly, he got the point, because he struck the steering wheel with the heels of his hands so hard it should have bent, making me jump. Then he cranked the motor and took me home in silence.

Block after block, I tried to stave off judgment of a man who would do that, then think it was a good idea to tell me, but I couldn't.

Judge not that ye be not judged, but I mean, *really*!

Still, I had asked him to be honest. And I was better off fore-warned.

The final insult came as we pulled into Canterbury Court. "Please," he said as he slowed at the entrance. "For Maryanne's sake, and for the kids, don't tell anybody."

Invoking his dead wife and kids to cover his ass? I stared at him in amazement, but managed to hold my tongue.

When he stopped, I didn't wait for him to come open the door. I got out, then leaned back down to tell him, "Wade, I don't think this is going to work. Our values are too different."

It was the kindest thing I could think of, under the circum-stances. Once again, I slammed the door and fled without looking back.

Feeling like my soul needed a bath, I stabbed the elevator but-ton over and over again till it opened.

Did Cindy know what he'd done? Please tell me Cindy didn't know.

Boy, would Mama get an earful tonight.

At least I could count on her discretion—for Maryanne's sake, and Wade's kids'.

I know I was being rigid, but infidelity was one area I wasn't willing to compromise.

If this was what was out there, I was doomed to live alone with crummy insurance.

Twenty-two

Jack

Jack sat in his mother's parlor drinking springwater instead of the lemonade Aunt Junie had made them. He could tell she was offended by his refusal of her hospitality, but he had more important things to worry about.

"Mama," he said, "I've found a really nice place for Aunt Junie to live. It's over by the Episcopal church. And the best thing is, she won't have to clean or cook or do laundry anymore. They do all that for you, so she can just relax and enjoy y'all's shows. They even have bingo night." If his mother thought she was looking at a place for Junie, she might just loosen up and say she liked it, too.

Aunt Junie brightened. "I love bingo. Ben and I used to play at the VFW every Friday night." She had already seen the photos he'd sent, swearing her to secrecy, and declared the place wonderful, probably because she'd be relieved of the chores and responsibility of taking care of her crazy sister.

"Great," Jack said. "I hear it's really nice." He'd seen for himself, and it was, sprawling on a huge, beautifully landscaped lot with a garden plot for the residents and two pools with hot tubs.

His mother acted as if he hadn't said a word, but he didn't push. He planned to let the new place do the talking for him.

When they'd finished their lemonades, Jack stood. "Okay. Who's up for a ride in the truck? We can go by Denny's on the way home." His mother never turned down a trip to Denny's.

Junie popped to her feet. "Oh, good."

Jack deliberately ignored his mother, fussing over his aunt. "It's a perfect day to go apartment hunting."

"Well, are y'all just going to go off without me?" his mother grumbled, rising to her feet.

Jack gave her a hug, holding on a little longer than necessary. *Please let her like it.* "Of course not. I need your opinion on Aunt Junie's new apartment."

She looked to his aunt in surprise. "Junie's moving out?"

"That depends," he said. "We're just looking today." Jack patted his mother's shoulder. "If you really like the apartment, maybe you could stay with her for a while, just till she gets used to it." The lie came out smooth as satin. He had to convince her, but she didn't have to know it would be permanent.

His mother stiffened. "But this is my home. I couldn't possibly leave my home, Jackson. How would Mama and Daddy and your father ever find me?"

"Don't worry about that, Mama," Jack said, shepherding her out the door behind his aunt. "Today, we're just checking things out."

If she didn't like the place, Jack had no idea what he'd do next. He couldn't stand the thought of having her dragged there, kicking and screaming.

By God's good grace, though, his mother was favorably impressed by the spacious unit with dual master suites. And she acted almost normal when they ate the sample meal the manager served them. She loved the common room they passed, especially the bingo game going on inside. Hallelujah, amen.

Mightily relieved, Jack winked a nod at the manager as they left, then helped his mother and Junie into the truck for the trip back to the house. With any luck, he could have them moved within the month.

They'd only driven a few blocks when his mother piped up with, "You said we were going to Denny's."

Jack flattened his mouth. She couldn't remember her parents, but she remembered that. "Mama, you just ate."

"Of course I didn't," she scolded. "I've been saving my appetite for the Grand Slam. You promised. Remember?" She waggled a long, bony finger toward the Denny's. "Turn left at the next light. It's three blocks down."

Aunt Junie giggled. "She's right."

God forbid his mother should ever forget the way to Denny's.

Jack let out a chuckle of his own and flipped the left-turn blinker. "Okay. Denny's it is."

Twenty-three

Cassie

A week from the following Thursday, I arrived at Dr. Patel's to find Jack in his usual spot on the sofa reading Elmore Leonard and looking a lot better. I noticed he'd shaved and had a fresh barbershop haircut that left his ears sticking out.

By now we'd gotten used to being on the same appointment schedule. "You're looking better today," I said as I took my place at the other end of the sofa.

"Thank you." He kept his eyes on the book. "How's the house going?"

Don't get me started. "Slow. Expensive. At this rate, I'll be bankrupt in less than five years." Now why had I told him that? Maybe because I knew he could commiserate. "Assuming there aren't any more major surprises, which is assuming a lot."

He closed his book, glancing over his reading glasses. "How did the date go?"

Rats. I'd forgotten I'd told him about the fix-up. "In an understatement of galactic proportion, not well. Let's just leave it at that."

One side of his mouth cocked back in criticism as he opened his book up again and glanced down. "Aaah. You're just too picky."

I clamped my lips into a tight line of indignation. Jerk!

Were they *all* jerks?

Refusing to give him the satisfaction of a reply, I snatched my pen and morning paper out of my purse, then started doing the Jumble. I was addicted to the Jumble and the crossword puzzle, which I did every day.

Jack let out a supercilious, "Women."

That did it. Pen poised, I leaned toward him. "I will have you know, Jack Wilson," I whispered low enough so the receptionist couldn't hear me over the air purifier, "that he got so drunk I feared for my life riding home with him. And when he talked me into giving him another chance"—I bent closer—"he told me he cheated on his wife while she was dying of cancer. Then he had the nerve to think I still might want to date him." I flung myself back upright. "If it's picky to consider infidelity a fatal flaw, then I guess I *am* picky."

I went back to my Jumble.

Jack let out a low whistle. "So much for fix-ups."

I straightened my newspaper, then wrote "gambit" in the third set of blanks. "If that's what's out there, I am done with dating."

He shook his head at me. "Do you always polarize things like this? One brief affair, and the guy's irredeemable. One bad egg, and you're off the whole gender?" He arched a newly trimmed brow. "Your sainted husband was a man, too, you know."

"One in a million," I shot back. I turned my attention back to the Jumble. Moeaba: "amoeba."

"Okay. One in a million." Jack faced me with a smug smile. "There are roughly a hundred and fifty million males in the U.S.

alone. For the purposes of argument, let's say a third of those are boomers, which leaves you with fifty million. And let's say that a third of those are single, which leaves you with about sixteen and a half million. So by your computation, there are at least sixteen good, one-in-a-million available men out there. Now all you have to do is find them before you go broke, and take your pick."

I smiled in spite of myself. He sure didn't talk like any mechanic I'd ever met. "You are impossible."

Next Jumble word: roocep. Poorec?

Croope?

Operec. No, operoc. No.

Brows lifted, Jack peered over at the paper. He liked to do the Jumble, too, and usually helped me when I got stuck, particularly on long, one-word solves.

Not today, not after that "picky" comment.

I shifted in my seat so he couldn't see it.

"Cooper." Of course. My own maiden name.

Jack let out a resolute wheeze. "You helped me with the house. Maybe I can help you find somebody, give you the male point of view."

Surprised that he'd offered, I turned back toward him.

He shrugged. "Did you ever try any of those legitimate Christian online dating services I told you about?"

"One of them. I filled out the questionnaire and joined for three months, but everybody who contacted me was from far away, and I specifically said I couldn't relocate."

He lifted a palm. "There you go, getting it all wrong. Maybe *they're* willing to relocate. Did you ever think of that?"

Please. "Well, we couldn't very well date if they're in Seattle and I'm here."

"No, but you could get to know each other by e-mail," Jack countered. "Dating is the last step. Get to know each other first."

"I don't trust e-mail," I said. "That idiot I went out with would have looked fabulous on a questionnaire. Double scotches by the pint don't come through on e-mail."

"Then ask for somebody who doesn't drink," Jack countered.

I wasn't buying it, but I realized I couldn't very well find another husband without dating. Unless . . . "The only man I'm interested in at this point is one the Lord God Almighty sends me Himself, and God knows where I live."

"Last time I looked," Jack chided, "things didn't work that way. That's like sitting on your butt instead of working and expecting God to provide a paycheck. We have to do our part, you know."

"That's not in scripture," I told him.

"Yes it is. 'If a man will not work, he shall not eat.' Second Thessalonians 3:10."

If he wanted to split hairs, I could split hairs. "Well, first, that's talking about a man, not a widow. And second, there are a whole lot more scriptures that command us to surrender our lives and needs to God. If God wants me to remarry, He'll provide somebody."

Jack rolled his eyes toward heaven. "So you're just going to sit back and let your money run out." He shook his head, then resumed reading without having to say, "It's your funeral."

I couldn't really expect him to understand.

"Mrs. Jones, the doctor will see you now."

There went another three hundred and fifty dollars. I got up and left Jack to his raunchy, violent book.

Two weeks later, Jack was there again, reading on the sofa, but in my regular spot lay a copy of *The Messenger*, the Southern Baptist regional newspaper, folded to the personals, with quite a few circled in red.

He didn't even look up. "I won't tell you what I had to do to get that," he muttered.

And I wouldn't tell *him* about the five fix-ups Mama had bullied me into trying since our last appointment. She'd enlisted all her friends, who'd arranged to have me invited to dinner to meet the following: one morbidly overweight accountant who talked about tax codes the whole time; somebody from the altar guild's nephew in Coke-bottle glasses who hadn't had a job since 1998 and liked it that way; another nephew who was a rabid NASCAR fan and took me to a sports bar where, after a few beers, he invited me to accompany him in his RV to the next big race; one well-built but fitness-obsessed personal trainer twenty years my junior (wrong!); and last but not least ("Such a handsome young man"), a gay gigolo from Arthur Murray (I don't think Mama's friend who set us up had a clue), who turned out to be the handsomest and most attentive of all, but uninsured.

So there I was, back at square one, with the poorhouse coming closer by leaps and bounds.

I picked up *The Messenger* and started to read the personals Jack had circled. "A minister? You did not circle a minister."

"What's the matter?" Jack said. "You have something against ministers?"

"No." Why did I feel compelled to explain myself to him? "I'm just not anybody's idea of a Baptist minister's wife. For one thing, I don't play piano. For another, I like my privacy." And the occasional R-rated movie or historical romance, if it's worthy and well done. "Plus, I'm rotten with committees."

"Bigot," he accused with a smug little smile.

"Male," I accused right back. I read the rest. Of eight, three looked interesting. They gave their e-mails.

Jack waggled a finger my way. "If you plan to answer any of those, I strongly suggest you set up a special e-mail address only for that, one that doesn't give away any personal information like your name. Just to be safe."

That made sense. Maybe I would.

Maybe I wouldn't.

He wasn't finished. "What you really ought to do is write a personal ad of your own."

"Why do you care?" I countered. It had become a code phrase between us, almost affectionate, over the past two months.

He shrugged. "You helped me. I help you. It's obvious you're clueless about men."

That was an understatement. All those years with Tom, I'd just assumed most men were like him. I'd actually felt sorry for the women who said men were dogs. And when the divorces had started breaking out all around us, I'd clung to my husband and found refuge in our circle of stoutly married friends.

The last two months had been proof of how little I did know about the realities of the opposite sex in the twenty-first century.

The receptionist stood and leaned over the counter. "I'm sorry, but Dr. Patel had an emergency. He's running about half an hour late."

"Somebody's face-lift fall?" Jack asked her, sarcastic as ever.

There was a certain freedom to having such a frank nonrelationship with a member of the opposite sex and not worrying about what he thought of me, or feeling responsible for him. "Are you always this obnoxious?" I asked.

He responded with an affable, "Only when I'm in a good mood."

As usual, he didn't elaborate about the cause.

Lord knew why, but I was beginning to like this guy—not a lot, mind you, but a little. At least he was consistent. It called to mind my daughter's gagging, eye-watering reaction when she was four and I'd made her try a bite of scalloped apples: "I like it a little, but I hate it a lot."

"So," I said, "what would *you* put in a personal ad if you did one for yourself?"

He turned the page in his book. "Only giant boobs need apply."

I laughed in spite of myself. "Incorrigible."

"So sue me, I'm a boob man," he retorted. "Anyway, I'm not looking for somebody to marry. Never will be."

"Good thing. No woman in her right mind could put up with you."

"Precisely," he said as if I'd just given him some great compliment. "But I have an idea what you could say if you did a personal."

"Oh, really. And what would that be?"

"Intelligent SWF Christian widow, very handy around the house, with a nice set of tools, seeks literate, reasonably attractive eligible SW Christian male. Object, the symphony."

Embarrassment sent heat up my neck. "I can't say that about the tools. Lord knows what ideas somebody might get."

"Only the ideas they'd have anyway," Jack said. "But I think the rest sums it up pretty nicely. You don't want to go for the health insurance in the ad. Way too mercenary."

I bristled. "You think I'm mercenary?"

"Aren't you?" he challenged. "You say you like honesty, then you condemn that guy for telling the truth. Once you meet somebody, you ought to be up front about your motives. As long as he thinks he's getting a ticket to Buckhead, it probably won't put him off." He cocked a cynical half smile at me. "After all, the insurance is what you're looking for."

I bristled. "No I'm not. I'm looking for a good Christian man with *great* health insurance. There's a big difference."

"Right." Again, the sarcasm.

I had half a mind to stomp the toes on his one foot.

Still, Jack had a point. I guess I couldn't very well expect God to drop a new husband on me from the sky.

Maybe I would try that I-Compatibility site. They always advertised a lot of marriages. Of course, the couples in the commercials all looked like they were in their thirties.

So maybe not.

I didn't have to decide that morning.

"Anything left from that garage sale you had?" Jack asked.

"A bit."

His interest perked up. "Like what?"

"A couple of upholstered Louis Quatorze–style chairs and a few occasional tables that were too nice to give away. Why?"

"A friend of mine likes furniture," he said. "Could I bring her by to see them?"

A female friend. Some women had no standards. "Sure. When?"

He groped in the pockets of his wrinkled shorts for his phone. "Let me see if I can get her." He punched a side button and the screen went white, then he held it out and said, "Call Frances Taylor, mobile."

A mechanical voice responded, "Call Frank Sisco, mobile?"

Jack scowled, then spoke louder. "No. Call Frances Taylor, mobile."

"Call Frances Taylor, mobile two?"

"No."

"No listing for Frances Taylor, mobile two," the voice taunted, then went back to the basic screen.

"Blasted thing," he grumbled, poking away at the buttons till he found the listing in his directory. He punched the green receiver button, then put the phone to his ear.

After a long pause, he all but shouted, "Frances! It's Jack. Found some good used chairs. I'll bring you to look at 'em in the truck. How about this afternoon?"

He looked to me in question. I nodded, hoping I could sell them.

He directed his attention back to the phone for a loud, "Okay. Pick you up at two." He hung up and dropped the phone back into his pocket. "We'll meet you there at two-thirty."

"I'll give you the address."

He waved me off. "Don't need it."

"Why not?"

"It's on the Internet. So are both your phones and bio. And your son Tom's and daughter Haley's."

I straightened, appalled. "What?"

Jack shook his head. "You have so much to learn."

Feeling violated, I had to agree with him. "You looked me up?"

"Sure," he answered without apology.

"Why?"

He shrugged. "Why not?"

"That's obnoxious."

Jack grinned. "You have a really limited vocabulary, don't you?"

I let out a huff, then went back to my Jumble. Pity poor Frances, whoever she was.

After my appointment, I had lunch, then picked up Juliette and took her home for some backyard time, lest she forget her roots, pun intended. Fortunately, I found the house locked and properly armed. The doors and windows were finally in, and the roof was done, lending a fresh look to the brick exterior despite the giant trash bin full of rejects that took up most of the driveway.

I put Juliette into the fenced portion of the backyard, noting the raw grading on the west side of the house where they were waterproofing the foundation. Then I let myself in, disarming the alarm. Inside, the air was hot and stale, smelling of sawdust and Sheetrock. The prefinished wood floors were down, but covered in fine dust, along with every other surface in the place. I bent down to swipe clean a patch of floor with my hand and was happy to see the rich cherry mahogany color. Just what I had wanted.

Then I stood up and sneezed for three whole minutes. So much for my meticulous cleaning before I'd left. What had I been thinking?

The existing kitchen cabinets and pine paneling had been re-painted in the soft white I'd chosen, making the room look much bigger, even without the new cabinet doors or Arctic White coun-tertops. But the outlets were all missing, and only a few new cop-per wires stuck out of the empty holes.

At least the electrician had started. After he and the HVAC people were done, the insulation people could foam the walls.

There still weren't any grates on the registers, but all in all, prog-ress had been made.

I decided not to brave the basement till another time.

What was left of my furniture stood jammed together under heavy white plastic drop cloths in the center of each room, giving the whole house a ghostly, abandoned look.

I spotted the flatness of the piano bench at one end of the pile in the living room and subsided to rest my artificial knees and hips.

To my surprise, I burst into tears like a weary child, wanting my house back. Wanting my life with Tom back. Wanting everything to be the way it was. Wanting, wanting, wanting.

I sobbed, wrapping my arms tight around me, and sobbed and rocked and sobbed some more.

Please, God, I can't do this. It's too much. Too much.

I cried till I was almost cried out, my breath coming in gaspy hiccups.

Then a creak from the back door brought me bolt upright. "Hellooo?" a raspy woman's voice called. "Are you there?"

Shoot!

I sniffed up, hard, but my nose was so swollen, I just made a pitiful Tim Conway, elephant-with-the-broken-trunk sound. Lord knew what I must look like. I swiped at my ruined eye makeup, then forced myself to stand tall and meet them in the kitchen. "I'm coming" came out "I'b cubbing."

Shoot, shoot, shoot.

The woman in the kitchen was dressed like a bag lady.

Jack's sharp eyes zeroed in on my face. "Frances, this is Cassie Jones. Cassie, this is my neighbor, Frances Taylor."

"Hello," the old woman said.

"I'm sorry," I offered, wiping my eyes again. "I was just having the required mid-renovation nervous breakdown."

"Think nothing of it," Frances said in a surprisingly cultured accent, her piercing blue eyes shining under her unruly mop of white hair. "That's a mighty fancy pig you've got out there. Took a real shine to me. What do you want for it?"

Juliette? "I'm sorry, but she's not for sale." I'd lost enough, already. Never mind the pet palace bill, the pig stayed. "If you'll follow me to the garage, I'll show you the tables and chairs."

Jack held the door for us without comment, then trailed us into

217

the garage. While I was uncovering the chairs, he stood by the door to the wood shop and asked, "May I?"

"Sure. But watch out for the mama cat."

He disappeared inside, then let out a long, low whistle of admiration.

I turned back to find Frances inspecting my chairs far more closely than I would have expected.

"Do you mind taking it out into the light so I can get a better look?" she asked.

"Not at all." Once we reached the afternoon sun, she said, "I'd like to check underneath the seat."

"Sure." She was probably only going to offer me twenty dollars for them, but I obliged anyway by tipping the back forward to rest on my thigh, so she could look underneath.

She pulled a long, thin little gooseneck flashlight from her tote bag, then threaded it under the black mesh beneath the seat, illuminating the top of the leg where it met the frame. "Hmph."

She carefully pulled the light back out, then pointed at me with it, straightening to all five feet of her with an imperious expression. "Jack neglected to tell me these were real."

As opposed to imaginary? I'd gotten them for fifty dollars each in a garage sale on Habersham just after we'd bought the house, then had them upholstered in a nice silk plaid that looked pretty with my grandmother's sofa. "I'm sorry?"

"Real Louis Quatorze," she clarified, pulling a huge wad of twenties from her tote bag. "I'll give you a thousand apiece, and not a penny more."

I almost choked. Real Louis Quatorze? "Are you sure?" I had no idea what real ones would be worth. Nobody at the garage sale had been willing to pay two hundred each, not even two for three fifty.

"Jack," she summoned. "Pull out that iPhone and tell me what they're asking for Louis Quatorze armchairs these days!" She eyed me. "I get first dibs."

It only took a minute for him to call back, "Seven thousand, give or take. Twenty, if it's original needlepoint," he called back. "Where did you get this slab of cherry?" he yelled to me. "I've never seen cherry that wide."

"From a farmer in Pennsylvania," I answered, my head spinning.

Frances frowned, then dug out a roll of hundreds. "All right, then, five thousand each, but that's my limit."

Whoa. Take it, quick, before she changes her mind. "Sounds good to me."

She counted out fifty hundred-dollar bills into my hand, then rummaged up another wad and added fifty more. "Done," she said with satisfaction, returning the rest to her tote. "Jack!" she hollered so loud it echoed from my neighbors' across the street. "Get out here and put these chairs in the truck before she changes her mind."

I peered at the bills. They looked and felt genuine, albeit well used.

Jack appeared with a strange grin. "Yes, ma'am, Miss Frances. Right away." I helped him carry the first one to his truck at the end of the driveway, then we came back for the other one. He nodded to the sheets I'd had them covered with. "Mind if I take those sheets?"

"Take, take."

Meanwhile, Miss Frances did a little dance of triumph, à la Zorba the Greek, singing, "Louis, Louis, whoa, baby, we gotta go," in a thready soprano.

Jack came back to collect her. "C'mon, Miss Frances. We need to get out of here before the traffic heats up."

She turned to me one last time with a cheerful smile. "You're sure you won't sell me that pig?"

Dumbstruck, I clutched the ten thousand dollars to my chest and shook my head no, then watched them drive away.

Then I corralled Juliette and went straight to the bank, forgetting to lock the house.

Once we parked at the branch on the corner of Peachtree and Pharr, I clipped on her leash and led her inside, ignoring the startled looks we prompted as I waited in line for a teller. I was so gobsmacked by my windfall that I'd completely forgotten my red nose, smeared makeup, and swollen eyes.

When I got to the teller window, I pulled the pile of bills from my purse and shoved the money at the surprised teller, pushing over the last few that had escaped. "If this is real, I want to make a deposit."

She regarded me with thinly concealed suspicion. "One moment, please, and we'll check on that."

A dignified manager promptly appeared behind her, probably summoned by a silent alarm. "How may we help you today, Mrs. . . ."

"Jones. Cassie Jones. I've been a customer here since you were Trust Company." I pointed to the money. "A woman just said my garage sale armchairs were real Louis Quatorze and paid me five thousand dollars apiece for them, cash. Please tell me this money is real."

The manager nodded to the teller, who began to inspect the bills and count them. When she was done, she told him, "Ten thousand dollars." She broke into a grin. "May I get you a counter deposit slip for that, Mrs. Jones?"

I finally came to my senses. "No." I groped for my checkbook in my purse. "I have one right here."

My hand shook when I filled it out.

"These funds will be available immediately," the teller said when she was done, handing me the deposit slip.

Guarding the deposit receipt with my life, I led Juliette back to my car and got in behind her. Adjusting the rearview mirror she'd knocked askew on her way to the passenger seat, I caught sight of my face and let out a gasp.

I looked like I'd been on a three-day bender.

Better get Juliette back to the porcine Plaza, then go to Mama's to repair the wreckage.

Then I planned to search for Jack Wilson's number, so I could find out what the heck had happened.

No way could I wait till our next doctor's appointment.

Boy, would the kids be shocked to hear about this.

As I headed up Peachtree, that still, small little voice inside me said, "The Lord worketh in mysterious ways."

Did He ever. I didn't know how mysterious till I talked to Jack.

Twenty-four

Jack

After Jack dropped off Frances and the chairs, he made it home and collapsed into his recliner, exhausted. He hadn't been there five seconds before his cell phone rang. "T. Jones" showed on the screen. He'd known Cassie would call, and he couldn't help smiling. "Feeling better about things?" he answered.

"The money was real!" Cassie blurted out.

"I figured it was. Frances worked for Sotheby's antiques division in New York for forty years. Made quite a killing with her own collection before she moved down here to raise horses next door to me. She's loaded."

"You're saying those chairs were really genuine?" Cassie asked in disbelief.

"I wouldn't have the slightest idea. Does it really matter?"

"What do you mean, does it matter? Of course it matters."

Please. Talk about looking a gift horse in the mouth. "Frances has those chairs on either side of her favorite 1753 Boston chest in her living room, and she's happy as a clam. She'll gloat over those chairs till the day she dies. Thinks she pulled a big one over on you."

A charged pulse of silence gave way to, "Did she?"

"Beats me." Groaning, he got up to fetch a cold springwater from the refrigerator. "Like I said, I don't know anything about the French stuff, just American."

Cassie's reaction was halfhearted. "I wouldn't want to cheat anybody."

Jack shooed D.I. out of his recliner, then clunked down into the seat. The trip to Atlanta had taken its toll, not to mention carrying those chairs. But it had all worked out so well. "In the immortal words of Woody Allen, take the money and run."

"I did," she said. "I just don't want to take advantage of anyone."

Why did women always have to complicate things so much?

The cat leaped into his lap and started pawing at his belly, which was smaller than it had been when he'd started Patel's diet.

Jack changed the subject. "That's quite a wood shop you've got there. I am seriously impressed."

Cassie didn't miss a beat. "Impressed enough to take some kittens?"

He frowned, exasperated. "I just made you ten thousand dollars, cash money, and you're trying to foist those kittens off on me?"

"Sorry. Reflex." After a brief pause, she added, "I probably ought to give you a commission."

He could use one. "Damn straight."

"How about ten percent?" she offered.

"How about fifty?"

She sighed. "Okay, fifty."

He was only kidding. "I was pulling your leg. Ten's more than fine."

"No. I wouldn't have made anything if you hadn't brought her. Fifty's only fair."

"I'll take ten, and not a penny more." He had his pride, after all.

"You'll take fifty, and that's that."

Not a pissing contest he'd expected. "We shall see, Mrs. Jones. We shall see."

"Exactly."

"Oh, by the way," he told her, feeling smug. "Did I mention that Frances is bat-shit crazy?"

"What?"

Jack smiled with consummate satisfaction. "Not legally, just absolutely." He hung up, then stroked the cat in his lap. "Let her put that in her Louis Vuitton and tote it."

She called right back, but he didn't answer, pleased that he hadn't activated the message feature on the new iPhone his son had sent him. And every time it rang, he grinned a little wider.

Twenty-five

Cassie

It soon became apparent that Jack wasn't taking my calls, so—spurred by a guilty conscience—I wrote out a check for five thousand dollars and sent it to him, registered. Mama said I was crazy to send him the money, especially after he'd said he wouldn't take it, but I had to sleep at night.

Maybe I *was* crazy to give it to him, but I did it anyway.

Heck, I hadn't done anything really crazy in my whole life, till lately. Maybe it was time.

The receipt came back, signed, a week later, but he still wouldn't answer his phone.

You'd think I was some collection agency, instead of the other way around. I hated it when people refused to answer their phones. It's so rude.

The Friday before my next appointment with Dr. Patel, Mama came home from bridge grinning like a reporter for *The National Enquirer* with a shot of Brangelina in the nude. "Guess what, guess what, guess what?"

Uh-oh. I looked up from my *Compleat Works of Elizabeth Barrett Browning.* "What?"

"Have I got a surprise for you." She actually rubbed her hands together.

I smelled another fix-up. "Tell, tell," I said according to script but without enthusiasm, doing my best to conceal my misgivings.

"Mary Johnson's daughter's husband's brother is single and sounds absolutely perfect. I gave her your number to give to him, and he's going to call."

Another fix-up. "And what do we know about Mary Johnson's daughter's husband's brother that makes him sound so perfect?"

"He's a real Renaissance man. Has two Ph.D.s from Emory, in anthropology and archaeology. Earned full tenure at Grantham." A small but prestigious school on a gorgeous campus just north of Atlanta. "But this year, after doing excavations all over the world, he finally decided to settle down and retire. So he moved back to town, and now he's just teaching a couple of anthropology classes at Emory as an adjunct."

There had to be a catch. "Divorced? Widowed? Confirmed bachelor?"

"Divorced. His wife left him after twenty years for one of his students."

My interest piqued. "That's a switch." But there are always two sides to every story, and I couldn't help wondering what his ex-wife's would be.

Mama went on. "After that, he threw himself into his work, but now, he's finally ready to meet somebody."

Must be terminally ill. Or maybe not. "Any other skeletons in the closet?"

"Only real ones," she said. "He *is* an archaeologist."

"Very funny." Actually, it was—till it turned out to be true.

Mama looked at me over her readers, nodding briskly. "It gets better." She rummaged in her purse for her cell phone, then pulled it out and started pushing buttons. "Let me see, first you go here, then you highlight that, then you choose that, and then . . ." Triumphant, she turned the phone to me. "And voilà." The screen showed a photo of a very attractive, laughing lanky man with thick, straw-colored hair and a deep tan.

"My, my." I took the phone for closer inspection. Humor and intelligence showed in his classic face, and he had that great Thomas Jefferson look of a well-aged redhead. As with a lot of men, he'd entered that appealing, ageless plateau of maturity. He could have been fifty or seventy, but whatever he was, he wore it well.

Finally, a good one!

Mama held out her hand, wiggling her fingers for me to give back the phone, but I wasn't finished looking. "I e-mailed Mary that nice photo of you holding little Ethan, for his sister-in-law to show him," she said.

A good choice, taken just before Tom died, when I still looked young and alive.

I studied Mr. Fix-up's face and felt a definite twinge of interest. "I hope you got my numbers right."

Mama clasped her hands, proud as a preschooler with her first sticker for perfect behavior. "Now all we have to do is wait for him to call."

We?

She poked in her purse again. "But just in case he forgets . . ." She produced a paper napkin with *Alexander Mathison* and two phone numbers written on it. "You can call *him*." She pointed to the name, then handed it to me. "He goes by Alex."

Maybe if I was thirty, but no way was I calling somebody's daughter's husband's brother for a date, cute though he may be.

Mama read my reaction immediately. "Now, don't go getting coy. At your age, you can't afford to fool around. This is a live one. Go for it."

"I'll give him a week to call," I deflected. "I don't want him to think I'm desperate."

Mama frowned as she reclaimed her phone. "I told Mary you'd be this way." She waggled a finger at me. "Shy doesn't work in this day and age, sweetie. Just remember that." She cruised off to her room.

Okay, Lord. This looks pretty good. If it's meant to be, please let him call.

That evening, I was slogging through several more dead-end e-mails on the Christian dating service when my cell phone rang. To my pleasant surprise, *A. Mathison* showed up on the caller ID. I straightened in my seat at the computer before answering, "Hello?"

A deep, resonant male voice said in a cultured accent, "I'm trying to reach a Cassandra Jones."

"This is she." My heart went pitter-pat. "But I go by Cassie."

"Hello, Cassie."

I loved bass voices, and his communicated both warmth and interest.

"This is Alex Mathison. My sister-in-law gave me your number and said we might enjoy knowing each other."

Straightforward. I liked that. "Hi. My mother just told me the same thing."

"So, where and when would you like to meet?"

Decisive, but deferential. I liked that he left it up to me, but suddenly couldn't think of a single scenario. "Do you have a favorite place for coffee?"

He chuckled, a low, rolling sound that made me want to hear him laugh. "Actually, I gave up coffee when I retired, but there's a nice little organic café just off campus at Emory called Pure Country. How about lunch, tomorrow?" Again, no beating around the bush. "We could meet there at, say, eleven-thirty?"

No messing around, just cut to the chase. Perfect! "Great. It's a date, then." Uh-oh. Shouldn't have called it a date. "I mean, a meet."

"No, it's a date," he corrected, "and I'm looking forward to it. I'll be the guy in the dark green fedora."

Oh, a fedora. Very nice. "I'll be the woman wearing a big, black rose."

"See you then."

Suddenly, I felt like a college girl, but in a good way, all expectation. "Bye."

I hung up and headed for Mama's room, where she had piled up in bed for her daily afternoon stab at the Sunday *New York Times* crossword puzzle. "He called," I announced, "and we have a date for lunch tomorrow."

Mama beamed. "Good for him. Good for you." She picked up her phone. "I can't wait to tell Mary." She waggled her fingers, waving me away. "Close the door on your way out, sweetie."

I realized I might as well reconcile myself to being the topic of conversation for the entire bridge group. And the altar guild. And the memoirs class at the senior center.

Oh, well. So what?

I was going to meet an intelligent, attractive man. Tomorrow.

Twenty-six

Cassie

Lucky for me, when date day rolled around, Atlanta was treated to a rare, breezy spell in the low eighties, so I didn't have to worry about sweating visibly when I met Alex. I found the restaurant without problem, thanks to MapQuest, then parked in the small graveled lot out back. Rather than enter through the beat-up screen door at the rear, I walked up the driveway to the front, where Alex sat under the awning, his fedora at an appealing angle, waiting at one of the sidewalk tables. He turned toward the sound of my footsteps on the sidewalk and spotted me, immediately standing to an impressive six one, at least, doffing his hat.

Hubba, hubba.

He was more attractive than his photo, and I *really* liked tall men. He was definitely into that whole Indiana Jones thing with the clothes, but it looked just as good on him as it did on Harrison Ford.

I did my best to act nonchalant, but failed miserably.

Approaching him at the table, I reached out to shake his hand. "Hi. I'm Cassie Jones."

He nodded as we shook. "Alex."

We smiled in unison, then both said at the same time, "You're even better looking in person."

Then I got to hear him laugh, and wasn't disappointed.

He pulled out my chair. "Please, sit." He thought to ask, "Or would you rather be inside? Either's fine with me."

"This is perfect." I sat, knees together and ankles crossed, slightly to the side, like a charm school graduate.

He took the seat to my right (my good ear) beside me at the small square table, not across.

Chemistry. There was definitely chemistry.

"So," he said, motioning for the waiter. "What would you like to talk about?"

"Anything but me," I said, honestly. "How about you?"

He grinned, turning a sidelong glance to the campus across the road. "Ditto, so already, we have a lot in common."

After all the disasters of my previous dates, this felt so smooth and easy. "I have a question, then," I said. (I had prepared.) "In all your years as a professor of anthropology, what's the most fascinating thing you've learned?"

He nodded in approval. "Good question." He thought, his eyes lifting unfocused into the middle distance. "So many things." Then turned back to me with, "If I have to pick, I'd say the discovery of mitochondrial DNA, and the fact that it proves that every human being on this planet is descended from a single female ancestor." He nodded. "As a Christian, I really love it when science proves scripture."

He was a *Christian*, and willing to admit it up front! Yay!

My excitement showed on my face, but I didn't care.

"Over the years in this business," he went on, "I've found that scientists can be so arrogant, sometimes, so sure they're right, despite the fact that much of what we think we know is later disqualified, or at least amended. Personally, I think science is a series of grand mistakes leading toward the truth, but I doubt we'll ever get there. God's creation is far more amazing than we could ever dream."

A+. A+++.

The waiter came and took our order (they had springwater and several organic veggies I could eat), then we talked on over lunch and beyond about archaeology and history and the state of the world and his many travels.

When the waiter brought the check, I volunteered to split it, but Alex insisted on paying, and I was glad to find him old-fashioned about that.

Unaware of the time, we kept right on talking as the rest of the patrons gradually disappeared. The man was fascinating: funny, interesting, wry. And he seemed genuinely interested in my thoughts and responses. It was well past two o'clock before he finally looked at his watch and said, "Wow. I've really monopolized you, here."

He looked at me with frank encouragement. "I think we need to continue this at dinner. How about tomorrow night?"

Yes! Yes! Yes! "Tomorrow night would be fine."

"What are you in the mood for? Pick a category, and I'll pick the restaurant."

Perfect, perfect, perfect. "Grilled seafood." I stood, wishing it was tomorrow night.

He stood, too. "Grilled seafood, it is." Suddenly, he seemed shy. "May I pick you up?"

I nodded. "Sure. My house is being renovated, so I'm staying with my mom at Canterbury Court, out on Peachtree. Do you know it?"

"Not yet," he said, "but I will." He took my hand into his callused one and gave it a squeeze, holding on just a split second longer than I did. "Seven?"

"Seven's perfect." Perfect.

"I'll walk you to your car." Such a gentleman.

On the way back to the lot, I asked, "So, how do you find Emory after Grantham?"

He raised his eyebrows. "Large. Urban." He shook his head. "But the students are pretty much the same." He made a face. "And the academic politics."

We reached the lot. "Of course," he said, "I didn't meet anybody like you at Grantham, or I never would have left."

Bull's-eye. Give the man a Kewpie doll.

That made me feel so good, I almost cried, and had to struggle to keep my cool as I approached my car. "This is it." I clicked the remote to unlock it, and he opened the door for me.

I was used to getting flak about driving a minivan at my age, but Alex seemed to approve. "Cool ride."

"Thanks. Comes in handy when you're a gardener, like me."

"Vegetables?" he asked, clearly hoping I'd say yes.

I shook my head. "Flowers."

He looked at my silk rose and smiled. "I could see you with flowers."

"I'll see *you* tomorrow night." I closed the door, prompting him to step back.

As I drove out, he stood there, watching me go.

Once I was safely out of range, I broke into the "Hallelujah" chorus at full blast, then sang myself all the way home with golden oldies from "Let the River Run" to "I Am Woman."

Happy. For the first time in more than a year, I was happy.

I couldn't wait for the next night.

Twenty-seven

Jack

Jack could tell that something wasn't right inside him, but since he was seeing Patel every two weeks, he figured it must not be major and tried to ignore it. He had felt worse than usual after trying to sort through some of his tools in the barn, but he was shaky with hunger and didn't have anything to eat in the house, so he forced himself to go to the diner and order lunch. Everything had been fine till he stood up to head for the bathroom before his food came.

The next thing he knew, he was flat on his back.

Mortified, he looked up from the diner floor—*definitely* not a place anybody would ever want to spend any time—and did his best not to focus on the food and assorted grime he saw from where he was lying. Or the huddle of worried patrons and waitresses gathered over him.

"Stand back, everybody," the owner ordered with authority. "Give him some air!"

That was the problem. He wasn't getting any air.

"I called 911," Jack's favorite waitress, Trish, announced in near panic. "The paramedics are on the way."

He'd paid her power bill a few times over the winters, so she was particularly nice to him.

Jack could hear the sirens from the firehouse only three blocks away.

He knew he could speak if he concentrated. The problem was, he had to breathe to do it, and that wasn't really happening.

A large, well-dressed black man loomed into the huddle. "I know CPR," he said with exaggerated enunciation, as if Jack had been felled by retardation or deafness. "Do you need me to do CPR?"

A real rocket scientist. Anybody who could ask for CPR probably didn't need it. Jack shook his head in denial, adamant, still gasping.

This was just a spell. He didn't have any pain or numbness in his jaw or arms. He just couldn't breathe.

"Just . . . give . . . me . . . a . . . sec," he managed.

It would pass. It always did.

Jack tried to relax when somebody yelled, "Back there." Then he heard heavy footsteps and the rattle of a stretcher.

"Please step back," the paramedics said, bending to take his vitals before the words were out.

"Sir, do you have COPD?" the first one asked him.

Jack nodded.

"Are you on nitro?"

Jack shook his head in denial.

"Push epi," the man told his partner, who had already put in an IV.

He felt the stimulant shoot through his body, and then he could breathe a little better.

Just another spell, thank you, Lord. Not his first, and not his last.

But something was definitely different. He would ask Patel.

Maybe it had to do with the vaccines.

Twenty-eight

Cassie

I braced myself for Alex not to be as perfect as I had thought he was at our first meeting, but when he rang the doorbell to Mama's unit, I opened the door to find him in a very nice suit, sans hat, and looking way too sexy for my own good.

Maybe he really was Mr. Perfect. For the first time since I'd met Tom, I felt desire for another man, and it felt mighty good, I can tell you. Only a lifetime of Mama's indoctrination kept me from grabbing him by his tasteful tie and kissing that perfect man-mouth.

"Hi," he said, clearly enjoying my obvious attraction to him. "I was hoping I could meet your mom."

This was definitely too good to be true. "Sure. She's—"

"Right behind you," Mama said, making me jump. "Please come in."

How had she snuck up on me like that?

She practically shoved me out of the way as I said, "Mama, this is Alex Mathison. Alex, my mother, Elouise Cooper."

Alex shook her hand with a slight, courtly bow. "It's a pleasure."

Mama all but dragged him into the sitting area. "Please come in."

Alex shot me a brief questioning look, and when I nodded, he did as Mama asked.

She steered him to sit in Daddy's chair, then perched on the one next to him. "May I get you something to drink? Scotch? Bourbon? Wine?" she asked in ascending order of respectability.

Alex grinned. "Actually, I've never been much of a drinker. Unless the alternatives are tainted well water or a muddy river, in which case, wine is a definite safety measure."

Not a drinker, but not rabid about it. Yes.

Mama aimed a coy point of her index finger his way. Then she embarrassed me by asking, "Are you always this adorable?"

He chuckled, coloring. "Every chance I get."

Mama stood, bringing him to his feet. "Well, in that case, I'll leave you two young people to your evening." She reached out and shook his hand again. "It's a pleasure to meet you, Alex."

"And mine to meet you."

Mama herded us to the door, then waved us off with, "Have fun. I won't wait up."

I shook my head, eyes skyward, as we made for the elevators. "Obviously, my mother is completely smitten with you at first sight," I said.

Alex grinned, looking adorably like a lankier version of George Clooney. "How about her daughter?"

No way was I stepping into that one. Not yet, even though I was. I just smiled and stepped into the elevator instead.

Dinner at the Buckhead Diner (far from a real diner) was noisy, but elegant and delicious.

As before, we talked about all kinds of things except my health, my husband, and our pasts. The more I liked Alex, the more I dreaded having to bring those things up, but there was time aplenty to get into all that. Or so I thought.

After supper, he took me to a cute little dessert café way out in North Fulton. Then he took the long route home, winding along the Chattahoochee, and I found myself wishing he'd pull over and give me a kiss.

He did pull over, but it wasn't to give me a kiss.

Some kind of animal streaked right in front of Alex's pickup, and I felt an ominous thump as I was all but jousted out of my seat. He braked, hard, but it was too late. We ended up almost sideways in the other lane. "Sorry," he said. "Do you mind if we take a little detour?"

Talk about odd timing. "I guess not."

"Thanks." He started backing up till the scene of the crime was in his headlights.

I looked away from the dark, bleeding lump in the road.

"This will only take a minute," he said, "if you can bear with me."

He backed onto the right-of-way, then stopped. "I'm a conservationist. I don't believe in wasting things."

Roadkill?

"Sit tight. I'll be right back." He got out and rummaged in the toolbox behind the cab, then pulled out a small shovel and a plastic bag. I winced as he walked up to the lump of ex-animal and scraped it up into the plastic bag, then tied it shut and threw it with a heavy thunk into the load bed, followed by the clang of the shovel.

Please tell me he's not going to *cook* it!

He's not going to eat it, I scolded myself. He's probably just going to put it in a compost heap.

But you're not supposed to put dead animals in a compost heap.

A cheerful whistle preceded his return. He got in, slammed the door, then started up the engine with a self-satisfied smile. "Beaver, poor thing." He looked over at me. "Okay to detour by my place?" he asked. "I promise, it won't take long."

I barely knew this man, and he'd just picked up a dead animal off the road. Now he wanted to take me—and it—home.

But then again, you can tell a lot about somebody by the way he lives. (Jack Wilson came to mind.) So I decided it might be a good idea to go along and see how Mr. Perfect lived. "Sure," I heard myself saying.

Maybe not the best idea, but too late, now.

He was right. It wasn't far. A remnant from another era, his small brick ranch house was down a little country road not a quarter mile from the turnoff by the river. The driveway wasn't even paved, just graveled. Full of weeds, like the lawn. Clearly, Mr. Perfect didn't do yard work.

Definitely creepy, and you couldn't see any other houses, and vice versa.

Danger, Will Robinson.

We pulled up to the carport filled with moving boxes. As if he'd read my mind, Alex said, "Sorry the place looks so bad. My landlady promised to have somebody clean up the yard, but now that I've signed the lease, she's conveniently forgotten."

A reasonable explanation. Maybe the inside was better.

He got out. "Would you like to come in?"

The fastest internal debate known to humankind raged in my mind for all of three seconds before my voice took over with, "Sure. Why not?"

He grinned at me without a hint of anything ulterior, then came around to let me out. Before we went inside, he scooped up the sack of dead beaver, then followed me to the front door, where a feeble lantern fixture lit the way.

Alex didn't bother with a key. "Welcome to my humble, and I do mean humble, abode."

Nothing prepared me for what was waiting inside.

I managed not to scream. Instead, I felt my smile freeze into a grimace.

Twenty-nine

Cassie

The inside of Alex's house looked like some abandoned museum from *The Twilight Zone*: bones, artifacts, skulls, and African masks and sculptures covered every square inch of the place, dust and cobwebs everywhere.

"How long did you say you've lived here?" I managed.

"Just over a year." He surveyed his treasures with pride. "This is my private collection. The rest, I left for the museum at Grantham."

There was *more*?

"Would you like to meet Rex?" he asked, clearly oblivious to my reaction to his house. Alex stomped his foot three times, and a leathery scrape from the back of the house drew my eyes to the hall, where a giant, olive-colored lizard with gruesome claws slithered in, then hissed and reared up, straightening its front legs to the max. The thing had to be five feet long!

On instinct, I fled behind Alex for shelter, inadvertently bumping into the bag of beaver.

Yuck! I levitated out of range.

Alex didn't seem to take offense. "Don't be scared. Rex is a

Savannah monitor. He's harmless, unless you're an earthworm or a snail. Or a boiled egg. That's what I feed him."

So much for Mr. Perfect. "You have a *monitor lizard* for a pet?"

Alex grinned. "They're very intelligent. And affectionate; he watches TV with me on the sofa every night."

"That's not loyalty," I snapped. "It's body heat. It's a reptile."

He reached down to stroke the lizard's neck, and the thing actually wagged its long, scaly tail. "Between Rex and Cindy, they do a good job of keeping anybody from stealing my collection." He nodded toward the back of the house. "I have six human Paleolithic burials in my daughter's closet, not to mention all these artifacts. They're worth a fortune."

Six human burials in the closet?

No, no, no.

Alex tapped his foot twice, and the lizard headed back from whence he'd come.

"If you'll excuse me, I need to get this ready to feed Cindy." Alex lifted the bag of beaver, which had started to leak. Gross! "It'll just take a sec."

I hated to ask, but felt compelled. "Who, or what, is Cindy?"

"My Burmese boa constrictor. She stays in the bathroom most of the time. It's got a tub and a heated floor." He set off for the kitchen, but I stayed where I was, not wanting to see the mess inside that bag.

This could not be happening. *God, I do not appreciate this wretched joke you have just played on me. I do not appreciate it at all.*

I heard the rustle of plastic, then a loud thunk that sounded like a butcher's cleaver, and shuddered.

Alex's voice came from the kitchen. "The tail and teeth might give her indigestion."

Another thunk. I almost tossed my cookies.

Needless to say, I did not kiss Alex good night when I finally reached safety at Canterbury Court.

Such a shame. He was such a nice man.

"It was a very interesting evening," I told him, shaking his hand just inside the main doors.

He shook his head. "You're not going to go out with me again, are you?"

"I'm sorry. You are a lovely man, Alex." Just way too weird for me. "But I have this health condition," I told him. "I'm violently allergic to mold and dust, so, given your collections and living conditions, I don't think there's any future in this for either of us, really. And I'm not into reptiles, so there you are." We wouldn't even mention the bag of beaver.

He sighed. "Story of my life." He gave me a peck on the cheek. "Sorry it didn't work out. You're quite a woman, Cassie Jones."

"And you are quite a man. It was nice meeting you."

He turned and left, and I headed for the elevator.

Enough with the divine irony! I complained to God. *Please send me somebody I can live with!*

Boy, was Mama going to get an earful tonight.

Thirty

Jack

Once the stuff the ER had given him that morning had all worn off, Jack was back in trouble, but he took it slow on his way up to Dr. Patel's office. The only reason he'd bothered to come was tucked under his arm. He'd put too much time and effort into it not to come.

Wheezing his way through the heat, Jack finally admitted that he had to do something about where he lived, now, but none of his options made sense.

He wasn't up to relocating to some strange place, alone. Atlanta was home. And he'd rather die than end up a burden on his children. They had enough challenges without adding him to the mix. Truth be told, he'd rather die than have to put up with the noise and the constant chaos of their young families. And their houses were probably almost as moldy as his.

For the first time in his life, Jack had no answers.

So he was actually glad for the diversion when Cassie showed up in the waiting room.

She scowled at him. "Why haven't you cashed my check?"

Uh-oh. Definitely crabby. Jack regarded her with raised brows. "I wasn't aware there was a deadline for cashing your check."

"Well, there is," she grumbled. "Please do it soon, so I don't have to carry it over for another statement."

Touchy, touchy. He wondered why, then came up with a distinct possibility. "So," he asked her, "how's your search for Mr. Right going?"

She regarded him through narrowed eyes. "Don't get me started."

"Okay. I won't."

After less than ten seconds of silence, she proceeded to tell him anyway about her latest fix-up, in hilarious detail. The only thing was, she wasn't laughing.

Jack managed to keep a straight face and waited till she was done to offer her the sheaf of e-mails he'd brought. "Good thing I got you these, then."

She picked them up and frowned, scanning the addresses. "Who is Mrs.Clean5000?"

"You," he said. "Or more accurately, me, pretending to be you on the three Christian dating sites I found that seem to be legitimate." It had given him something to do between appointments.

"What?" She looked at him as if he'd just dropped trow. "You did *what*?"

"I got you some legitimate prospects." He pointed to the e-mails he'd printed out. "Those are all screened, most of them widowers. I stapled the correspondence for each one together, so you'll know what's been said. Eight in all." He was very proud of himself. "I put the Web sites and your user names and passwords at the top."

Cassie's mouth dropped open. "That is the . . . I don't . . ."

Finally, at a loss for words.

She colored up in fury, shaking the e-mails at him. "That is the most egregious invasion of privacy anybody has ever perpetrated on me in my life! I ought to have you arrested."

This is what he got for helping her? "I don't think there's a law against impersonating a Christian widow," he responded with amusement. "But I might be wrong."

"You *are* wrong," she accused. "So wrong, I cannot begin to address it."

Of course, she *would* address it.

"First," she scolded, "nobody asked you to do this."

No, she'd just asked him to help her find Mr. Right, which was what he'd done.

"Second," she went on, "this is unforgivably underhanded. And third—"

He didn't need to hear the rest. There was no sense addressing her objections, so he shut her down with, "Last time I looked," Jack interrupted, "Christians are supposed to forgive even their enemies. And I am not your enemy. I was only trying to help. By your own accounts, you're not doing so well with the fix-ups."

She threw the e-mails into his lap. "Lord knows what you told those men."

"Only what you told me," he retorted. "And told me and told me."

Before she could lay into him again, the door opened and the nurse stuck her head out. "We're ready for you, Mrs. Jones."

Cassie pointed a manicured finger at him. "We are not done with this." Then she stomped off, slamming the door behind her.

As soon as she was out of earshot, the fluffy, gray-haired bookkeeper appeared from her cubicle behind the receptionist and asked over the check-in desk, "If she doesn't want those, can I have them?"

Jack laughed. And laughed, and laughed, setting off a coughing spell, but it was still worth it. Then he wiped his eyes and, when he had the breath to speak again, replied, "I'll leave them here on the coffee table. If Cassie doesn't pick them up on her way out, you can have them. But I'll bet you a dime to a dollar, she'll take them."

He was right.

Thirty-one

Cassie

The whole office had heard my conversation with Jack, so there was no point in trying to hide it. The man was great at putting up boundaries for himself, but completely incapable of respecting mine—or anybody's, for that matter.

Idiot.

Dr. Patel schlepped into the exam room on his tire-tread extra soles. "So, how are you feeling today, *physically*," he qualified, lest he set me off about Jack, I was sure.

"Better. But I'm looking forward to getting back into my house. Mama has carpeting, and her friends bring their little dogs with them to visit, so I'm still coughing and sneezing after I've been there for a while."

"How long will it be before the house is ready?"

"The mold man said another week, if everybody comes when they're supposed to."

"You will feel much better when you're in a safe environment," the doctor promised.

"What about the diet?" he asked. "How are you doing with that?"

"Fair. I'm not eating things I'm not supposed to, but the rotation part is really hard, especially while I'm living with Mama."

"Did you try the dietitian I recommended? She's very good."

For his other patients' sakes, I decided to tell him the truth, straight out. "Yes, I tried her, and no, she's not good. She faxed me menus and recipes that included stuff I'm not supposed to eat, then charged me $150 for a phone consult without even asking what foods I liked or hated. I told her anyway, then asked her to send me some menus and recipes that were safe for me to eat, and she didn't. So I feel like I got stiffed, and I'm not calling her again. Why pay her, when she's no help? I'll just do it myself."

That made two referrals he'd given me that I couldn't trust.

"Of course, that is your prerogative," he said, not even addressing the issues I'd raised. What was it about men and conflict? "Many of my patients have found her quite helpful."

Maybe it was just me, then, and another one of those cosmic jokes God kept pulling.

By the time Dr. Patel had scoped my sinuses and checked the yeasty beasties on the base of my tongue, I was calmed down enough to behave myself.

I checked out ($451.49), then headed through the waiting room, where the stack of Jack's illicit e-mails lay on the table, daring me to take them.

When I'd first realized what he'd done, I'd sworn that hell would freeze over before I looked at them. But I was getting desperate. Tom's insurance money was going out so fast, I had no idea how I would survive beyond the next year.

So I swallowed my pride and picked them up. If Mr. Right was in there, I couldn't afford not to. And as it turned out, he was.

When I opened the outer door to leave, I could have sworn

I heard somebody from the little office behind the desk say, "Damn."

On the way home, I swung by to pick up Juliette, then took her to the house for a visit, wondering if she was as homesick as I was.

She seemed like it. When I let her loose in the backyard, she had a sniff fest to end all sniff fests, then peed prodigiously, followed by a happy munch fest in a patch of wild clover that had grown up in my absence.

Letting myself into the back door, I was pleased to see that everything looked finished. Registers in place. Cabinet doors hung. Rich, new wooden floors. Streamlined French doors and windows, lacking the old mullions, let in much more sheltered light.

I tried the new white wall switch and was rewarded with a warm glow from the simple chrome chandelier I'd picked out for the kitchen. There were still footprints on the floors, but most of the dust was gone, and the painting had been done, giving the whole place a new lease on life.

My heart twisted inside me, catching me unawares. Seeing my home without the reminders of Tom and our family made me sad on a level I couldn't plumb. I needed for things to be where they were supposed to be. Then I could work on finding someone, but only when my past was back in place.

I returned Juliette to her Hog Hilton, then went back to Mama's for another week, where I passed my time corresponding to the men in Jack's e-mails. Actually, he'd done a pretty good job of being me, because none of the men seemed to notice the switch. As the communications progressed, one stood out: CarMan335, a retired auto executive from Detroit who was looking to relocate in the Atlanta area near his two married daughters.

I reread his most recent e-mail: "Dear Cassie, You sound like a woman I could care for, but I'm glad you're willing to take it slow. I'm an old-fashioned man with old-fashioned values who loved my late wife deeply, so the idea of starting over with someone new feels disloyal, somehow, but I am not cut out to live alone. I need someone who will be a companion and helpmate—not a servant— with a kind heart, who can laugh with me and live our lives to the fullest." I wondered what he meant by "the fullest," but kept reading. "In exchange, I will cherish and protect her, and provide for her. If that's what you're looking for, please reply, so we can get to know each other better."

After my past experiences, I forced myself not to get my hopes up. I just kept exchanging e-mails with him about life and our common faith, and he came across as a really nice man whose tastes and values meshed with my own. Intelligent, too, but with a nice sense of humor. We liked many of the same books and movies and shared memories of the milestones we had lived and the children we loved (I said only nice things about Haley, which were all true.)

If the e-mails were accurate, he was definitely a Tom kind of man.

By the time two more weeks had passed—not the one week my contractor had promised—I was still at Mama's and seriously considering meeting the man. But first, I had to get back into my house.

The next Monday, a crew came in and HEPA-vacuumed the whole place, top to bottom. Then, safely clad in my respirator, I spent a whole day directing the movers to put the furniture back in place. Then I wiped the furniture down again with the mold cleaner, just to be safe.

On Tuesday, Juliette and I presided over the delivery of the leather-upholstered pieces I'd bought or had recovered. (Yes, they make coral-colored leather, so Nana's sofa looked surprisingly good back in its place. And, as luck would have it, Juliette took major offense at the patterned pigskin I'd selected, so she wouldn't have anything to do with it.) Then Mama and I spent Wednesday and Thursday cleaning and putting back all the personal touches that made my house my home.

Only then did the remediation team suck the ducts and fog the whole house.

When Juliette and I moved back in on Saturday morning, the place smelled fresh and new, but looked like an updated version of the home I knew and loved. All I had left to do was demold and put away what I'd taken to Mama's. I was done by four, then cooked a legal supper and watched *Andy Griffith* and *Dick Van Dyke* reruns on the cable, as grateful for the restoration of my independence as I was for my house.

That night when Juliette and I scrubbed away in the shower, I was exhausted, but in a good way. Before Dr. Patel, I wouldn't have had the strength to do any of the things I'd accomplished in the past week. Make that five weeks. And when I finally got into my safely encased bed and under my mold-free sheets and seersucker spread, I snuggled up on my encased pillows and let loose with a long, deep sigh I'd been holding in since I left. "We're baaaack," I whispered to Juliette, who responded from her corner with a satisfied grunt.

Then I started to cry, and cried and cried and cried, as much from relief as from loss.

I was home again. Now I just had to find someone to help me keep it.

And maybe, just maybe, CarMan335 might be the one.

Thirty-two

Cassie

A week later, I woke up on the morning of my next appointment with Dr. Patel feeling better than I had in years. Fall was in the air, and I was finally alive again. "Good morning, Miss Juliette," I called across the room. Juliette let out a grunt, then lumbered over to my bedside and oinked briefly, as if for reassurance that this was still home.

I sat up and swung my legs on either side of her, then bent over to give her jowls and neck a good scratch. It didn't even hurt to do it. Boy, did I feel better! I couldn't believe the energy I had.

Since we'd been home, even Juliette seemed more animated and content. As soon as I got over being sore from the move, I'd stopped waking up in pain every time I turned over in the night, and Juliette stayed put in her mold-remediated dog bed till I got up. Not that I'd trust her to roam the house, but at least she seemed content.

Best of all, my e-mails to CarMan335—whose name was really Howard Gustafsen—had been like writing to a wonderful old friend I just hadn't met yet. And meet him, I would. It was all arranged, much to my mother's dismay.

Speak of the devil, my phone rang, showing Mama's number. She didn't bother with hello. "Please tell me you've thought better of this cockamamie scheme to go to Detroit all by yourself and meet some total stranger you haven't even talked to."

"Mama, Howard is not a stranger. We've been e-mailing several times a day for weeks. He's a very nice man."

"So he says. Hasn't anybody explained to you that people lie on those dating sites?"

"Yes, you. Twice a day, every day for the last three weeks." I headed for the kitchen to let Juliette out, then feed us both.

Mama wasn't giving up. "For all you know, he could be some serial killer."

Which is why I'd taken precautions. "Tommy got somebody to run a background check on him, and the man hasn't even had a parking ticket in the past seven years. He's a decent, upstanding citizen."

Mama swooped in for the coup de grâce. "Then why isn't he married?"

"For the third time, Mama, his wife only died two years ago." I punched on the coffee maker, then crossed to the rolling bin of Pig Chow that I'd spray-painted white, with a row of pretty little pink pigs stenciled around the top.

"How do you even know he is who he says he is?" Mama prodded.

Why couldn't she leave me alone about this? "Mama, are you afraid I'll end up moving to Detroit? Is that what this is all about?"

"Of course not," she grumbled. "You just had your house redone. I know you're not going to move. I'm just worried that this man isn't who he seems to be. That he's only marrying you for your money."

"I haven't even *met* the man, and you keep talking about our getting married." I pulled out twelve pick-a-size white paper towels and folded them, zigzag, into a thick cushion, then put them on a plate. "In case you've forgotten, I hardly have any money left." I carefully laid four thick slices of market bacon across the towels, then topped them with six more sheets of towels. "If, and that's a big if, we end up getting married, I'd be marrying him for *his* money, not the other way around." Or, more accurately, his health insurance, and then only if he's a truly good man.

Mama knew better. "I know you're lonely without Tom, sweetie, but so much could go wrong, here. A woman alone in a strange city in a hotel . . ."

I put the bacon into my new built-in microwave over the stove, then pressed the minute button four times and sent it spinning slowly on the carousel. Then I had an inspiration. "You know, Mama, you're right." That ought to shock her. "Why don't you go with me? You can even make a copy of his driver's license before we go out."

That took her aback. "Well, I . . . well, I'm supposed to count the offering on Mondays, and there's bridge on Wednesdays and Fridays, and altar guild . . ."

"They can manage without you, and there's plenty of time to find somebody to fill in for you. It's not for two more weeks." I appealed to the one thing guaranteed to help her make a decision. "If you decide today, I can still get those seventy-nine-dollar tickets Airtran is offering."

Thrift was Mama's middle name. "I don't know."

"Okay. That's fine, but here's the deal: either you decide to go with me before noon today, or you keep your worries to yourself. I don't want to hear another word about it, okay?" Let her put that in her trick and trump it.

Mama exhaled in exasperation. "I'll have to think about it."

"You have till noon. And remember, not making a decision is making a decision."

She hung up without saying good-bye.

A Canadian front had blown through, so the sun was shining down on another perfect, mid-seventies day, allowing me to enjoy my trip to the doctor's, and even the hike from the handicapped parking. When I got to Dr. Patel's office at ten, though, I straightened outside the door and took a deep breath to make room for the humble pie I was about to eat. Then I went inside, and sure enough, Jack was sitting there on the sofa, looking at me with a sharp gleam in his eye.

Why did it annoy me so that I owed him, big-time, for connecting me to CarMan335, devious though his methods had been?

I sat down. "Jack, I apologize for what I said about the e-mails. I know you were only trying to help."

He tucked his chin with a smug smile. "CarMan335, isn't it?"

How I would love to swat that smile from his face. "How could you tell?"

"You don't look so desperate today."

What nerve. "Did I seem that desperate before?" I snapped.

"Only to anybody who paid attention."

"Thanks a lot," I retorted.

"Now, don't go getting all snippy," he said, reopening his copy of *The Book of Marie*. "So, when are you going to meet him?"

That was really none of his business, but then again, he had found CarMan335 for me. "In two weeks."

"When's he coming in?" Jack asked. "Would you like for me to pick him up at the airport? Check him out for you, man to man?"

"He's not coming here. I'm meeting him there."

Jack tucked his stubbled chin, scowling. "Is that wise?"

"Now you sound like my mother."

As if summoned by the mere mention of her name, my phone rang, and Mama showed on the screen. "Hi, Mama."

"All right, I'll go," she bit out. "But only if we can see a show while we're there."

"I'll find out what's playing." Maybe we could all do a matinee on the last full day, when Howard and I had had a chance to get to know each other better.

"Okay, then," she said. "I'll start packing right away." As I said, Mama prolonged the anticipation of all her trips by dithering *ad absurdum* over what to wear and what to take.

"Good. And bring a sweater. With luck, it'll be cooler there." August and September in Atlanta were often the worst months of the summer, sending the mold and pollen counts to the stratosphere, and October wasn't much better.

I had barely hung up when Jack mused over his book, "Good idea, taking her along. Of course, if he's a serial killer, it won't do any good."

"Have you been talking to my mother?" I accused.

He just shook his head.

The nurse came to collect him. "Mr. Wilson, the doctor is ready to see you now."

It wasn't until Jack stood up with a gravelly groan of effort that I realized he didn't look a whit better than he had that first day I'd met him.

Maybe I should be the one looking for somebody to take care of *him*.

The idea appealed to me immensely. When I saw him again in a month, I could bring a bunch of e-mails from eligible Christian women who thought I was Jack.

Assuming I wasn't too busy courting Howard. But I still had two weeks left to find Jack some women before I left for Detroit. That would be plenty of time, especially since single women outnumbered single men our age by the drove.

The first thing I'd have to put was "Full-breasted women preferred." It sounded so much nicer than "Only big boobs need apply."

Thirty-three

Cassie

This was it. I was finally going to meet Mr. Right.

Mama fluffed the black rose pinned to my fake St. John's hot-pink jacket. "There. I think that's straight."

"Let's just pray we can say the same thing about Howard," I added, more nervous than I'd been about meeting somebody since I'd met Tom in college.

Mama assessed me with a critical eye. "You look at least ten years younger than you really are."

"Thanks to your good genes," I said, then gave her a hug.

Mama pointed to my bag. "Cell phone on and ready?"

"Check." I pointed to hers. "How about yours?" Mama never kept her cell phone on, but for tonight, she'd agreed to turn it on and stay close by it for security purposes.

"Check."

"All charged up?" I asked.

She made a face at me. "You ought to know. You did it." She followed me to the door. "Now remember, you promised to make a copy of his driver's license and give it to the desk clerk."

I promised yet again. "I'll call if I'm going to be late."

"You'd better," Mama said. " 'Cause if I don't hear from you by midnight, I'm alerting the law."

On that note, I went downstairs to meet Howard.

When I entered the lobby, a tall, handsome man with a nice head of hair stood up and zeroed in on me.

He looked different from his picture. Better. Definitely better.

I walked over and extended my hand. "Howard?"

He took my hand even as he shook his head no, but didn't release his grip. "Sorry. And I do mean sorry."

That was when I saw the wedding band on his left hand. I jerked free of his grip, electrified by the sharp current of my embarrassment. Of course, I was still wearing my wedding ring. "Sorry." I scanned the room, praying the real Howard hadn't seen that.

Lucky for me, he hadn't. Within seconds, I watched the real Howard come in through the revolving door, a small bouquet of roses in his hand. Conservatively, but expensively, dressed.

He made straight for me, a genuine smile on his face. "Cassie?"

"Howard?" He was nice-looking enough, and pretty is as pretty does, as far as I'm concerned.

He handed me the flowers. "For you. Welcome to Motor City." Then he reached inside his suit jacket and pulled out his driver's license, clipped to a color copy. "My daughter suggested this might put you more at ease."

A+ for the daughter. I was monumentally relieved that I hadn't had to ask. "Thank you so much. That's very thoughtful. Just one moment." I made sure they matched, then took the copy over and left it with the desk clerk, along with my name.

When I got back, Howard said, "I made reservations for the

restaurant here, if that's okay with you, so we could get to know each other a little better before we go out somewhere."

Yes, yes, yes. Perfect.

This guy wasn't as handsome as the fake Howard, but he radiated goodness. I felt like a nineteenth-century deb at her first ball. "Great."

Relief showed on his face, and I breathed easier, seeing his transparency. He guided me toward the elevators to the rooftop restaurant. "They have great steaks here, and really good salads. Actually, everything's good." He eyed me with approval, not having to say, "including you."

The maître d' led us to a window table overlooking the lights of the city, and we compared notes on the menu. They didn't have any hors d'oeuvres I could eat, so I declined, but encouraged him to have something.

"I'm saving my appetite for a T-bone," he said. "So why don't we choose our main course?"

Grateful, I selected the grilled boneless chicken au jus on a bed of shredded, sautéed summer squash (hold the pepper), with springwater, and he had the T-bone with oven-roasted vegetables and sweet potatoes, and iced tea.

That done, I started the conversation with, "So how are your granddaughters in Alpharetta doing?"

He smiled as only a doting grandfather could. "Taking ballet and karate and soccer and gymnastics. Honestly, I don't think they do anything but sleep and eat breakfast at home." There was no harshness in what he said. "But that's how the parents have to do it these days. It's not as if they could let their kids out to play the way we did."

"We let Haley and Tommy ride their bikes to day camp at the park in our neighborhood, and to the municipal pool when they were older. No way would I do that now."

Howard shook his head, wistful. "Things were different back then, but not necessarily better for everyone. There was still a lot of racism and repression among the poor."

"Which we've exchanged for gangs and drugs," I said. "But none of that is new. I'm a student of history, and there's nothing new under the sun, really. The technology is different, but the weaknesses are all the same. Power corrupts. Tribalism kills. That's why I rarely watch the news, which isn't new, at all. Most of it is just rehashes. It's just depressing."

Howard laughed, not in derision but amusement. "I might have to try that."

Oh, good. He was flexible. Very good.

"If they do come up with something really new," I said, "would you let me know?" I smiled. "But not Facebook or Twitter. I'm a bit of a technophobe."

"I can be technical enough for both of us," he said. Then he placed his hand on mine, giving it a brief squeeze before retreating. "But I sure am glad you do e-mails."

"Me, too." My heart went pitter-pat at his touch.

I decided to test the waters further. "Tell me about your wife. How did you meet?"

Howard grinned. "Only if you'll tell me about your husband."

Good answer. "Okay. You go first."

As naturally as if I were an old friend, he told me their story. We laughed over the funny things and sighed together when he told me about losing her. But when he spoke of the present, he seemed at peace.

Then I shared about my life with Tom and the kids, including some of the less harrowing incidents with teenaged Haley. Howard laughed at the mishaps and commiserated when I told him about losing Tom. But I stopped short there. If all went well, there would be a time to tell him about my condition.

By the time we'd finished our dinners and fresh berries with Splenda, I felt as if I'd discovered a real friend. One I would definitely like to kiss.

Howard smiled. "And where is this famous Mama you've told me about?"

I felt a bloom of heat in my cheeks. "Well, actually, she's downstairs in our room."

"Smart," he said. "I could have been Jack the Ripper, for all you knew."

A tiny zing of disquiet shot through me. "But you're not, are you?"

He shook his head, meeting my gaze with a calm, lucid one of his own. "No. I'm just a man who had a happy marriage and hopes to have another one before I die."

Before we got up, Howard once again took my hand. "If things work out between us, you know there will be four people in this relationship."

I nodded. "As there should be. It would be so wrong to try to erase them."

Howard exhaled. "I couldn't have put that better." He stood. "Come, my lady. I'd like to meet your mother."

"How about coffee in the bar downstairs?" I suggested. I knew Mama was still up and dressed, waiting to hear how things had gone.

Howard grinned from ear to ear. "Perfect. If you'll excuse me, I'll be right back."

While he headed for the loo, I called Mama.

"What's the password?" she demanded without saying hello.

I'd completely forgotten about our safe word. "Chicken," I said. (It had been Mama's idea. If I'd said "salad," she would have called the cops.)

"Was that the good one or the bad one?" she asked.

"Good." Very good. "Are you still dressed?"

"To the nines," she answered.

"Great, because Howard wants me to invite you to have coffee with us in the bar on the mezzanine," I said. "If you're up to it."

"Be there in five," Mama said. "I take it he's a keeper."

"One in a million, from the looks of it."

I had just hung up when Howard came back with a single red rose for me.

"It's a keepsake for our first meeting," he said as he handed it to me. "The first of many, I hope."

I blushed from the chest up, and fiercely. "I hope so, too."

There really was a Mr. Right, and I had met him.

Mama thought so, too. Jacked up on the coffee she'd drunk meeting Howard, she talked my ear off singing his praises when we finally got to bed.

Finally, I had to get rough with her. "Mama, if you don't hush up, I can't go to sleep and dream about him."

"Hushing up, now," she said, and did.

But I didn't dream of Howard. I dreamed of Tom, when we were young, and it was fine.

Thirty-four

Jack

Another cardiologist, and a bunch of new tests. Just what Jack needed, but Patel had insisted.

A week later, Jack sat in the sunlit office that overlooked St. Joseph's Hospital where he'd had the tests.

The doctor breezed in with his files and shook Jack's hand. "Mr. Wilson."

Jack could tell from the brisk tone that the news wasn't going to be good.

He waited till the doctor took his seat to say, "Let's have it, Doc. And no sugarcoating."

The man's brows lifted, his expression somber. "I wish I had better news for you, but you have what we call a lazy heart."

Perfect. Something else wrong with him. "Is there anything you can do?"

"We can try you on coenzyme Q10, which has been of help in some cases."

Jack zeroed in on the key words "try" and "some cases." Not looking good.

If God wanted him to die, why was he doing it by degrees?

Jack would have had a hissy fit, but he lacked the energy. "Will you give me a prescription for that?"

"It's available over the counter," the doctor dismissed.

Jack glared at him. "Would you give me a *prescription*, which will be covered by my insurance."

"Sure." The doctor capitulated. He took out his scrip pad and started writing. "If this doesn't help, we can give you an IV treatment. But let's try the pills, first, and see what happens. I'd like to see you again in a week."

Perfect. Another doctor to see on a regular basis.

Not that Jack had a lot to do. He'd taken a leave of absence from work till January, but it still irritated the schmoo out of him that he had to see this guy so often.

Thank the good Lord, his mother's move had gone well, at least, two weeks sooner than Jack had expected. The facility had recommended movers who were pros at that kind of relocation, and they'd also sent an LPN over every day for a week in advance, to help his mother pack her personal belongings and prepare her for her "visit" with Aunt Junie. At home with the familiar nurse, his mother hadn't balked a bit when it came time to go.

Jack punched the speed dial for her number, which she'd been able to keep.

His mother answered the phone with, "Junie Belle Snyder's apartment, her sister speaking."

"Hey, Mama. How are you?"

Her voice lowered to a loud whisper. "I'm so glad you found this place for Junie. She just loves it, and they do all our chores and our meals, and they treat me just like a member, even though I'm only a visitor." She reverted to a normal tone, which was half shouting. "Couldn't be nicer. They even have bingo, if you can imagine that. And a shuttle to take us to the library and the store. We're quite the gadabouts."

So far, so good. Jack heaved what passed for a sigh of relief, given his condition.

Thirty-five

Cassie

The next three days were out of a dream. Howard showed me the city, invited Mama to go with us for just enough outings to make her feel included, and all in all, left me smitten.

He kissed like a dream, too.

When our last full day rolled around, I hated to see it come, but he'd promised to fly down to visit me and his daughters in Atlanta very soon, so I sucked it up and tried to make the best of it.

Things were moving fast—far faster than I would ever have imagined—but we seemed so well suited to each other that I decided to put him to the final test on our last night out and tell him about my health, before I got more physically or emotionally involved.

I knew he'd pass the test. He wasn't a shallow man, and he had two married daughters in Atlanta, and his son in Detroit was being transferred to California, so he had no reason to stay in Michigan.

After we dropped Mama off from our matinee of *Mamma Mia!*, Howard took me back to his house in Grosse Pointe for supper. The place was wonderful, a solid Georgian brick with a welcoming interior, but not that much bigger than mine. His late wife and I shared similar taste in decorating, so I knew Howard would feel at home in my house, too.

Howard made a great salad, which we ate with grilled chicken breasts and fresh green beans sautéed in a little olive oil.

The man could cook, too. Perfect, perfect, perfect.

After dinner, I waited till I was helping him wash up to say, "Listen, Howard. There's something I need to tell you before this goes any further."

He paused at the sink, his expression suddenly wary. "If it's about your past, we're both adults, and I don't think either of us needs to—"

"It's not about my past. It's about my present, and my future." I put down the dish towel and patted the bar stool beside me. "Why don't we sit?"

"Uh-oh. She wants me to sit down," he said as he obliged.

I sat facing him. "You see, I have this condition—"

Instantly, he put his head in his hands. "God, no. Not again."

"I'm not dying, Howard. It's called chronic fungal arthritis," I hastened to clarify.

Howard looked up at me through his fingers. "You scared me half to death." He straightened, shaking his head. "I thought you were going to say you had cancer, or Alzheimer's or something."

"No. Nothing that dire." Encouraged, I forged ahead and dumped it all out there. "It's just I'm allergic to almost everything except what you've seen me eat this week, and I have to live in a mold-free bubble, and take vaccines every week and stay on this really strict sugar-free, carb-free rotation diet, and I have the joints of a ninety-year-old, so I've had twenty-four surgeries, including both knee replacements, and both hips, but I'm okay as long as I stay on my diet and in my bubble. There. That's it." I remembered one more thing. "And my body looks like a road map from all the scars. But that's everything." I nodded, hopeful. Except the bite guard, but that could be dealt with later, along with the stress incontinence. "No cancer. No Alzheimer's."

Howard got up and strode to look out the windows. Not a good sign.

Please, God, let him understand. Please let him want me still. This one's a keeper, Lord. Please.

But God never intervened to take away our choices, and I knew it. This choice was Howard's to make.

Howard stood staring into space for a long time. At long last, he dropped his head and murmured, "Cassie, I'm going to have to think about this." He turned to face me with a look of conflict. "I like you so much. But I had planned to travel in my retirement. Hike. Ski. Finally to be able to be spontaneous, and what you just told me . . ." He dropped his gaze.

Not good. Very, very not good.

I fought to mask my disappointment. "I see." He liked me, but he didn't want what came with me. "Maybe you'd better take me back to the hotel."

I could tell he didn't want to hurt me, but I could also tell he thought I'd cramp his style, which I would, and it unglued the pieces of my heart I'd pasted together since Tom had died.

Mr. Perfect only wanted Mrs. Perfect, and I was anything but that.

Mama was right. Men our age didn't want someone to take care of. They wanted someone to take care of them.

The trip back to town was long and silent. When we got to the hotel, Howard parked under the porte cochere, then came around to let me out, waving off the valet. "I just need some time to think about it," he lied. "I'll call you soon."

Lie, lie, lie.

Two could play at that game. "Oh, well. It was fun while it lasted." I wrapped my silk shawl tighter around me against the crisp autumn night. "Good-bye, Howard." I didn't bother to shake his perfect hand.

I walked away without looking back, my head held high, and I managed to keep from crying all the way up to our room. Then I cried, off and on, all night.

Furious, Mama threatened to go give him a good talking-to, but I managed to dissuade her. What would be the point? He didn't want somebody with my complications. It was that simple.

Shoot. I'd turned into a real bawl-baby.

Cried out and stuffed up, I flew back to Atlanta in sunglasses to cover my swollen eyes, then took Mama home and holed up in my house, licking my wounds, with only Juliette to console me. I didn't want to talk to Mama about it, or my children, so I quit answering my phone. No surprise, there were no missed calls or messages from Howard.

Except for my trips to Whole Foods and the drugstore, I didn't go out again until it was time for my November visit to Dr. Patel.

As always, Jack was there waiting on the sofa, his khaki slacks the only concession to the change of season. He eyed me with assessment. "Obviously CarMan335 didn't work out."

I sat with a plunk. "I don't want to talk about it."

He leaned forward with a scowl. "No clamming up now. I'm your matchmaker, here. I have a right to know."

I knew he wouldn't let me alone till I told him, so I relented. "He was perfect. Absolutely perfect. It looked like a match made in heaven. There was only one catch." Feeling my mouth tremble, I looked down at my hands till I could safely speak again. "He wanted somebody perfect, not somebody with my problems."

"Sorry-assed sumabitch," Jack muttered. His gaze sharpened. "Where does that leave you?"

Might as well tell the truth. "Going broke at ninety miles an hour, with no health coverage by the end of next year." I leaned back into my seat and let out a long sigh. Then I realized I hadn't asked about Jack. "How about you? You look rode hard and put up wet."

"If something doesn't happen immediately, and I mean immediately, I'm going to be forced to permanently move in with one of my kids, which I consider a fate worse than death. My son made me come to his place after I had a spell, and it made me even sicker."

"Bummer," I said.

"The kicker is, their houses are just as moldy as mine," he said. "My son's basement is worse than the farmhouse ever was. But even though he tried to clean it and used the spray, I'm still croaking, and now it's official."

"I'm so sorry."

We sat there, deflated, for several minutes before Jack perked up abruptly.

He regarded me through narrowed eyes, and I could almost see a lightbulb going off in the air above his brain. "Listen, I've got a business proposition for you."

"And what would that be?"

Nothing prepared me for what was coming next. "Marry me," he said, his voice even. "Strictly platonic. Under the terms of my retirement, my spouse qualifies for full health insurance until Medicare kicks in, and then a good supplemental, after that. Even if I die. In exchange, I'll get a safe place to live. We can set up the house rules in a prenup. If it doesn't work out for either of us, either of us can have it annulled."

What? "Listen, I need health insurance," I said, "but that's not exactly the kind of marriage proposal I had in mind," I snapped. Or the man I wanted.

"Think about it," Jack said. "You have your room, I have mine. You leave me alone, I leave you alone. Most of the time when I'm not . . . busy, I read or do my e-mails. We could just live in the same house."

"That's not a marriage," I argued.

"Who says?" he retorted. "We're both well beyond the shady side of middle age, not love-struck teenagers. Who says marriage can't be what we decide it is?"

I hadn't thought of it that way, but this . . .

"I'm talking respect, companionship, and the same wretched diet."

When I didn't respond, Jack raised his eyebrows and went for the jugular. "You know you'll never really be happy with anybody besides Tom. Admit it." He leveled a frank stare at me. "Nobody's perfect, Cassie, until they're dead. You're a one-man woman, and nobody could ever live up to Tom. And if you slept with somebody, you'd feel like you were cheating on Tom. Admit it."

That was hard, but hearing it, I realized he was right.

"If you married somebody else with romantic expectations, consciously or unconsciously," Jack argued, "you'd spend the rest of your life trying to make him over into Tom's image."

Struck right square in the solar plexus by the fact that what he said was true, I sputtered, "That is insulting!"

Jack didn't even bother to address that. He just kept on negotiating. "And you know nobody would have me, so it's not as if I have a lot of other options. I can't live with my kids, for a lot more reasons than the mold. But what if I promise to clean up after myself and only bring my clothes?"

Why was this starting to look even vaguely possible to me? "Jack, listen, I know we're both desperate, but this is not the answer."

"Why not? I'll even promise to be agreeable, but only if you don't talk to me before ten in the morning."

The whole thing was so preposterous, I didn't know where to start. "This is crazy. I can't marry a mechanic I barely know just for health insurance. It's—"

"I'm not a mechanic," he said with a mixture of triumph and criticism. "I'm a Ph.D. professor emeritus in English and American literature. Until this quarter, I've taught two English lit classes a week at Oglethorpe as an adjunct."

That was a shocker!

"What about all that *stuff* at the farm?" I heard myself objecting. "You can't bring—" What was I saying? I was negotiating terms! When did I go from *no* to negotiating terms?

Jack's closed-mouth smile lengthened his stubbly chin. "Admit it. This could work."

To my amazement, I found myself actually considering his proposal.

Respectability would be served, if we were married. And he'd promised a prenup, stating that either of us could get an annulment if it didn't work out. The house was in trust for Tommy and Haley, so I didn't have to worry about that.

"I'd have to see all this in writing before I even *think* about considering it," I told him.

285

Jack pointed to me in triumph. "E-mail me your list of terms as soon as possible. I'll do one, too, and we can hammer out a final deal. Then I'll get everything drawn up. But don't drag your feet. I don't know how much longer I can survive where I am, and that's no joke."

I knew it wasn't, and I certainly didn't want him to die for lack of a safe place to live.

I began to smell divine irony of the first water, and frankly, it stank.

The nurse appeared. "Mrs. Jones, the doctor is ready to see you now."

I looked at Jack in challenge. "I'm not changing my name."

He grinned. "Wouldn't dream of asking you to."

As I rose to leave, he issued his parting shot: "With any luck, I'll die, and you'll get my life insurance, too, as well as widow's benefits. Think about it."

Believe it or not, I did.

Jack had a point. Who said marriage had to be what we'd thought it was as kids?

At our age, with our needs, couldn't we define it as we pleased?

The idea was shocking to me, but appealing, as well.

So after I got home, I sat down to make out my list of house rules. Starting from my first waking moments of the day till my last at night, I laid out what I could live with, and what I couldn't.

I wasn't saying yes, mind you. I was only setting the ground rules if I did.

Thirty-six

Jack

From the minute Cassie walked out of the waiting room, Jack couldn't decide whether his bright idea had been totally insane or preternaturally clever.

Married? He'd asked that woman to marry him?

All his traditional sensibilities reared up and said he'd gone stark raving loco.

But his practical side said it just might work. On his way back to the farm, he realized he'd have to be very strict with Cassie about the house rules. And the financial arrangements. When he died, the farm would go to his kids—not that it was much of an inheritance, the way things were, but he wanted them to have it. If he married Cassie, he'd want to contribute what he could to her property taxes and utilities, even though the farm was a huge drain on his limited resources.

Of course, now that his house was clean and straightened up, he might be able to find a decent tenant to bring in some extra cash. He'd keep the rights to the barn and the garden, of course.

Just lease out the house. With a trial period at first, so he could kick them out if they were destructive.

Whether he married Cassie or not, he couldn't live there anymore.

He wondered what he could get for rent. No college students. And first and last months' rent, with a substantial damage deposit. That would weed out the transients. He'd do an online credit and background check, too.

Heck, maybe one of Frances's grooms next door might want to rent it. He dialed her number, and she answered on the second ring with, "How did you know I was thinking of you?"

"I didn't. I was thinking of you." Jack knew better than to beat around the bush, or he'd be stuck on the line for hours. "Listen, Frances, do you think any of your staff would like to rent my farmhouse? It's making me so sick, I have to move out."

"How much are you asking?" she shot back. Frances was crazy, but the canny businesswoman in her occasionally made an appearance.

"Whatever's fair," he told her. "Why don't you check the listings in the area and come up with a figure for me?"

"I sure will hate to lose you for a neighbor," she said with genuine affection—probably as much for his vegetables as his presence.

"I'll still have my garden," he reassured her, "so you won't lose me entirely. Or the vegetables."

It occurred to him that he might reduce the rent in exchange for the tenants' maintaining the garden, if they were willing. For that matter, he could use the first month's rent to pay for an irrigation system from the well, so he'd only have to go out to check on things when he felt like it. Even with the drought, watering food crops was allowed.

When Frances didn't bite on finding out what the place was worth, he offered, "I'll call around and find a real estate agent to give me some comps. You check with your people."

"Right. I can think of two who might be interested." She barked a laugh. "Of course, whether they'll want to have *me* for a next-door neighbor remains to be seen."

A valid point. But if they would, it would solve a lot of potential problems. At least he'd know they had a job. Frances was devoted to the people who worked for her and paid them well, even with the recession.

As Jack turned onto his driveway thirty minutes later, he decided it wouldn't be crazy to marry Cassie. Just eminently practical.

As long as she didn't interrupt his reading or computing to talk at him.

That would be condition number one.

Thirty-seven

Cassie

Jack had given me a lot to think about. A whole lot, most of it things I'd rather not admit, but in the end, I had to accept the fact that what he'd said about Tom was accurate.

I had been looking for a perfect man, but there was no such thing. And no man would be Tom, the only one I really wanted.

It wasn't fun, seeing my illusions for what they were, but it was honest. Jack was nothing, if not honest. Blunt though he'd been, I knew he hadn't told the truth to hurt me.

Or even to manipulate me, because I still had a choice.

As I pondered the idea of accepting practical reality instead of fantasy, I realized yet again how much Tom had protected me. But now that he wasn't there, I found myself leaning toward the truth.

For the first time in my life, I didn't ask my mother or my children or my friends what I should do. They wouldn't be living with the consequences of my decision; I would.

Instead, I sat down at the computer and reviewed what I thought would be fair for both Jack and me.

Number one on the list was, he had to keep his person, his room, and his bathroom immaculate.

Number two: he could bring his cats with him, but couldn't let them into the house. Heck, we could keep them all, even the kittens in the workshop, but they'd have to be fixed and live outside. I could build them a heated, insulated cat hotel, with a separate cubby for each, and mount it on the side of the garage.

Number three: if he wanted to watch sports—besides Georgia Tech football or the Braves—he'd have to do it in his room, at a reasonable volume.

Number four: I would cook for both of us, but he would do the dishes immediately following the meal, unless he was too ill to stand up. (I knew all about that passive-aggressive man-trick of leaving chores so long undone that the wife finally stepped in and did them.) Not that Tom was that way—I hadn't wanted or expected him to do any housework—but that was then, and this was now.

A thought occurred to me, so I looked at the list and went back to do another number one: there would be no unwelcome physical contact. Jack would sleep in his room and I would sleep in mine, and each of us would respect the other's privacy, as long as he kept his room clean.

Definitely number one.

I renumbered the rest, then proceeded to items like only playing classical music or mellow golden oldies in the common areas—no heavy metal or country western salutes to bad women and/or drunkenness.

I agreed to wash his clothes with mine, but only if he put them in the laundry room every Monday and Thursday morning by ten

A.M. (my wash days), then promptly put them away when they were folded.

Oh, and my tools: Jack couldn't use my tools or workshop without specific permission, and he had to put everything back the way he found it as soon as he was finished, or pay a twenty-five-dollar fine. For twenty-five dollars, I wouldn't mind cleaning up my tools.

I looked at that one and felt a little sheepish, because it might have been a mother talking about her kids, but this was my life, and my tools. If he wanted to share them, he had to act like a grown-up.

Maybe I ought to raise the fine to fifty dollars. Yep. Definitely a better incentive.

By the time midnight crept up on me with a yawn, I'd written twenty pages, single spaced. This was my life, after all, and I didn't want any unpleasant surprises. Satisfied with the stipulations, I added one more rule: if any disputes arose, I agreed to discuss them with an open mind, but retained the final say, as it was my house.

There.

I did a grammar/spell check, then sent it to Jack as an attachment.

The next morning, his e-mailed list was waiting for me. I clicked on the attachment and printed it out. You can imagine my embarrassment when I found only a few requests from him—most notably, "no talking to Jack before ten in the morning unless he initiates the conversation," and "no interrupting Jack's reading or computing except in the case of genuine emergency." The rest were his agreements to abide by an impressive number of the very rules and conditions I had requested. He'd even thought to say that neither of us had to go to the other's family events unless he or she wanted to, something that hadn't occurred to me.

I checked the time sent and saw that he'd e-mailed his list less than ten minutes after I'd sent him mine, so he couldn't have written it as a response.

Typical of his gender, his points were fewer and far more global, while mine were many and much more detailed. Yet his "conditions" showed a generosity of spirit I never would have expected.

At the end of the list, he suggested I call him the next morning so we could arrange to go over them at the restaurant of my choice.

It was the next morning, so I called.

Jack coughed into my ear, then wheezed out a strangled, "Hello."

Whoa. He needed to get out of that place, and pronto. "How soon can you be at the Original House of Pancakes on La Vista?"

"Thirty minutes. I need to shave."

That was a good sign. He wanted to shave before we got together. "Okay. See you there. Be sure to bring your copies of both lists, so we can compare notes. I'll bring mine."

A tight spate of coughing preceded his "I'll bring my laptop, too."

I got to the restaurant early, so my favorite waiter entertained me with a detailed narrative about the new Tom Cruise movie he'd seen the night before (regardless of Tom's Scientology and unadulterated nuttiness, my waiter had a *huge* crush on him).

When Jack came crawling in fifteen minutes late, I felt a new urgency to get this thing hammered out.

Eschewing my favorite—now deadly—Dutch apple pancake, I ordered coffee (not made with springwater, but what are you gonna do), three poached eggs, and bacon, crisp. Jack just said, "Ditto," maybe because he didn't have the breath for much else.

"Okay, Jack," I said as the waiter walked away, pushing up the sleeves of my beloved old red merino Ralph Lauren cardigan, "let's hammer this out so we can get you out of that farmhouse." Somewhere along the line, I'd made up my mind to give this a try, so there wasn't any point in dillydallying.

He paused, tucking his chin, eyebrows raised. "You're going to marry me?" He looked genuinely surprised, which set me back a bit.

"Isn't that what you wanted?"

"Yes," he said. "I just thought you'd"—he paused for a labored breath—"take longer."

"Do you want it to take longer?"

"No." This pause was briefer. "No." Hope dawned in his eyes.

"All right then. All we need to do is come to an agreement on the terms."

He nodded, almost smiling.

"Okay, then." I laid the two lists side by side. "Item number one . . ."

Three eggs, four crisp bacon strips, and five cups of coffee later, Jack closed his laptop. "I'd say that does it."

Already, he was breathing and talking better.

I nodded. We hadn't been that far apart, to start with. "I think this thing could work."

I could hear God laughing.

Jack actually smiled. "All that's left to decide is when." His optimism clouded. "And how."

I had to chuckle. "Don't worry. No veils or guests or ceremonies."

His expression cleared. "How about a judge? The clerk can be the witness."

Visibly relieved, Jack nodded. "How about I buy your breakfast, then we can get some rings and a license?"

Too fast, too fast. But I was impressed by the fact that he was willing to wear a ring. "Okay," I heard myself say. "I'll follow you in my car."

Definitely not the conventional way for the bride and groom to travel, but this wasn't conventional by anybody's standard.

Mama and the kids were going to have a *fit*!

I followed Jack to Kay jewelers, where we picked out the most economical convex gold bands we could find. I felt like a traitor when I slipped off Tom's band to have the new ring sized, but quieted my conscience with a promise that I'd wear it around my neck on a chain after the ceremony. We left the rings to be sized.

Due to the limited parking at the county complex downtown, we left Jack's truck at my house, then I drove us to get the license. We had our blood tests done at the AnyTest lab near Houston's on Peachtree.

"I know a judge," Jack told me over a club salad at Houston's afterward. "He'll do the ceremony up in Cumming."

Cumming suited me. At least I wouldn't have to worry about bumping into anybody I knew. "Okay."

"I'll even wear shoes," Jack said with a spark of mischief.

"Shoes, plural?" Until that moment, I'd completely forgotten he was missing the bottom half of his left leg. "I am honored, indeed, Sir Flip-flop, but I was thinking of going barefoot, myself."

"Very funny." At least he knew I was kidding.

The next day, Jack picked up the rings, then took me to the

bank to have the prenuptial agreements notarized in duplicate. I'd read through both copies, and everything was in order.

The notary looked at the top page and couldn't help smiling. "Goodness, what a clever idea." She glanced at us both. "A lot more marriages would work out if people were this practical in the first place."

To my embarrassment, I felt my neck and cheeks go hot, but so did Jack's, so I figured we were even.

We stopped by the lab next and got the test results: neither of us had a social disease. So we took the results downtown to the marriage license bureau, and the wedding was on. But Jack was so sick, he had no business driving, so I convinced him to let me pick him up for the ceremony in Cumming two days hence.

On the second wedding day of my long life, I knocked on Jack's door, and he answered it looking like Mr. Corporate America in expensive dark mustard gabardine slacks, a navy silk-and-wool-blend blazer, a crisp white shirt with a tasteful tie, and shiny black wingtips. He'd even gotten a decent haircut. But his lips were almost blue, and he was working hard not to erupt with that telltale wheezing cough.

My senses sharpened by life in my own bubble, I could smell the mold in his house.

"We can come back by for my truck and my things," he said, suddenly awkward.

How long would it be before we got used to each other?

I told myself we would, in time. And that was all we needed to do: get used to each other.

If not, no harm, no foul. We'd go our separate ways. My signed, notarized copy of the prenup was in my safe-deposit box if I needed it.

Dear Lord, we were really going to do this.

I had prayed about it incessantly since Jack had proposed, but I prayed one more time, just in case. *God, if you don't want this to happen, please don't let my car start.*

The car started fine, so I carefully backed up and turned around, unsure whether by the laws of nature or the will of God.

Either way, this was it.

I headed for the street. "Okay, here we go." The second the words were out, I realized they were just stating the obvious, which was one of the things Jack had asked me not to do. "Sorry."

"That's okay," he said equably. "We're both nervous."

Major understatement.

At the mailbox, I turned toward Cumming and reviewed my preparations.

I had given Jack Tommy's old room, the larger of the two that overlooked the garden in back, and farthest from the master. After cleaning it yet again from the chandelier to the baseboards, I'd made his encased double bed with mold-free linens and four fluffy new hypoallergenic encased pillows, then left my portable travel air filter doing its thing on the nightstand. I'd even sprung for a nice flat-screen atop the dresser, with its own DVR box for the cable. And mold-killer shampoo and soap in the adjacent bathroom.

I was betting Jack didn't have the big, expensive air filter the doctor had recommended, but that could come later.

Everything was ready at home. And, to my amazement, everything was ready with me.

After all, Jack was just a housemate with benefits.

I colored.

Medical benefits, that is.

"Did you tell anybody?" Jack asked.

"Oh, gracious, no. I didn't want the hassle. Better to present them with a fait accompli."

"My sentiments, exactly."

I merged onto I-400 north, finding it surprisingly free of traffic. Another divine omen?

Jack pointed to the radio. "May I?"

"Sure."

He turned it on to public radio, and classical music filled the strained silence with soothing tones.

By the time we got to the Cumming courthouse, I'd almost relaxed.

Fortunately, we only had to wait a few minutes in the judge's outer office. When we finally entered his chambers, the portly man stood and eyed me with approval. "Good Lord, Jack. How'd you ever get a pretty lady like this to marry you?"

Both of us blushed. Realizing we weren't in the mood for kidding, the judge asked his secretary and a clerk in to witness the ceremony—if you could call it that.

The whole thing took less than three minutes, insultingly brief, to my sensibilities. But then again, it was really only a formalization of a business agreement. And the "love, honor, and obeys" wouldn't have been honest.

Even so, the judge insisted his secretary take pictures for our kids on both of our cell phones.

Before we left, Jack shook the judge's hand and leaned in for a confidential, "I'd appreciate it if you didn't mention this to anybody at the diner. I told Frances I had to move for my health, so that's okay, but I'd rather not have to explain this to every Tom, Dick, and Harry in town."

The judge pumped his hand. "Mum's the word."

I knew better. I'd seen the look in the secretary's eye. She couldn't wait to advertise this small-town exclusive.

Jack nodded. "Thank you, Your Honor."

I took Jack's arm and sailed out like a duchess, feeling anything but married, yet wanting to preserve his pride.

Then we had an early (legal) dinner at the Golden Corral. After that, I took Jack to pick up his truck, then he followed me home and parked in Tom's space outside the garage without comment.

At least I didn't have to worry about some robber hiding in the bushes anymore. Not that Jack could do anything about it if there was, but he was there with me, and that was what counted.

As I passed his truck on the way in, he pulled a duffel bag and a copy of *To Kill a Mockingbird* from the passenger seat.

I unlocked the back door, then disarmed the alarm and let him in. "Welcome home."

From the minute Jack Wilson walked into my house, Juliette acted as if he were the only human in the world. She leaned against his good leg, then followed him around like a dog, fluttering her blond piggy eyelashes for all they were worth.

Maybe it was the testosterone, but suddenly, I ceased to exist. Not that I minded that much. With Jack there, I didn't really need a pig anymore.

"If it's okay with you," I told Jack, "I'd like to wash all your clothes and clean your stuff before you put everything away. I know it's a violation of our privacy agreement, but it's safer for both of us, that way."

Jack nodded, petting Juliette. "Fine, for just this once. I don't have any pajamas, anyway."

I decided to ignore that remark.

"There are clean towels in the bathroom for your shower." I

looked at my pig. "If you don't want her in there with you, hogging all the hot water, pun intended, I suggest you put her in my room and close the door. It's metal, so she can't root it open."

Jack arched a single brow. "Any more instructions?"

Ouch. "You're contaminated, Jack," I said mildly, "and so are your things. I spent too much time and money making this a safe place for both of us to let you bring mold inside."

"Fair enough." He actually smiled. "See? It's easy when you're honest with me."

"Can I get you anything else?"

"Nope. I'm good. And I'm going to bed as soon as I get cleaned up."

It was only five, but already getting dark outside.

Jack didn't have to say it had been a long day. It had for both of us.

After putting his scant collection of casual clothes and boxers into the washer along with the duffel bag, I wiped down his portable CD player, his cell phone, and his toiletries with mold cleaner, then dried and put them in a plastic bag to leave outside his room. When I laid the bag at his closed bedroom door, a muffled, "Get back, you beast," came through the bathroom door over the noise of the shower.

Maybe I did need a pig, after all.

Smiling, I went to watch HGTV in my room till it was time to put Jack's clothes in the dryer.

Things shook out very nicely after that. Jack started getting better immediately, and he never failed to do his chores or thank me for taking care of the food and laundry.

We fell into our routines like brother and sister, which suited both of us fine. He soon felt well enough to take over a class for a teacher who'd had a baby, so he spent his spare time working in the yard or reading or grading papers. I did my housework and shopping and volunteered and visited Mama, keeping up with the kids by phone.

And, to my amazement, neither of us had to tell our families anything. We just didn't mention each other in our conversations, which was easy, since we led our separate lives.

Till Jack got that fateful phone call.

Thirty-eight

Jack

Full and happy from the supper Cassie had made, Jack had just settled on the sofa afterward to watch *Jeopardy!* when he heard his cell phone go off in the bedroom. Too comfortable to move, he let it pass. Then it rang again. Annoyed, he didn't answer. Whatever it was could wait.

When it started ringing for the third time, Cassie quietly got up and brought it back. "Here." She handed it to him. "Either turn off the ring or answer it. I don't care which."

Jack sighed, then looked at the screen. Three missed calls from his mother. Might as well get it over with. "Be right back." He headed for the kitchen, so as not to disturb Cassie further.

Once there, Jack pressed the call-back button. It wasn't his mother who answered, but his aunt. "Oh, Jack," she sobbed. "I'm so glad you called. It's your mama."

A thin thread of fear slid through him, like the blade of a hacksaw.

"Calm down, Aunt Junie," he told her. "What's happened?"

"She's *dead*," his aunt told him, drawing the word out.

At first, Jack didn't assimilate what she'd said, then it began to sink in.

"She had a bad evening," Junie wailed, "and I had to fuss at her to go to bed. And when I got up to go to the bathroom, she was *gone*." Another spate of tears. "It's all my fault. I should have kept better watch on her."

"Aunt Junie," Jack soothed, "you have to sleep. It's not your fault."

She moaned into the receiver.

His mother was dead. Why didn't he feel anything?

Part of Jack didn't want to know the details, but part of him did. "Please tell me what happened."

"She got out, somehow, and she was walking up that big road that goes to Denny's, right in the middle of the lane, and a drunk driver hit her."

Poor Mama. Poor drunk driver.

Junie paused to blow her nose, then collect herself. She sounded better when she came back on the line. "We were still searching for her here at the place when the police came and told us."

She blew her nose again. "They said it was instant, that she probably didn't even feel it. Lord, I pray that that's true. I feel so awful about letting her get out—"

"Aunt Junie," he interrupted, "I want you to listen to me carefully. This is not your fault, and it's not the home's, and it's not that driver's, even though he was drunk. Our days are numbered by the Lord, so it was just Mama's time. You know she was ready to go home to heaven a long time ago. At least it was quick."

"Oh, Jack," she said, starting to cry again. "You are so good."

"Tell the people at the place to call the funeral home. Then I want you to get some rest. I'll be down there tomorrow, okay?"

His aunt started sobbing again, but managed to get out a drowned, "Okay," then hung up the phone.

Jack just stood there with the phone in his hand, staring sightlessly at Cassie's immaculate kitchen as he tried to get his arms around the fact that his mother was dead, and how it had happened.

"Jack?" Cassie came in with a concerned expression, then halted when she saw him. "Jack, what's happened?"

He looked up at her, cocking his head. "My mother escaped the assisted living and got hit by a drunk driver. She was going to Denny's." It seemed so unreal. "She's dead."

As he said it aloud, his body jerked briefly up and back, as if someone had slammed him with an uppercut to the diaphragm.

Tears threatened, but he kept them back and stared at Cassie, finally beginning to feel the loss, even though the mother he loved had been erased by degrees over the past few years as her Alzheimer's had advanced.

Yes, she was old. Yes, she was crazy. But she was his mother, and now she was gone.

Cassie rushed over and enveloped him with a hug. "Oh, Jack, I'm so sorry." He knew she meant it, and it felt good to have the comfort of her arms around him. "So sorry."

He held on to her, tight, not wanting to let go, so they stood there, slowly swaying like a worn-out couple at the end of a dance marathon from a thirties movie.

He didn't know what to say, or what to feel.

Cassie patted him and stroked his back. When both their legs began to give out, she said gently, "Why don't you sit down? I'll make you some decaffeinated tea, that spiced green kind you like."

Jack nodded and gratefully went to the banquette, where Juliette reared up and nudged her snout under his arm, as if in comfort.

In suspended animation, Jack tried not to think or feel. There would be time for that later, once his mother had been laid to rest.

The microwave dinged, and Cassie brought the tea and fixings to the table, then sat down across from him. "Do you need any help with the arrangements?"

He shook his head. "No, thanks. When Mama first found out she had Alzheimer's, she picked out her coffin and paid for the service in advance. She even made arrangements with the minister she wanted, and wrote her own eulogy, which should be interesting."

"I can't imagine what you're going through," Cassie said. "If I lost Mama . . ."

Jack took a sip of tea, savoring the sweetness and the scent of oranges, then sighed. "It's not the same. Your mother is still herself. I lost mine over the years by degrees. She hasn't been the woman I knew for a long time."

"Oh."

The shock began to wear off, bringing him back to himself. "She's whole again, now. And it was quick, so she didn't suffer. I'm grateful for that." Her ordeal was over, at last.

Cassie nodded. "Will you be leaving tonight?"

He shook his head, raking his fingers through his hair. "I can't. Too worn out. I told Aunt Junie I'd be there tomorrow."

"I'd be happy to drive you."

Cassie's generosity made him smile. For all her faults, she was kind. "No. I'm going to fly this time and rent a car."

She hesitated, considering, then ventured, "Would you like for me to go with you?"

Jack shook his head with a wry smile. "Lord, no. But thanks." The pall lifted somewhat. "Nobody knows we're married, and I don't think this is the time to tell them."

"Of course," she said, apologetic. "I wasn't thinking."

Awkward, she braced her hands on the table to push herself erect. "I'll just leave you to set everything up, then. I don't want to intrude."

Jack grasped her hand and held it. "You're not intruding. I'm really glad you're here."

Cassie covered his hand with her other one and gave it a squeeze. "What are friends for?"

Jack was just beginning to realize what a good friend she'd become. "Thanks, Cassie. For everything."

"Anytime." She herded Juliette back to her bedroom and closed the door.

Only after he'd booked tickets home and a rental car did Jack go to bed himself and start calling the kids about their grandmother. Not that they would care that much. They hadn't even bothered to visit her in ages. To his surprise, though, they all wanted to come to the funeral—as long as he paid for the motel.

Oh, well. What were fathers for?

It was eleven before everything was done, and Jack fell into a black, dreamless sleep, grateful that when he woke up, it would be at Cassie's.

Thirty-nine

Cassie

The house seemed so empty with Jack gone. Cooking for myself was a drag. And I was surprised how much I missed him and looked forward to his phone calls.

Somehow, that single, long consoling hug had narrowed the distance between us significantly. There wasn't anything sexual about it, but it had taken us from being talking friends to touching friends, and that was good. Friends ought to be able to hug each other. Not that I meant to abuse the privilege, of course.

Still, I missed him, even though he called me often. His recaps were characteristically brief and to the point. Times, places, what they ate and where. (Definitely not doctor approved.) If he did mention the family, he talked about his aunt and his kids and the grandchildren, so I ended up with a much clearer picture of who was who. I even wrote it down for future reference.

The son in Chamblee came as a surprise, but Jack hadn't been obligated to tell me about him in the first place. We both knew that our two families would remain separate, and that was more than okay with me. Our plates were full without stepchild issues.

As usual, I had to read between the lines, but he seemed to be at peace about his mother's passing.

Maybe I shouldn't use that word, since she'd been hit by a passing truck.

I made a mental note to avoid the term when he got home.

Five days after he'd left, he called me when his return flight landed, and I picked him up just outside baggage claim. He looked tired, but not exhausted, and glad to see me.

"Whew." He tossed his duffel into the backseat, then flopped into the passenger seat beside me and slammed the door. "It sure will be good to get home."

"Home will be glad to have you back," I said as I navigated the lane changes to access I-85 North. "It's been way too quiet since you left."

He smiled at me with what could have passed for affection. "You're the one who does all the talking."

I chuckled. "Would you like me to put you out here, or at an exit ramp?"

Still smiling, he laid his head back and watched the road ahead.

The silence between us was safe, so I didn't fill it up with questions. He would tell me what he wanted to, when he was ready.

Things were back to the way they should be. Jack was home.

Forty

Cassie

With Jack home, I felt a new peace, a new contentment that had nothing to do with my financial or physical security, and everything to do with gratitude. I was grateful for his company and our lives, just the way they were. And ourselves, just the way we were. Barring some major catastrophe, I could see our friendship stretching into the future, and I hoped his life would be a long one, now that he was so much better.

Surprising though it was, I had come to depend on him. And he depended on me.

I savored each quiet, orderly day with uncommon satisfaction, enjoying taking care of him.

He never did mention his feelings about losing his mother, and that was okay. Jack didn't share his feelings about much of anything, except what annoyed him, so I didn't push.

The holidays rolled around, and I had Thanksgiving dinner at Mama's while Jack went to his son's in Chamblee. The next day, I cooked a legal feast at home for Jack, who appreciated good food as much as any man I'd ever met.

Then, as I was finally lying down to watch TV in my room after our feast, the phone rang, and everything changed.

"Hi, Mama," Haley gushed. "Guess what? I'm getting married, and we're all coming to your house for Christmas to have the wedding. Don't worry, though. We both want it really small, just the families. His name is Mark, and he's a lawyer."

Forty-one

Jack

Jack had never had it so good in his life, and he made sure Cassie knew it. First and foremost, he was feeling human again, thanks to her mold-free house and her cooking, cleaning, and laundering. Second, she kept to their agreement far better than he'd expected. Now that they were together so much, she didn't chatter the way she had at the doctor's office.

And speaking of the doctor's office, Jack wished he'd had a camera when Cassie had showed them her new insurance card that listed her as Cassandra Jones Wilson. Standing behind her, he'd eyed the shocked receptionist. "That's confidential information," he'd warned, "and if one word of it gets out, I'll sue for HIPPA violation."

The receptionist had nodded, her chin lengthening behind clamped lips.

Apparently the warning worked, because the doctor and his nurse both waited till each of them was in respective exam rooms to congratulate them individually in whispers.

As for his kids, he'd simply told them he'd found a room in a safe place to live, then resumed their relationships as they'd been before he moved.

Thanksgiving dinner at his son's was okay, at best. Charlene couldn't cook for squat, so it was easy for Jack to stick to his diet, eating only the turkey and canned green beans. He told them he was having dinner the next day with Cassie, and they accepted it without question.

A Christmas dinner with Cassie at his son's would be the next step. At least they knew he was seeing her, which should ease the way when he finally had to tell them they were married.

Jack definitely didn't look forward to that. His kids critiqued his life enough, already. This would probably send them beyond the pale.

But as it happened, the day of reckoning came sooner than he'd wanted.

The afternoon of Cassie's post-Thanksgiving feast, he was still digesting the turkey, gluten-free gravy, fresh pole beans, mashed red potatoes, low-carb homemade cranberry sauce, and sugarless apricot soufflé Cassie had served him at two. For the record, it is absolutely true that the way to a man's heart is through his stomach, but there are limits, even to that. So Jack left his room at halftime for some cold springwater and a couple of Tums from the kitchen drawer Cassie kept stocked with over-the-counter remedies.

But when he got to the kitchen, he found her at the breakfast table with her head in her hands. "Cassie? What's wrong?"

She looked up, and to his relief, she hadn't been crying. She just looked deeply troubled. "The jig is up. I just got a call from Haley. She's coming for Christmas to get married, and she invited Tommy and his family to stay here, too."

"Uh-oh. Guess I'd better go to a hotel."

Cassie sighed in exasperation. "Hotels are full of mold, and you know it. And anyway, I have no idea how long Haley's planning to stay. When I asked for particulars, she said she'd quit her waitress job so she would have time to get the wedding together, but she didn't give me any dates."

To Jack's surprise, Cassie started leaking tears. "Her father was supposed to walk her down the aisle."

Grief and weddings were a potent combination, and definitely out of Jack's purlieu. But he couldn't stand to see Cassie so wounded, so he crossed to pat her shoulder, referring to condition one. "Welcome?"

Cassie dropped her face into her hands again and sobbed out, "Very welcome."

Jack pulled up a chair and put his arm around her shoulders. In his experience, there was no point in reasoning with a crying woman or trying to offer solutions. The best thing to do was simply hold them and say the magic words: "It's going to be okay, Cassie. We'll get you through this."

Of course, if you do that, they're liable to fall apart completely, which is what Cassie did. She leaned against his shoulder and wailed, "No it's not. Tom's dead, and Haley's getting married without him, to somebody I never even heard of." Like mother, like daughter? "It's never going to be okay."

Jack just held on and let her cry it out, stroking her hair with his free hand. "Yes it will," he murmured. "You're going to get through this." How often he had consoled his own daughters this way when they were dating.

Even though Cassie had been holed up alone in this house for a year before he came into the picture, she obviously had more griev-ing to do. Jack was glad he could be there for her. She'd done so much for him. And it had to be hard, forced to marry somebody she barely knew, even though they got along amazingly well, all things considered. She was much quieter on her own turf.

But she was definitely a crier.

Eventually, her sobs subsided into childlike gasps. She gripped his Hawaiian shirt. "How am I going to tell the kids?"

Now it was time for solutions. "Simply. Honestly. And defi-nitely by e-mail, not phone."

"They'll just call and yell at me," she said, her voice thick from crying.

"Then ask them not to in your e-mail. Ask them to wait for at least twenty-four hours and try to see things your way before they call you."

She nodded against his shoulder. "Good idea."

Suddenly, the contact between them went awkward. They both drew back to their separate spaces at the same time.

Cassie wiped her eyes. "Thanks so much, Jack. It's really nice to have somebody to hug me when I need it."

"Any time." Jack decided he should probably follow his own advice and e-mail his kids with the news, too. "I might need a hug, myself, after I tell mine."

Cassie laughed and headed to the fridge for a springwater. "Who'd have ever thought the two of us would end up where we are?"

"While you're up," Jack said, "would you mind tossing me the Tums? That dinner was amazing, but I overate."

Cassie opened the drugstore drawer and obliged. "The best part is, we have leftovers. Screw the rotation. It's Thanksgiving."

"Amen to that, sister." Jack poured a handful of Tums into his palm.

"Whoa, whoa, whoa," Cassie said, lifting a staying hand. "Those have sugar in them. Try a couple, first."

"Do they make them without sugar?" Two Tums were a mere drop in the bucket after he'd eaten so much.

"Why don't you go online and see?" she suggested. "I'm going to write my kids and tell them that I've married a semiretired English lit professor I met in the doctor's office." She shot him a wry glance. "Think that'll satisfy them?"

"Tommy, maybe. Haley, probably not. Women always want the details."

She pointed her water bottle at him. "That's a bald generalization and a sexist remark, you know."

"Absolutely. But it's true."

"Change the 'always' to 'usually,' and I'll agree."

"Usually, then." He stood. "You're not going to try to make me politically correct, are you? Because it's not going to work."

"How well I know. But I reserve the right to call you on it when you say stuff like that."

At least she was smiling when she said it.

"Fair enough." He turned back toward his room. "I'm going back to my game."

"And I'm going to my computer to write the kids." She followed him through the living room, then headed for the master with a parting, "Don't forget about the sugar-free Tums."

"I won't." When he opened the door to his room, Juliette leaped up and came over for a lean and a scratch. Then he took his laptop into bed with him and wrote the kids during the commercials.

By the end of the game, he'd finished:

*Dear kids: Guess what? I have just married a very nice
lady named Cassie Jones who is a great (diet) cook and lives in
a mold-remediated house in Garden Hills. We are good friends.*

He hadn't realized that was true till he'd written it, but they
had become friends, and it felt good. Very good. Despite her femi-
nist noises, Cassie accepted him as he was, which was more than
he could say about the other women of his life. Of course, he *had*
cleaned up his act, but that suited him fine, too. It was good to be
surrounded with order and cleanliness.

Still, the terms of his and Cassie's relationship were none of the
kids' business, but he didn't want to misrepresent things, hence his
reference to friendship.

*We have the same medical condition, so it works out very
well for both of us. She is keeping her name, and I am keeping
mine. She has a son in Charlotte and a daughter from New
Orleans who's getting married here this Christmas, so we will
be very busy over the holidays. Please don't call me about this,
as it is done and I am happy and feeling much better, now that
I don't have one foot in the grave and the other on a banana
peel. I hope all your Christmases will be blessed.*
    Love,
    Papa

In the "to" slot, he selected *groups*, then *FAMILY*, then hit the
send button. He'd just logged out and turned off the computer and
his cell phone when he heard a tentative knock on his door.

Jack stood, awkward with the idea of lolling in bed in front of

Cassie, even though he was fully clothed. Juliette immediately got up to lean against his good leg. "Come in."

Cassie opened the door and shot a baleful glance at the pig. "Traitor." Then she lifted a printout. "Do you mind if I run this by you first, before I send it to the kids? I waited till the game was over."

"Read away."

" 'Dear Tommy and Haley: Guess what? I met a very nice man at the doctor's office who has the same condition I do, and we got married. He is a semiretired literature professor who has great health insurance, and we have become good friends.' " She looked to him for approval. "Is it okay to say that?"

"It's true, isn't it?" he asked. "I think of us as friends."

She smiled, clearly pleased by his response. "Yes, we are."

"Okay, then."

She focused back on the printout. " 'He has two grown sons and two married daughters who live in Chamblee, Orlando, and New Orleans, and five grandchildren.' " She paused to qualify, "I didn't mention your children's names, because I think it would only complicate things if Haley tried to contact your son in New Orleans, and I know she would."

"Wise," Jack ruled, his earlier assessment of women confirmed by Cassie's more detailed account. "Go on."

" 'Things are working out very well for us, but I'd appreciate your waiting until you've had time to digest this before you call me about it. I love you both almost as much as I love your daddy. That will never change.' " She looked to Jack to assess his reaction.

"Take out the 'almost,' " he said.

She scratched it out, then added a few more words and read, " 'I

319

love you both as much as I will always love your daddy. That will never change.' "

Jack nodded in approval. "Good ending." He wasn't trying to replace Tom, and never would. "Good job. That it?"

" 'Love, Mama,' " Cassie concluded with obvious relief.

Jack walked over with his arm out to hug her shoulders. "Welcome?"

Cassie nodded, a new peace in her eyes. "Welcome."

He gave her a brief squeeze and a parting pat on the arm. "I said almost the same thing, only mine was shorter."

"Figures."

"That's sexist," he teased.

"Duly noted." Focusing on Juliette, Cassie patted her thigh. "Come on, you traitor. Back to Mama."

The pig regarded them both, then gave Jack's leg one last lean before she followed Cassie back to the master bedroom. As Cassie closed the door behind them, he heard her say, "You're gonna end up pork chops if you don't give me a little affection, at least."

Jack smiled and flopped back onto the bed, then searched the cable listings for the next game.

Five o'clock and all's well, an imaginary town crier called in his mind.

Well, indeed.

Until Haley arrived two days later with all her earthly goods.

Forty-two

Cassie

To my pleasant surprise, I didn't hear a peep out of the kids about my e-mail bombshell. Maybe they were too shocked. But Jack had just settled down to watch the Tech-Georgia game with me when I heard a car drive up, then a door slam, followed by a clatter toward the kitchen door, then a repetitive thud. I went to see who was there.

"Oh, shoot." My daughter Haley stood there, her back toward the door, loaded down with a motley collection of duffel bags, totes, and shopping bags. "Mommmm!" she called, her hands too full to ring the bell.

I leaped sideways fifteen feet, back into the living room. "It's Haley," I told Jack in a harsh whisper. "What should we do?" Shoot, shoot, shoot!

"Open the door?" he said calmly, with an encouraging nod.

"I'm not prepared for this," I whispered, panicked.

More thumping. "Mommm! Open up!"

Jack shook his head. "Calm down. It's okay."

Not!

He made to rise. "You want me to do it?"

I motioned him back into the black leather wingback recliner. "No. No. I'll go." What I would say, I had no idea. "She might have called," I complained.

Jack chuckled, his calmness contagious. "You asked her not to."

"Oh, yeah." I braced myself and mustered up a welcoming smile. "Okay, then."

I went back to the kitchen and opened the door. "Haley, sweetie. What a pleasant surprise." I grabbed a couple of the closest shopping bags. "Here, let me help you."

Haley stepped inside, regarding the kitchen as a personal affront. "Everything looks different. It doesn't even look like our house."

"The place needed a lot of repairs, so I decided to remodel while they had everything torn up for the mold remediation." I gathered up the baggage she'd dropped in dismay. "Why don't we just stow these in the laundry room till we've had a chance to sort things out?" I didn't want them contaminating everything, but that could wait for later.

Scowling, Haley took in the new décor, opening a couple of drawers to see what was inside. "Nothing's where it used to be."

"I figured I might as well reorganize. I had to get rid of a lot of things."

She glared at me. "Yeah, like all my stuff. Which is still in boxes that take up my entire apartment, I might add."

Saving that battle for another day, I came over and gave her a hug, but it was like hugging an armful of coat hangers. Haley remained rigid and aloof, confirming my fears about her reaction. "Would you like to meet Jack?"

Her deadly expression said no, but she shrugged. "I guess I might as well."

"We were just about to watch the game." I kept my arm around Haley's shoulder and led her into the living room, where Jack was standing, ready.

"Jack, this is my daughter Haley. Haley, this is Jack." I didn't call him my husband. No sense rubbing salt into the wound.

Jack shook her hand, making direct eye contact. "You're even prettier than your pictures."

She arched a dark brow, suddenly looking just like her father when somebody said something unacceptable in a lady's presence. It took me aback.

Jack noted my expression and came to the rescue. "Cassie and I were just about to have some turkey lettuce wraps and taro chips. Are you hungry? They're really good."

At last, Haley yielded a bit. "I'm starved."

"These are great," I told her. "Low carb, with low-carb mayo and cranberry sauce I made myself." I headed for the kitchen, and the two of them followed with a calculated distance between.

Give her time, Jack's expression told me. *You're doing fine.*

"Can I still stay here?" Haley asked as she plopped into the banquette in the breakfast nook. "Or have you converted my room into something else?"

Ah, yes. The sarcasm.

"Your room is still your room," Jack said equably. "But Tommy's out of luck. His room is now my room, and I'm staying put."

I straightened in surprise, my jaw dropping behind closed lips. So much for subtlety.

Haley was just as surprised as I was. "You don't . . ." She looked to me as I busied myself getting out the ingredients for the lettuce wraps. "Y'all have separate rooms?"

I smiled. "I told you, sweetie. We're friends."

323

I could see Haley's mind spinning a mile a minute. "Then why did you get *married*?"

I allowed myself a sigh. "Did you even read my e-mail?" I started peeling off whole lettuce leaves from the outside of the head.

"Yes. Well, yes and no," Haley confessed. "After the first part, I just went into shock."

Jack smiled and came to my rescue. "Your mother and I have the same condition. I needed a safe place to live and she needed better health insurance, so this seemed the most logical solution. I was dying, with no other place to go."

"That he was," I added, touched that he would bare himself that way to help me out.

"But you were dating other people," Haley protested to me.

Jack and I chuckled in unison. "I'll tell you about that fiasco later," I said, spreading my homemade version of low-carb Miracle Whip inside the lettuce leaves.

It seemed the perfect time to turn the tables. "Speaking of dating, why haven't I heard anything about this lawyer of yours?"

Haley colored, shifting in her seat. "Well, it all happened sort of suddenly."

Jack and I looked at each other and laughed.

"Been there, done that," he said, defusing the moment, God bless him.

I weighed my words carefully to keep the questions nonjudgmental. "How did you meet?"

"He was one of the angels for the theater group I was working with. We met at a fund-raiser two months ago."

Uh-oh. *Young* lawyers couldn't afford to be angels. But I took it slow and easy. "Is he from New Orleans?"

Haley shifted in her seat, clearly holding something back. "No. Actually, he's from Conyers. His parents still live there. That's why we decided to get married here."

"That makes sense." I started slicing strips of turkey to put into the center of the roll-ups.

Haley began to relax a little. "His dad's retired from GM, so they don't have a lot of money. That's why we want to keep it small. That, and . . ." She frowned over at me.

"He's been married before?" *Please, Lord, let her say no.*

Haley let out a sigh, her posture defensive. "Yeah. But she was a real witch about the divorce. Took the kids and moved back to Conyers, so he could hardly ever see them."

Oh, no. The plot thickens.

Jack shot me a warning glance, but I couldn't help myself. "How old is he, sweetie?"

Haley squirmed. "Old enough to know who he is, which is more than I can say for the men my age."

"And how old would that be?" Please tell me she's not looking for another father figure, now that hers is gone.

Haley did a slow inhale, then blurted out, "Forty. Only eleven years older. But I really don't see how that matters."

"Only when you're older," I said, trying desperately not to judge her situation by my own prejudices. I topped the turkey with a dollop of cranberry sauce made with agave nectar, then rolled the first leaf into a cylinder and secured it with a toothpick.

Finally, Jack chimed in with, "So, have y'all picked a date?"

Haley's expression shouted *none of your business*, but her taut answer at least bordered on civility. "December twenty-ninth."

Whoa. How many days did that leave? "Goodness. I guess you'll be pretty busy between then and now." At least the house was clean. I finished another roll-up, then put some taro chips on her plate and handed it over. "Here you go."

Haley regarded me, and her plate, with suspicion. "You're not going to try to stop me?"

I kept filling and rolling. "Nope. But I do have one request, and it's a request, not a demand, but it's a very important one." *Please, Lord, God of truth, let her do it, and let her see the truth.*

Haley clearly didn't want to know what I was going to ask of her, so she took a bite of her roll-up, then said with her mouth full, "Wow. This is really good."

Jack leaned over for a better look at my preparations. "Your mother is the best cook I ever tasted." He sneaked a piece of turkey.

"Ahh-ahh." I lightly smacked his hand with the flat of the knife, struck by how *marital* the whole vignette seemed.

I finished our plates, then served us all artificially sweetened iced tea and sat with both of them in the breakfast nook, Jack on one side, Haley and I on the other.

"What's his name?" Jack asked.

"Marcus Macomber Williams, Esquire," Haley said with pride. "He's a defense attorney, and a great one. He's just taken a great job with King and Spalding, downtown, so we're moving back here. He's out looking at condos to rent till his place in New Orleans sells, even as we speak."

Without her?

Oh-kay. "Haley Williams sounds very nice," I said.

"Oh, I'm not taking his name," she said as if the mere suggestion were absurd.

Uh-hunh. Shift the subject to something less controversial. "So, have you thought about what you want to wear?" Haley definitely wasn't the white-gown-and-veil type.

She grinned (finally!). "I already have it. Red peau de soie, very demure Jackie Kennedy in front, very Dior, but with a really low back."

I nodded. Very Haley.

"Our costume designer made it for me to wear to the gala where Mark and I first met."

I'd long since abandoned any hopes of being the mother of a traditional bride. Frankly, I was surprised she'd chosen to marry at all. At seventeen, she'd told Tom and me that she didn't believe in our "stuffy" views about premarital sex, or marriage in general, and her subsequent behavior backed that up. My only consolation was that she'd promised to practice so-called safe sex.

Better she should wear red than black to her wedding. "Red's your best color," I told her, "and very festive for the holidays."

Jack's only comment was an arched brow.

I wondered what the groom's parents would think when Haley walked down the aisle (or wherever) wearing scarlet. Probably that she was a total hussy, but what are you going to do? Haley wasn't a kid; she was twenty-nine and her own woman.

That didn't mean she wasn't about to make a horrendous mistake, but I'd deal with that later.

"Flowers?" I asked.

Haley began to warm up at last. "Just a bunch of daisies with a red ribbon, if I can get them."

"Nice. Simple." Cheap, thank goodness. "I'm sure we can order some."

"Where were you thinking of having the ceremony?" Jack asked.

Haley looked past me to the living room. "Well, I'd thought of having it here, but everything looks so different. So . . . plain."

"I like to think of it as simple and elegant, like your mother," Jack commented, and it felt good to have him come to my defense. "The most important thing is," he went on, "your mom's feeling better now." He aimed a challenging glance at my daughter. "Did you have any idea how very sick she was this summer after she took those treatments?"

Haley straightened, defensive. "Mama's never been healthy."

It stung, being dismissed that way.

"Your mother was dying until she found Dr. Patel," Jack said evenly, "who finally diagnosed what was wrong with her all those years."

He paused to let that sink in. When Haley reacted with skepticism, he added, "You came mighty close to being an orphan."

Haley looked to me, still unconvinced. "Is that true?"

"According to the doctor, yes. But the important thing now is that I'm better."

I could tell she didn't buy any of it, but I was content enough, just knowing it was true. And having Jack as an ally.

I went back to the wedding. "How many people were you planning to ask?"

"Counting us and y'all," Haley said, casting a disparaging look at Jack, "and Tommy's family, it would be twenty-one."

Jack being the odd man out, in more ways than one. I almost laughed.

Amazing, how calm I felt simply because he was there, so I wasn't facing this alone. "I know the house looks different, but we have plenty of room for that many here," I offered, grateful to God that I felt well enough to take on something that momentous.

"I'll talk to Mark," she said, as if he would have any input. Haley got up and took her plate to the sink, then rinsed it and put it into the dishwasher, maybe for the first time in her life. Usually, she just left her messes for me to clean up.

I watched in amazement, but just as I was about to comment, I felt Jack's hand on my forearm. He shook his head with a wry smile, so I held my piece.

Haley came back and took our empty plates. "I'll clean up in here." She aimed a pointed look at Jack. "Why don't you go watch the game?"

"Good idea." Jack rose and left in record time for a one-legged man.

Haley closed the swinging kitchen door. "What happened to his leg?" she asked in a stage whisper.

I shook my head. "Some sort of accident. He doesn't like to talk about it."

Haley shrugged, her tone reverting to normal. "What was it you wanted me to do?"

I braced myself and hoped for the best. "All I want is for you at least to talk to Mark's ex-wife before you marry him."

Haley looked at me as if I'd asked her to strip naked and run down Peachtree Road. "What? That's crazy."

If I had a nickel for every divorcée who'd told me she wished she'd talked to her boyfriend's ex before she'd married him, I'd be a wealthy woman. "If Mark is the man you think he is, it won't make a difference," I told her. "But if he's not—and his ex isn't the witch-bitch he told you she was—wouldn't you rather find out before the wedding than after?"

"But she *is*. She took the kids—"

"So Mark told you, but trust me, there are two sides to every

329

story. Don't you want to know both sides before you make this final?"

Such hostility she sent my way. "Mama, she probably wouldn't even want to talk to me. Or she'd spend the whole time slandering him."

"You won't know until you find out." I took her hands in mine. "I have complete confidence in your ability to evaluate the situation."

She looked away, clearly resentful and noncompliant.

"If your daddy were here," I said softly, "he'd be able to size Mark up with one good conversation, but he's not."

Haley turned a sidelong glance my way, her eyes welling, causing mine to do the same.

"Dear Lord, how I wish he were here." I tightened my grip on her hands. "Do you believe I love you? That I only want the best for you?"

Haley's gaze dropped. "Sure."

"Then do this thing, but not for me. Do it for yourself, your own happiness."

My daughter was clearly exasperated, but I could tell she was thinking about it. "Oh, all right. I'll try. But she still may not see me."

"Do you know how to get in touch with her?"

Haley cocked her mouth to the side. "No."

I got out the metro residential directory. "What's her name?"

"Cynthia Williams."

I looked it up, and there it was, in Conyers. I wrote the number on my scratch pad, then tore it off and gave it to Haley. "If this isn't the same Cynthia Williams, let me know, and Jack can track her down on the Internet."

Haley took it with obvious reservations. "This is going to be *so* embarrassing."

"You don't know that," I said, giving her back a pat. "I'm proud of you for being so sensible."

Haley tucked the number into her hoodie. "I'm going to unpack first."

"Well, actually," I said, "I need to wash everything in mold killer and wipe down the rest before you bring them into the house."

She frowned. "Isn't that a bit *extreme?*"

"Nope." I kept my tone light. "It's what I have to do to stay well, so I'm going to do it."

Haley rolled her eyes as if she were fourteen instead of twenty-nine. "*What*-ever."

Forty-three

Jack

Jack waited till he heard Cassie in the kitchen before he ventured out of his room. He knew from his own daughters' nuptials that the whole Haley/estrogen/wedding thing was dangerous territory, compounded by the complications with the groom's age and history.

Fortunately, he hadn't heard a peep out of Haley's room since he woke up and went to shave.

When he dressed, he put a thick sock on his artificial foot as well as his real one, to keep from waking the dragon daughter.

When he got to the kitchen it wasn't ten yet, but he poured himself a cup of coffee, then sat and asked a silent, drawn Cassie, "So, how did it go after I left?"

She glanced at the clock. Nine-thirty. Then she shot him a brief look of gratitude. "I don't know. Well enough, I guess. I got her to promise to talk to his ex before she goes any further with this."

Jack shook his head. His own ex thought he was the worst husband in the world, when in fact, he was just not *her* idea of a good husband, meaning perfect. "You think that's going to help?"

Cassie got up and started breakfast by cracking six eggs into the frying pan. "I think Haley's intelligent enough to assess the situation accurately." She put the bacon into the microwave, then punched the minute button four times.

He liked the way she did the bacon. It came out crisp, but not hard, and most of the fat went into the garbage with the paper towels. Thanks to her cooking, he'd already lost six pounds without even trying or feeling the slightest bit deprived. Maybe there was something to this high-protein, low-carb thing.

As for having Haley talk to her fiancé's ex, Jack didn't comment, because Cassie wouldn't like what he was thinking.

She poured them both some diet cranberry juice. "I know what you're thinking, that his ex's opinion of him is probably way too subjective to mean anything."

The long way to say "wrong."

Jack focused on his coffee. "Mmmm."

He wasn't sure when they'd fallen into being able to read each other, but they had. Still, the last thing he wanted for breakfast was a disagreement, so he kept mum.

Cassie went on without him. "I just think every woman who marries a divorced man should talk to his ex. There are always two sides to every story. Ditto for a man who marries a divorced woman. He should talk to the ex, too."

Before he could stop himself, Jack said, "You didn't talk to mine."

Cassie plated up the eggs and bacon. "Actually, I did."

What?

Jack watched her cross the kitchen to set their plates on the table, then sit facing him.

She bowed her head. "Would you please bless it?"

"No," he said, indignant. "Not till you explain yourself." He jerked his napkin open across his lap. "How in blazes did you find my ex? And when were you planning to tell me?"

Cassie glanced up at him with a condescending expression, then bowed her head and said, "Lord, thank you for this food and all your many blessings. Please help Haley to make the right decision. Amen."

"You didn't answer my question," he scolded.

"Questions, plural," she corrected, then took a bite of eggs. As usual, they were perfect over-medium.

"How did you find her?" he repeated.

"Easy." Cassie took a sip of juice. "I just called and asked your daughter Jeannie."

"*Before* we got married? Jeannie didn't tell me anything about that."

Cassie took a sip of coffee. "I made up a name and said I was an old friend from school who wanted to get back in touch."

"You lied?" Jack had always thought of Cassie as a total Goody Two-shoes, by-the-book prude.

She met his gaze straight on. "Oh, absolutely," she said, unruffled. "It wasn't any of your daughter's business, and I certainly didn't want to start some big brouhaha."

"And what, pray tell, did you tell Millie?" It felt weird, even saying his ex's name.

"Her, I told the truth: that I was considering seeing you, but I wanted to get her opinion first."

It galled the schmoo out of Jack to think of his ex doing a hatchet job on him, which he knew she must have. "And what did she tell you?"

Cassie remained placid. "Nothing I didn't already know."

Blast. She was going to make him drag it out of her. "Like what?"

"That you always had your nose in a book, instead of relating to the people around you. That you were a male chauvinist slob who expected her to wait on you, hand and foot, without ever saying thank you."

"I said thank you." He had! Well, sometimes. But he had made the money so Millie could stay home. Wasn't it her job to take care of the family? You shouldn't have to thank people constantly for doing their jobs. Lord knew, nobody ever thanked him, including Millie.

"She also said you worked too much and didn't know how to have fun." Cassie seemed to be enjoying this way too much. "That you were a prude and a total loner, oblivious to the effect your behavior had on those close to you. Et cetera, et cetera."

He'd heard Millie's version a hundred times before the divorce. Never mind that he'd tried to include her in the things he enjoyed, but she'd preferred to gamble or go on cruises where she could gamble—spending his hard-earned money that should have gone to the kids. But she was still the mother of his children, so he didn't mention the gambling to anyone, not even Cassie.

"So, why did you marry me, then?" he had to ask Cassie.

"Because I don't care if your nose is always in a book, and you're not a slob around here. We covered that in the agreement. And because, in the past twenty years, I think you've figured out how to have good, clean fun." She pointed her fork at him. "Except for the boob jokes, of course, but as long as you don't impose them on me, it isn't a problem."

Jack shifted in his seat, angry despite the fact that Cassie obviously hadn't been negatively affected by his ex's character assassination. Never mind that some of it had been accurate.

Cassie sized up his reaction, shaking her head. "Now, there's no cause for you to get your knickers in a knot. It was obvious that the two of you weren't suited for each other. And I wasn't looking for a soul mate; I was looking for a housemate, so what she said didn't worry me. What I knew of you was more important."

"And what was that?" he asked.

"That you're capable of compassion."

How would she know?

Cassie went on. "As far as the Stepford wife part, as long as you abide by our agreement, I don't mind taking care of you one bit. It makes me feel useful. I always enjoyed taking care of my family."

After all his sick, sorry years alone, it was nice having a real home and somebody to look after him. "I do appreciate what you do for me."

"I know. That's essential," she told him.

"What else do you know about me?" he asked, frankly fishing.

"That you're intelligent, with a sharp wit."

It had always been enough for him to know that, but for some reason, it pleased him to hear her say it.

She continued without prompting, "And it's okay that you're a loner with your nose in a book, because that way, we don't stay tangled up in each other's *stuff.*"

A good point. "Anything else?"

Cassie smiled. "And last, but by no means least, I married you because you were as far up the creek as I was without a paddle, thanks to the same condition, so we'd be on the same regimen and benefit equally from the arrangement."

Appeased, he focused on his eggs and bacon, appreciating the fact that he didn't have to say any more, and she'd be okay with it.

They finished eating in companionable silence. He was just

about to pour his third cup of coffee when she asked him, "And why did you marry me?"

"Like I told you: I needed a safe place to live, and pronto."

She arched her brows, leaning back and circling her cup with both hands. "And that was it?"

He felt he owed her honesty, at least. "Look, I don't want to hurt your feelings, but it's not like I had other options. You were it."

She let out a short sigh. "Ditto. Divine irony, of the worst kind. God did this to both of us, you know."

He couldn't help smiling. "I figured. But the nice thing is, we're not doing so badly, are we?"

She peered at him in assessment, a slight smile on her lips. "Not bad at all."

"Okay, then." He stood, taking both plates, then putting them in the dishwasher. "I'm going to go out to check on the farm. Then I'll probably drop by the library at school." Anything to kill time. He didn't want to get stuck in the middle. "Be back around five."

"You don't have to leave just because Haley's here," she said.

"I know. See you at five." He didn't like being displaced, but he disliked drama even more, so he was out of there.

Forty-four

Cassie

Haley didn't get up till almost eleven. When I heard her turn on the shower, I headed for the kitchen to make her favorite: silver-dollar pancakes.

Ten minutes later, she came in wearing her robe and toweling her thick, dark hair. "Hey."

"Hey, yourself." I stirred the pancake batter, praying for strength not to eat them once they were done. "How about some silver-dollar pancakes?"

She shook her head no, yawning hugely. "I don't do breakfast anymore. Any coffee?"

"I thought you drank tea." I set down the bowl.

Haley shook her head, finger-combing her hair. "Nope. Switched to coffee when I started working at night."

I started a fresh pot. "Do you like working with the theater?"

"Love it, but the funding crisis is as bad with us as with the rest of the arts. Good thing Mark and his lawyer friends stepped up, or the theater group would have had to fold six months ago."

She went to the fridge and poured herself a glass of diet cranberry juice. "I hated waiting tables, though. So many drunks, and every one of them thought they had the right to touch me for the price of a tip." She shuddered. "I certainly won't miss that."

So much for her degree in theater arts. "I'm so sorry you had to endure that, honey."

She shrugged. "Paid the rent." I handed her the cup of coffee. "But no more," she went on. "After I marry Mark, I'm going for my master's, then Ph.D., so I can teach."

Not "after we get married," but "after I marry Mark." Or was I just splitting hairs? "Sounds like a good goal."

"He already has two kids," Haley said, loosening up, "but he said I could have one if I wanted."

Again, it sounded like a solitary option, as if the baby would be hers alone, not his.

The next question came out completely on its own. "Did you have a chance to set up that meeting with his ex?"

"Mama, I haven't even finished my coffee," she complained.

Don't push her. She'll only balk. "Sorry. I'm just anxious to hear the results."

"It's not like you called *Jack's* ex before you married him," she accused.

"Actually, I did. So there."

Haley looked at me with a mixture of surprise and curiosity. "So, what did she say? Tell, tell."

Perfect. I smiled. "Only after you tell me what yours says. Deal?"

Haley frowned. "That's dirty pool."

"I think it's perfectly fair." My daughter was nothing, if not curious.

"Oh, all right," she grumbled. "But only if you tell me the whole truth and nothing but the truth, so help you God."

"Ditto. Deal?"

She sighed. "Deal." She got up and took her coffee back to her room, calling over her shoulder, "I'm going to call her and set things up on my cell."

I closed my eyes. *Thank you, Lord, for making a way where there was no way. And please let her know if this is a mistake.*

Forty-five

Jack

All the way back out to the farm in his newly clean truck, Jack couldn't keep from contrasting his old life and his life with Cassie.

He'd always thought his independence was the most important thing, but there was definitely something to be said for having someone provide a clean, welcoming home. Someone who accepted him as he was and took good care of him.

He'd never felt the peace he felt at Cassie's when he was married to Millie. Maybe because Millie had kept complaining, day in and day out, and never given him any credit.

Grumpy, Jack exited I-400, then headed cross-country toward the farm. He'd missed his garden. But when he finally pulled into the dented carport, the neglect and debris he'd left behind struck him afresh.

How could he ever have wanted to live like this? *Why* had he ever let himself live like this?

And in that instant, he didn't care about a blasted thing in the whole place.

Not the tractors or tools in the barn, or the collectibles nobody wanted, or the moldy books he'd amassed. None of it mattered.

What mattered was that he hadn't been the father or the husband he should have. Millie was past history, and good riddance, but the kids were another matter. Now that he had the peace and safe haven of Cassie's, he could be a better father.

A better friend to Cassie.

Jack looked at the farm and knew he didn't want to come back. He pulled his cell phone out of his pocket and dialed Frances. She answered on the second ring. "Hey, lady. It's Jack. How would you like to rent my whole farm for pasture, and the house for your groom?"

"I thought I was still going to get some vegetables," Frances complained.

"You will, if you let your groom work the garden. It'll grow anything if you water it."

"How much you want?"

"What will you pay?"

Frances considered for less than a minute. "A thousand a month, and not one penny more."

"Deal. I'll send you the papers." He remembered one thing just in time. "Only one condition. If I die, all bets are off. You'll have to deal with my kids."

"That sounds reasonable." She let out a dry chuckle. "Who'da thunk it? You, settling down in Buckhead with the raccoon lady."

"And a lady she is, my friend," he admitted to both of them, "the genuine article."

"I could tell for myself," she scolded. "Don't be a stranger, now."

"I'll come take you to lunch at the diner every now and then," he promised.

"See that you do." Frances snorted. "Now git back to Buckhead, before I start blubberin'."

Jack hung up, then gazed at the dry, cold acres around him. "Good-bye."

He was actually looking forward to going home.

Forty-six

Cassie

Jack had been gone for two hours when Haley returned to the kitchen for more coffee, looking pensive.

"What's up?" I asked, pretending to be nonchalant as I refilled her mug.

"She said she'd be happy to talk to me."

So the ex was game. Good for her. "When?"

"We're meeting for a late lunch at a restaurant in Conyers."

"Neutral territory. That sounds promising."

"*Today.*" Haley held her mug with both hands, peering into the garden without focus.

There in the warmth of the kitchen, woman to woman, I sensed a softening of the barrier she'd put between us.

She gave a slight sigh, the way she used to when she was little, then looked to me, serious and grown. "Now I don't know what to say."

"Just tell her you're seeing Mark, and you'd like to know what happened between them, if she doesn't mind talking about it."

"The thing is, I haven't really asked Mark what happened,

either. I mean, he griped that she'd moved the kids away from him, but I never pursued it."

"Sounds like you and Mark are overdue a conversation, then. But that can wait. I think it's smart to talk to his ex first. Then you'll know what to ask him."

She turned sideways in the banquette, then drew her knees up close. "What if I don't like what I hear?"

I crossed to stroke her hair, wishing there was some way I could spare her from the hard realities of her relationship, but knowing I couldn't. "I'm really proud of you for having the courage to do this." I placed my hands on her shoulders in solidarity.

Her right hand covered mine. "It's never simple, is it?"

"No. But it's worth the risk, loving someone." We sat there in a brief bubble of communion, mother-daughter, woman to woman, and it was good.

Then the bubble burst. "Do you love Jack?"

I laughed before I could catch myself. "No, but I like him very much. That's enough. We don't interfere with each other's lives, and we get along just fine."

"I still can't believe you actually *married* him," she said, "without even warning us. Tommy is still in shock."

"He'll get over it." I looked at the clock and changed the subject. It was almost noon. "What time are you supposed to be there?"

"One thirty."

"Then you'd better get hustling. It's quite a ways to Conyers."

Haley slid out of the banquette and stood. "I know." She surprised me with a long hug, her head on my shoulder. I could feel the fear in her embrace.

"Do you want me to go with you? I could wait in the car."

She sniffed, then drew back. "Gosh, no. I'm a big girl, Mama, or I wouldn't be doing this."

I smiled into her lovely face with pride. "Yes, you are." Then I swatted her tush. "Now scoot."

She left half an hour later and hadn't been gone but a few minutes when Jack came back looking smug about something.

"That was quick," I told him. "I thought you were going to be gone all day."

"Plans changed," he said. He went to the fridge for a bottled water, his damp sneakers squeaking on the wood floors. He'd taken to wearing real shoes lately, even on his running foot.

Jack sat down, then announced, "I made a decision. I've rented the whole farm to Frances for pasture, and the house for her groom. She's paying me a thousand a month, which will definitely help with the medical stuff."

"Won't you miss being there?" I asked him.

"Nope. I talked to the Fulton County extension office and signed up for their master gardener service. Between that and teaching and reading, I'll be plenty busy."

I nodded to the mess where my garden had been out back. "I could use your services right here, if that's okay with you. Between Juliette and the foundation work, my backyard has seen better days."

Jack nodded, taking it in. "Sure. If you had that oak in the corner taken out, there would be enough sun for a vegetable garden."

"How much would that set me back?" I asked.

"I know a guy in Cumming who could come down and do it for three hundred, if we give him the wood."

"Bonded and insured?"

"Not for three hundred. If you want bonded and insured, it'll cost you three thousand."

349

"Well worth it," I argued, "if the tree gets loose and falls on the house or the garage."

Jack grinned. "It won't. He'll top it out, then lower the branches and trunk segments to his helper below. I've seen him do it a dozen times without a single slip."

"I'll have to think about it."

"Well, don't think too long," he said. "We need to get the stump out clean so I can level the plot and start tilling in the soil amendments as soon as possible so they can leach out over the winter." He smiled. "I'll have to bring my tiller from the farm. The one that works," he qualified.

It was the first time I had seen Jack really happy, and that made me feel good. "Just as long as you don't mess with my hydrangeas and camellias or my gardenias."

He shook his head, looking like an impish little boy. "I won't mess with those, but the abelias will definitely have to go."

"Why?"

"Because they're a waste of space. Gobble up plant food, and only put out those wispy little flowers you can't even see. I can't stand 'em."

He was definitely going to enjoy this project. And thanks to his health insurance, I could afford to have the tree taken out.

But I didn't want to make it too easy for him, or he'd never feel that he'd won out over me—very important to his male ego. "I don't know. I don't want everything all torn up."

"You've got to break a few eggs to make a cake," he said.

Good. That gave him something to do.

Now, if I could just get Haley to delay her wedding . . .

Forty-seven

Cassie

Jack was out measuring the backyard for his garden plan and I was cooking dinner when Haley came back and hurried past me with a brief "Hi," then holed up in her room. I'd tried to read her expression as she went by, but she didn't look upset. She seemed to be concentrating, more than anything else, which I took as a good sign.

So I shoved my raging curiosity back down into its sack and tied the top shut. Maybe I'd make some Toll House cookies, her favorites. That always helped her open up. But, then again, it would probably tempt Jack beyond endurance, so I decided against it.

Haley would talk to me when she was ready.

When it started getting dark, Jack came in, nose to his plans and pen still scribbling, and headed for his room.

I nuked the French-cut green beans, then added salt and ghee, topping them off with toasted almond slivers. Then I grilled the chicken breasts I'd marinated in lemon juice, mustard powder, Splenda, and olive oil. When everything was ready, I went back to Haley's door to tell her, but the moment I raised my fist to knock,

351

it swung open to reveal my surprised, but grim, daughter, dressed to the nines.

"Supper's ready," I said.

"Actually, I'm having dinner with Mark." Her expression said she wasn't looking forward to it. "We need to have that talk."

I knew better, but couldn't resist asking, "How did it go this afternoon?"

Haley didn't look me in the eye. "She was very nice. Very forthcoming."

I couldn't help myself. "Any bombshells?"

My daughter faced me squarely. "Actually, no. But I realized there were a lot of things Mark and I haven't talked about that we need to before we get married."

So she hadn't ruled it out. I covered my disappointment with an honest "I'm really proud of you, honey, for being so realistic."

Her face crumpled for just a moment. "Mama, I love him, and I want to get married. I don't want to be realistic."

I gave her a brief hug. "I know, sweetie. I know. But you're a grown-up, and it comes with the territory."

She exhaled heavily as I let go and stepped out of the way, literally and figuratively. "I hope everything goes well. Really, I do."

She nodded. "Thanks. Don't wait up."

I always did, just like Mama waited up for me, but I kept that to myself. After all, she was a grown woman.

I stood in the hall praying after she left. *God, please show her the truth and reveal your will for her in this. I beg you, with a mother's love.*

Then I knocked on Jack's door. "Supper's ready."

"Be right there," came from inside.

I went back to the breakfast nook and sat, wishing, wishing,

wishing that Tom were there to counsel our daughter. It was times like these that I missed him the most.

Jack appeared, rolling up his sleeves. "Smells great, as usual." He sat, his expression as lucid as a little boy's as he looked inside the serving dishes on the table. "Yum."

"Would you please bless it?" I asked.

Jack bowed his head. "Dear Lord, we thank you for this food, and I thank you for the hands that made it. Open our eyes to the needs of those around us so that we can be your hands and heart in this world. And please be with our children, especially Haley as she talks to Mark. Thy will be done, amen."

I've always been a sucker for a man who prays so eloquently, especially when he includes my children. Emotion thickened my voice as I said, "Thanks, Jack. That means a lot to me."

"You're welcome." He took the top off the Corning Ware casserole that held the chicken and got down to business without further ado.

After we finished, he started carrying the dishes to the sink. "Why don't you go put your feet up? You've had a full day."

"Thanks, but I'd rather help. It keeps my mind off Haley."

He took an empty casserole from me. "She'll be fine. Haley's a smart girl. She can figure this out."

"But what if she doesn't?"

"She'll get married and deal with that. Worst case, she'll realize it was a mistake and get a divorce."

"I hate divorce," I admitted. "So does God."

"True, but He gave it to us because of the hardness of men's hearts." Jack rinsed the dishes, then put them into the dishwasher. "Actually, divorce was a protection for women in Mosaic times."

"Oh, right." I handed him the silverware and a glass.

"No, really. Check it out in your study Bible."

"How did you feel when you got divorced?" I countered.

Jack turned off the water and looked me in the eye. "Like a failure, as a husband and a father. But Millie had somebody else, so what was I supposed to do?"

"Fight for her? And your family?"

He didn't seem to take offense. "That battle was long over, and so was the war. I admit, a lot of it was my fault. I knew we were in trouble, but I withdrew into my work and my books. I don't know if it would have made any difference, even if we'd tried counseling. The truth was, we didn't really like each other, and when I tried to get her to stop gambling, she said she hated me."

"Gambling?" I tucked my chin. "This is the first I've heard of any gambling."

"And it'll be the last." Jack rinsed the sink with the sprayer. "I don't bash my ex. Out loud, anyway, even though she has a serious problem. She's still the mother of my kids."

"Definitely two sides to the story," I muttered.

"There was never any peace in our home." Jack put soap in the dishwasher, then closed it and dried his hands. He turned it on, releasing a soft swish. "That's one of the best things about being married to you," he said, facing me. "This home is always a place of peace. And you accept me for who I am."

I was so shocked, I didn't know what to say. A meager "Thanks" came out automatically.

"Want to watch a movie?" He headed for the sofa. "You pick. *It's a Wonderful Life* or *Christmas Vacation*?"

"Oh, definitely *Christmas Vacation*." No matter how many times I saw that movie, it always made me laugh.

We sat on either end of the sofa, just as we'd done at Dr. Patel's.

When the movie was over, I felt better. "Thanks, Jack. That was just what I needed."

He regarded me with an odd expression. "I'm glad you didn't marry any of those yahoos you were dating."

"So am I." Since it seemed to be a night for honest confessions, I added, "I don't know what I was thinking, anyway. It's way too ugly, what happens when I go to bed at night, to think of going to bed with anybody."

"Amen to that," Jack said. He raised his artificial leg. "Aside from the obvious"—he tapped his teeth—"two bridges in a glass by the bed."

I chuckled and topped him with, "Bite guard. I look like an alien."

He smiled and pointed to his nose, "CPAP."

That was a surprise. "I didn't see a CPAP when you moved in."

"I brought it in when you weren't looking," he said. "But don't get all het up. I demolded it right away."

I could top that. I pulled up my Chico's pants to expose my knee-replacement scars. "Road map, times twenty-four."

"You want a road map? That's not a road map." Jack lifted his Hawaiian shirt to reveal a network of jagged scars across his pale pink skin. "I tangled with a combine, the one that took my leg. *That's* a road map."

I don't know what came over me, but I felt compelled to bare my deficiencies. "Oh, yeah? How about stress incontinence?"

Jack pooh-poohed that with a wave of his hand. "Prostate. Can't go when I want to."

"I snore like a chain saw."

"I know. I've heard you," he said, much to my embarrassment.

He topped me with, "Even if I wanted to have sex with somebody, I'm not sure I could, thanks to the blasted blood-pressure medicine."

Whoa. He'd really bared his soul with that one. I decided humor would be the safest way to respond. "So my honor's safe with you," I told him with a smile.

"Maybe. Maybe not." He didn't seem too upset about it.

I leaned back into the sofa. "So here we are, a couple of rejects."

"Yep." He chuckled. "Two misfits who fit just fine."

Then I realized that God had answered my prayer exactly as I had asked it: He'd sent me a good Christian man to marry, one who wouldn't—couldn't—try to replace Tom in my life. One who could protect me and be my friend without making me feel unfaithful to Tom. One who needed my home as much as I needed his health insurance.

Talk about divine irony!

I started laughing and kept on laughing.

"What's so funny?" Jack demanded.

Laughing so hard that tears came to my eyes, I barely managed to get out, "We are."

He considered, then cracked a smile. "I guess we are."

Then Haley walked in.

Forty-eight

Cassie

Haley looked at us with a mixture of embarrassment and confusion. "What's going on?"

I did my best to sober up. "Hi, honey. You had to be there."

"I haven't seen you laugh like that since Daddy died," she said with more than a hint of accusation.

Jack came to my defense. "Aren't you glad to see your mother happy?"

"Of course," Haley backpedaled. "Mama, could I talk to you, please?" She frowned at Jack. "In private?"

"Sure, honey." I stood. "G'night, Jack. It was fun."

He looked from me to my daughter with a smile. "Ditto." He headed for the kitchen as I followed Haley to her room.

She closed the door behind us, then motioned toward the bed. "Sit. Sit."

I sat. "Tell, tell."

"I'm so glad I talked to Mark's ex, and even more glad that I'd done it before I talked to Mark. He really opened up and told me how he'd put his work ahead of his family, and how much he

357

regretted that now. That's why he wanted to move back here, so he could be a real father to his kids." She sat against the pillows. "As for work, he's finally realized that family is more important. He wants to have a baby with me, but I'm not sure I'm ready for that."

Good insight. I nodded, not wanting to interrupt.

"We talked about things we'd never even addressed before, and Mark was completely transparent with me. We discussed visitation and how he'd handle the kids when it came to discipline and respect for me, and he promised to be firm but fair with them, even though we both know they'll try to test things out at first. Frankly, I want to see how he manages with the kids he's already got before we have one ourselves."

"I think that's very wise."

"But Mama, I do love him, and nothing I heard today has changed that. It's only made me face up to what I'm getting into. Mark's wife said they both contributed to the breakup, but the main problem was his putting work first. She's glad he wants to be in their children's lives again, but she's worried that Mark will dump them again. I told her that as long as I had anything to say about it, he wouldn't."

She looked at me with trepidation. "I know you wish I'd fallen for somebody less complicated, but I didn't. You always told me you can't love people in pieces, and I love Mark the way he is, with all his past mistakes. At least he admits them and knows better, now."

Peace and respect welled in my heart, and I knew we'd both gotten God's answer. "Okay then. Tell me what you'd like me to fix for the reception. I want everything to be just perfect."

Haley laughed. "Nothing's perfect, Mama. And nobody, least of all me."

I said a prayer of thanks. "Or me."

She's going to be okay, Tom. And so am I.

I went to tell my new husband and friend about the wedding. But when I got to the kitchen, my heart turned over inside me. "Jack!"

Forty-nine

Jack

On his hands and knees, like a dog. Jack couldn't believe he'd been reduced to this. He crawled across the spotless kitchen floor, then managed to pull himself up onto the banquette, but no sooner had he done so, than he found himself facedown on the breakfast table, arms slack at his sides.

He lifted his head, but got so dizzy, he turned it and lay with his ear to the polished wood for a long time.

This was different, something new. Something that scared the juice out of him.

He heard someone coming, then Cassie cried out, "Jack!" She rushed to his side, grabbing his hand. "What is it?"

He tried to speak, but couldn't.

Not now, God. Not when he was finally happy.

"Jack, stay with me," she said, her voice desperate. He watched her grab the cordless phone on the table and punch in 911. "Oh, God, do *not* put me on hold." He felt a tear fall on his cheek. "Yes, yes, I have an emergency. We need an ambulance at—yes, this is

Cassie Jones—yes, that's the address." She was crying now. "I think my husband's having a stroke or a heart attack!"

"Mama?" Haley called from the living room.

"Haley," Cassie shouted, the phone still tucked to her ear. "Come help me get Jack onto the floor and raise his feet."

Cassie bent to kiss his forehead. "Jack, keep your eyes open," she ordered. "Don't do this."

Haley rushed over, and the two of them slid him to the floor on his back, then Haley went for a blanket to cover him, but by the time she got back, Jack was rising from his body, looking down on the three of them.

The pain stopped.

Light. He was weightless, and it was so quiet, the scene below him getting smaller and smaller.

"Jack, no," Cassie screamed in a tinny voice from the bottom of a well. Then she thumped his chest so hard it sucked him back into his body, bringing the pain with it, along with the sound of dying sirens.

Jack gasped.

"Good. Breathe!" Cassie ordered as she started doing rapid chest compressions, so hard he thought his ribs would crack. "You cannot leave me, Jack. Not when I've just gotten you broken in."

He would have laughed if he could.

"I mean it, Jack," she said with iron in her voice, hair flying with every compression. "Don't leave me. I need you."

"Mama," Haley yelled, "they're here."

He closed his eyes, then opened them again to a clatter of equipment and activity. EMTs in navy, Cassie sobbing into Haley's shoulder.

Haley glared at him. "Don't die, Jack," he heard, though her lips weren't moving. "Mama can't take it. Not so soon after Daddy."

Something really wrong in his chest. Not pain, just wrong.

A strange black man loomed over him. "We think you're having heart failure, Mr. Wilson. We're going to take you to cardiac at St. Joe. Stay with us, now."

Oxygen mask, hissing moisture in his face. Cassie crying. "My wife," he managed to get out.

"Mrs. Wilson, he's asking for you."

She didn't even correct him, just rushed over, her face tortured, to grip his hand. "Okay," he told her. "Be okay."

Please, God, not now. This'll destroy her, and she doesn't deserve it. She needs me.

I need her.

I *like* her!

Like her? I—

And then it all just stopped.

Fifty

Cassie

Haley tapped me on the shoulder, and I raised my head from my arm on the back of the sofa in the waiting room. "Here's your Diet Coke, Mama," she said gently.

Cried out and exhausted, I nodded, not caring what I looked like. I took a long swig of the drink, hoping it would settle my stomach and wake me up. Outside, the lights of the intersection of 400 and 285 sparkled in the darkness, and a TV murmured away from its mounting on the wall. "Did I miss anything?"

She sat beside me, close, and stroked my back. "Nothing. They said they'd call us right away if anything happened, so no news is good news, right?"

Odd, to have her taking care of me for the first time, but I was glad.

By now, I was just numb and stopped up. When Jack's eyes had glazed over in the kitchen, I'd felt enough grief and denial to last a lifetime. Far more than I ever would have imagined. For the moment, though, I'd shut down to survive.

This couldn't be happening again.

"You kept him alive, Mama," Haley told me for the fifth time. "The EMT said he never would have made it without the CPR." She gave me the same worried look I had given her so many times. "They'll fix him. He'll be okay. Jack said so. I heard him."

Jack wasn't okay to start with; that was the problem.

Please, God, heal him. Let him live.

If he didn't, I . . .

I genuinely didn't know what I'd do.

My cell phone rang, causing us both to jump. I snatched it from my lap to my ear. "Hello?" Please, no bad news. Please!

"Mrs. Wilson?" an unfamiliar voice asked.

This was no time to get into technicalities. "I'm Jack Wilson's wife."

"This is Dr. Rosenburg. Your husband is stable in CICU. We've discovered that he has a lazy heart that may have been caused by the blood-pressure medicine he's been on. They've just recalled it from the market for that reason."

Relief and anger bubbled up inside me, but I focused on the moment. "So he didn't have a heart attack?"

"Not a clot. His heart just slowed to the point that it almost stopped."

"Is there anything you can do?" Please, let there be something they can do.

"Yes. We can discuss the options in the morning when I make my rounds. For the moment, he's stable and the prognosis is fairly good."

Thank God. There were options. And "fairly good" was a lot better than "poor." "Can I see him?"

"Only for a moment, and only if you don't upset him."

"I won't upset him. I just want to see him. He looked so awful when they wheeled him into the ER." I closed my eyes, as if I could block out the awful image.

"I'll tell the nurses," the doctor said. "But he needs his rest, so I'd advise you to get some sleep, yourself, after you see him. We'll talk in the morning, say, around nine."

"Thank you, Doctor. Thank you so much."

"You're very welcome." The call went dead.

I closed my eyes as relief flooded through me. There were options.

"Mama?" Haley's voice was anxious. "What did they say?"

I nodded as I spoke. "He's okay for now. We can be grateful for that." I grabbed my purse and started to stand, suddenly hollow and a bit weak in the knees, but I made it erect. "He's in CICU. They're going to let me see him. Just for a minute, but I can see him."

Haley took my arm and started in that direction. "Good. Then we'll get you something to eat, and I'll take you home."

I nodded, tearing up just a little, and grasped her hand. "I'm so glad you're here. I don't think I could face that house again, alone."

"I'm glad I'm here, too, Mama."

We walked in silence toward the cardiac intensive care unit.

"You really care about Jack, don't you?" she asked.

"I had no idea how much, till I found him slumped on that table."

"Then I might like him, too," she mused.

I took a deep breath, strengthened. "You will, when you get to know him. He grows on you." He'd definitely grown on me.

Haley smiled as we neared the double doors to the CICU. "I can see that."

She stayed behind as the nurse led me into the unit and Jack's room, blinking with telemetry and hung like Tarzan's jungle with tubes and wires. They were giving him red cells.

Jack was pale, but a lot pinker.

I touched his hand, not wanting to disturb him, but needing to make sure it was warm.

It was.

He opened his eyes and frowned at me, unfocused, and his low heart rate went up a little.

I stroked his hairline. "Hey. That's some way to get a girl's attention."

His scowl went deeper. Jack still being Jack, he grumbled, "I'm still alive?"

"It appears so." Thank you, God. "I'm no angel."

He let out a gravelly cough, wincing, then a half strangled, "I know that. You broke my rib."

"Saving your life," I said calmly, remembering the doctor's admonition. "But you can thank me later."

His eyes closed again, but he was smiling. "I intend to. For a long, long time."

"That suits me fine."

He gave my hand a squeeze, then fell asleep.

The nurse came in and motioned me to leave.

I left that room feeling 300 percent better than I had when I went in. Jack was going to be okay, and so was I. And so was Haley.

It wasn't a hope. I knew it in my soul.

I would get to take him home again.

Who knew what might happen then, once he'd been off that blood-pressure medicine for a while?

We might just fit even better than we thought. Or not. Either way, I would be happy with Jack.

The pieces of my heart started to settle back into place.

In the waiting room, I greeted my daughter with open arms. "Come on, honey. Let's go home. Everything's going to be okay."

And it was.

Acknowledgments

This book is my gift for all the boomers out there who find themselves falling apart, and for their descendants, who will relate to my characters and live, learn, and laugh with them. First and foremost, I'd like to thank the good Lord for allowing me to do work that brings hope and humor to my readers. Second, I am deeply blessed to have a son and daughter-in-law who love and care for me nearby. I am so grateful and proud of them both for not only putting up with me but also providing for me with love and generosity. My four grandchildren are icing on the cake, and being with them takes me out of whatever troubles or crises I might be facing.

Thanks, too, to St. Martin's Press and my editor, Jennifer Enderlin, for their continued support of my career.

As a single woman, I deeply appreciate the help of Maaco car repair in Lawrenceville, Georgia, for their honesty and the unfailing quality of their work. My son is right when he says I *cannot* back up properly, so I'm a regular customer in the minor dent-and-scratch category, but all my collisions are under three miles an hour with stationary inanimate objects, so no humans or animals are in any danger. Unless I try to back up in the electric cart at the grocery store, in which case, look out!

I'd also like to thank my bookkeeper Liz Fortson for doing the numbers thing for me, because I'm so bad at math that two personal bankers (at separate institutions, after trying to help me straighten out my checking accounts) have told me that I should *never* have a debit or ATM card, or nobody would *ever* get it straight. Hand to my heart, that is absolutely true. (Fortunately, I do keep all my receipts.) Thank goodness for Quicken and my trusty bookkeeper.

Thanks also to Debbie McGeorge, Cheryl Espenlaub, my pals Doug Jackson and Ken Miller, my housemate Sandi Grimsley, my favorite sculptor Julie Brogdon, and my sweet neighbor Celia Dasher for being such wonderful friends, in spite of my many shortcomings. Also to my precious, amazing Red Hat Club friends, Joan Boudreau, Vickie Fortson, Bonnie Henderson, Mary Jane Kremenski, Liza Kremer, Lois Love, Sara Moran, Holli Moore, and Rosie Peck. What amazing, wise, and wonderful friends you are. Thanks, too, to my pals at Stonehedge Garden Club for their friendship and understanding over the years. My yard (and my life) wouldn't bloom without all you've taught me.

I'd also like to thank Anna DeStefano and Anna Adams for the wonderful work they have done leading our published authors in Georgia Romance Writers for the past year. "Our Annas" spent many hours and much care and effort, and we in GRAN appreciate it. With all the changes in the book industry, our published authors can help each other immeasurably by sharing information and reliable referrals as we enter the era of the e-book.

I also appreciate the warm welcome and acceptance I've re-

Acknowledgments

ceived at the Atlanta Chapter of American Penwomen, and also
the Sugar Hill WORD chapter of ACFW, a wonderful group of
Christian writers who don't hold my romance novels against me.

I want to be clear that all the characters in this book are fictional, figments of my imagination, even though Cassie Jones
shares my weird health condition. In real life, I owe a deep debt of
gratitude to my doctor, Donald Dennis, ENT, for diagnosing and
treating my allergies and rare form of arthritis. The only charac-
teristic Dr. Dennis shares with my fictional doctor in this book is
his genius. Dr. Dennis is a kind and generous man who has helped
me through some really bad times, for which I thank him from my
heart. For anyone with chronic problems with yeast or fungal infections, he's the man to see. If I got any of the technical things
wrong, the errors are mine, not his.

Also, the dates and fix-ups in this book are cobbled from dozens of horror stories friends and acquaintances have shared, plus
hours of watching *Divorce Court* and *Judge Judy*, so no character
represents any one person, and any similarities to any real people
are purely coincidental. (I haven't really dated, to speak of, since
my divorce in 2001. For one thing, nobody asks me out. For the
other, I'm too darn busy.)

I'd also like to thank my church, Blackshear Place Baptist, in
Oakwood, Georgia, for helping me so I could get my prescriptions
filled when the well ran dry. What a mighty and merciful ministry
we have there. And thanks, too, Ken, for the help.

To my sister Elise, you are Christ's hands and heart in this
world. What would I do without you? And also my sisters Betsy
and Susan, you are such blessings to me and all of us who love you.
And to my mama, who is still great company and always makes me

laugh. Love you, love you, love you. For my brother Jim and his sweet wife, Charlotte, and my amazing, beautiful niece Elizabeth, I love you all so much.

Last but by no means least, special thanks go to all my readers who posted to my Facebook and Twitter pages or e-mailed me, and especially those who gave me wonderful reviews on Amazon.com and Barnesandnoble.com or Goodreads.com. With the demise of so many bookstores, publishers are relying more and more on Internet traffic to gauge our success as writers, so I welcome any positive tweets and posts, or direct e-mails to me at haywood100 @aol.com. I answer them all myself, and cherish each one. For those of you who don't like my books, God bless you. Books are like food: everybody likes something different, which is what keeps all of us writers in business.

Watch for *Queen Bee Goes to College* next year, a sequel so many of you have asked for to my bestselling *Queen Bee of Mimosa Branch* that takes feisty Lin Breedlove to community college at sixty, where she gets more of an education outside the classroom than in.

mL

1-13